Indecent Exposure

by Erik Dolson

Indecent Exposure

Published by Gnome de Plume LLC.

Thank you.

The artist is simply a channel. Characters speak, seemingly of their own accord. Events occur as if in a logical universe. It often feels as if the author does not create, but recreates. If there are flaws, it's in the transcription.

Indecent Exposure is fiction, and the characters within are fictional. But some of them appeared, as if by magic, with their own voices, attitudes, and demands. A few were in fact quite demanding. The theme of this book is the result.

Sensuality is not a sin. Coercion is. Sexuality can be a treasure, a joy, a source of power, or a corrosive force, and sometimes all at the same time. That makes it complicated.

Sex has also been a currency forever. But there are differences between an embrace, an exchange, and extortion. Most of us know where a relationship sits on that line, though it may be hard to draw at times. It is not only the act that matters, but also the intent.

Every artist knows, in that place from which art flows, that we are not solely the source. In that place, there are mysterious connections that seem to draw together elements of what will be become the art. There are many influences.

As an author, and a man, I have to thank the many strong women I've known over the decades who helped me reflect, grow, and change. I'm not finished with that, God knows. I'll never be finished. But as a result of their input, sometimes thoughtful and sometimes justifiably outraged, I hope I'm a better man than I used to be.

I'd also like to thank Tom Robbins, while I'm at it. To travel in his books is to travel with a mind so sharp, so funny, and so in love with what I'll call the Female Essence that he made it okay to embrace all She has to offer. At least for me.

Finally, *Indecent Exposure* is just a story. It doesn't have to be any more than that, either.

~ Erik Dolson

Chapter 1

Americans often introduce themselves by asking "What do you do?" as if that defines who we are.

So I'll start there. My name is Jessica and I'm a lawyer, though I lost my law license for a while after I landed in jail. In some ways jail was a good thing, though I certainly didn't think so at the time.

I've been told I don't look like a lawyer, and don't act like one. What should a lawyer look like and how should a lawyer act, outside the courtroom? Lawyering is what I do, not who I am. All those "shoulds" are just forms of oppression.

That's not to say I'm opposed to dressing for my role, nor that I'm opposed to good manners. Manners are condoms for social intercourse.

Being direct saves energy. It cuts through the bullshit, and it outs bullshitters pretty effectively. Maybe that's the edge some say I have.

Like everybody else, I'm a mix of biology, psychology, and happenstance. Biology is being born male or female, straight or gay, brown eyes or blue, ugly or beautiful. Psychology is the ever-changing wiring of our brains. Happenstance is the stuff that just happens: where we were born and brought up; the fight a jailer has with her drug-addled son before coming to work, mean and wanting to get even; an Iranian taxi driver who just arrived in Seattle and drives around, lost, making us late to a job interview.

These divisions are a little arbitrary, but we all carry marks from where we've been that determine where we're going. Some of us even carry what I call "totems of childhood," something concrete that reminds us why we are who we are.

My totem is a teacup from France. It was my grandmother's. I broke it when I was a little girl, but I wear a piece of it now as a necklace to remind myself who she was, what she was to me, and that a lot of life, good and bad, is the result of happenstance.

My parents are still alive. James and Janet Jones named my older sister Jordan. They considered Joanne for me, but decided instead on Jessica. If they'd had a son he would have been named Jason. They thought all those Js would be cute, I guess.

When my dad finished his second tour in Vietnam, he and Mom were married. Everyone said Vietnam changed him. Mom told me recently that when he returned, he smelled burnt and tasted bitter.

I asked her why she still married him. She said women marry men thinking they can change them, men marry women thinking they will never change. That sounded like something Grandmama would say, probably in French.

My parents are still married, though only because my mother is afraid of the dark. She's one of those women, even in this day and age, who opts for domestic tranquility over honest self-expression. I've only seen her stand up for herself once, and that time she was actually standing up for me and my grandmother. I was awed and grateful, but wish she'd found that resolve to improve her own life.

She was assistant to the city manager in the small town where I grew up on the north Washington coast. Assistant to several city managers. One time she told a friend that she was training the third "idiot man" to be her boss. I was in middle school then and asked afterwards what she meant.

"Never mind, Jessica. They do the best they can, and a job's a job."

The job was important. My father had been a carpenter, then decided he shouldn't be pounding nails for other people but build houses and sell them himself. That worked until the recession around 1980. He'd borrowed a lot and then interest rates went to over 20 percent. My folks lost everything.

They lived with my grandparents for a few years and scraped by. Eventually they were able to buy a house — a box that he'd built and sold years before. He absolutely hated that, especially given that he'd built it fast to sell and workmanship wasn't the best.

After that he worked as service manager at the local Dodge dealership. Unfortunately, we lived in a town that favored Fords. So maybe he has some reason for the bitterness, the anger, and the sarcasm that seemed to lurk like a creepy stalker just outside the edge of every conversation. Or maybe that's just who he is and what life gave him in return. Biology, psychology, and happenstance.

Forget the clichés. I had a normal childhood with nothing more than the usual traumas suffered by a smart, pretty girl full of curiosity.

Maybe my childhood wasn't completely normal. I was raised mostly by my grandmother. She was born in France, fell in love with my dad's father during World War II and came back with him to Washington. My grandfather died when his fishing boat sank in 1983, and I don't much remember him, except sometimes he made me uncomfortable.

Grandmama lived not too far away in the same town. She walked over to take care of my sister and me when we were babies and my mother was at work. Later, we went to her house after school and Mom would pick us up on her way home. We spent a lot of time at my grandmother's house.

Grandmama had blue eyes but thick dark hair and an olive complexion, different from most people in the area who descended from Swedes and Norwegians. She never lost her heavy French accent, which made her exotic to my friends. My mother said I looked more like my grandmother than like anyone else in the family, which also explains why I never really fit in with kids in my hometown.

There were other reasons, of course, but in a way those too can be attributed to my grandmother. When girls in school all wore the same skirts and blouses and uncomfortable shoes, I wore jeans and hiking boots when I could. I loved a blue wool sweater I found at the Salvation Army made for someone three sizes larger than me, but wore another sweater underneath made of the softest cashmere. Other girls said that also probably came from a dead person, but I just loved the feel of it against my skin.

They pretty much ostracized me, which hurt at first when kids I'd been friends with since grade school decided they liked new friends better than me.

I asked my grandmother one day what was wrong with me.

"Jessica! There is nothing wrong with you!" she said. "These girls do not own who they are, unlike you. They are mirrors for each other, always looking at glass to see themselves and how they should feel. You look out, through windows."

A day or two later she found an old copy of *The Ugly Duckling* at the library and gave it to me to read. "Lessons here for you to remember," she said with a smile to my frown at the children's book.

Once I asked if she ever wanted to go back to France and see her family.

"When I told them I would marry your grandfather, they said I was betraying the family and should never return."

"But that was so long ago!" I said. "Maybe they changed their mind!"

"*Tout passe, tout lasse, tout casse*," she said to me, her blue eyes looking into mine. "Everything passes, everything wears out, everything breaks. This is life. We make choices. We live with them."

That would be one of the most important lessons she taught me, though I didn't know it at the time.

I lost my virginity when I was fourteen with a boy about my age, and it was one of those typically awkward, messy first times for each of us. No big deal, I won't go into details.

It was a bigger deal when I was caught having sex a year later. Sam was nineteen. He'd missed a year of school because he'd been sick, but lied to me and said he was seventeen. I'd lied to him, too, and told him I was seventeen. He believed me because I'd skipped third and seventh grades.

We'd been kissing and touching for a couple of months, but neither of us had an orgasm. At least with each other. I'd masturbated of course, and I'm sure he had, too.

That night we'd gone to a dance at the high school. One of his friends had given us a joint, and another friend gave us hits from a bottle of vodka a bum had bought for him in Everett. We were a little high, pretty relaxed, and like most kids that age, extremely horny.

We parked his hand-me-down pickup truck in the cul-de-sac of a subdivision that hadn't yet been built. Sam had already unhooked my bra, and every time his fingertips brushed my breasts, a little zip of electricity shot from my pelvis to my brain and back. I finally said fuck it, I wanted him right then and right there.

"We're doing this," I said, as I scooted my ass out of my jeans.

"Are you sure?"

"Yes! I'm sure!"

That was all the encouragement he needed.

"Jessi, I just love you," he said. His shirt came off and he yanked his jeans down to his knees. I sat on his lap facing him. Oh, God, did that feel good. I pulled my sweater off and the bra came with it, so I was naked in the pickup and that was so hot and erotic all by itself that every nerve in my body was on fire.

Sam got off first, but not by much. Feeling his cock pulsate, knowing he was filling me, I came right after he did. I collapsed on him, resting my head on his chest, my arms wrapped loosely around his waist.

That's when the cops shined a flashlight into the truck and rapped loudly on the window.

When they saw our IDs, they skipped the customary warning and drove us to the station.

They took us to separate rooms. I still remember the dingy walls, covered with gray paint left over from repairing warships at Bremerton, and buzzing fluorescents. While waiting for my parents, the woman cop, Officer Deborah Riddle, started talking to me about consequences, older boys, alcohol, and all that.

She started asking questions, then started answering for me, too, putting words in my mouth, confusing me.

"It's all they want, and they will tell you anything to get it," she said. "They will tell you they love you. They will tell you they want to marry you. They will promise to buy you things. Did he say these things?"

"Well ..." I was trying to figure out if Sam's "Jessi, I just love you" fit the description. I'd already decided to fuck him when he said it, but he did say it. How was I supposed to answer?

"I know how these things go," she said to my hesitation. "Did he make you take your clothes off?"

"We were parked and we were kissing. It just kind of got out of hand." I was trying to take some of the responsibility without taking all of it.

"But was it his idea to park?"

"We talked about it. We just decided to," I said.

"But he drove?"

"It was his truck, he drove," I said.

"Well then, he decided where the truck was going, I'd say. Older boys can make girls believe things. They seem so much smarter and more mature," she said.

By the time my folks arrived, she had changed my story into something resembling rape.

I repeated her story — to myself and everyone else — that I was pressured into it, that maybe it was almost rape. I knew deep down that wasn't true — that I was the instigator — but told myself it really didn't matter.

Sam completely disappeared. He didn't come back to school. His friends told me he'd gone into the service, and they said I'd really fucked him over. I tried to defend myself, but they said I lied about what happened. It did no good to say those weren't my lies.

Things weren't so good at home after that. I developed a bit of an attitude. Mom was anxious about my period. But typically, she didn't come right out and ask.

"I'm going to the drug store, Jessi. Do you need anything?" she would ask. Finally, one Saturday afternoon, I'd had enough tiptoeing around the subject.

"Either some tampons or a pregnancy test, do you mean?" I asked.

"Oh no, dear, I was thinking maybe soap or shampoo …" her voice trailed off. "Of course, if you need one or the other …?"

Unfortunately, my father heard just the wrong part of the conversation. He'd not been able to look at me since Sam and I had been caught. But now he did, and the expression on his face was ugly.

"You pregnant?!"

"Mom and I were talking about going to the drug store," I said. "It doesn't concern you."

"Don't use that tone of voice with me."

"Yeah. Okay." Yes, I was adding gasoline to his burn.

"You think you can go be a slut and then stand there and talk to me like that?!"

"What did you call me?"

"A slut. And it's not just what *I* called you. Other people are talking."

"Wait a minute. Didn't you date Mom when she was 16? You never touched each other until you were married?"

"That's not the point. And you're 15."

"So the point would be …?"

"You letting that boy have sex with you. Acting like a shameless slut. A streetwalker."

"I thought I was your daughter."

"Not when you act like that."

"You turn that daughter thing on or off just any old time?"

"Go to your room."

"Excuse me? 'Go to your room?' That's your response?" My attitude was now embellished with my laughing at him. Since I'd had sex and everybody knew it, I figured I'd achieved a certain status. It's a powerful discovery for a girl, young enough to be wanted, old enough to say yes.

"This is my house! Go to your room or get out!"

I ended up where I always did, at my grandmother's.

Grandmama did not judge me. She did not scold me. All she said was something about "These Americans, obsessed with what they fear, fearing their own obsessions," or something like that; she said it in French, so I didn't understand every word, but her meaning was clear.

Chapter 2

What we see depends not just on what we look at, but also upon experiences we bring to the looking.

Instead of my mother's constant fear that something bad was going to happen, or my father's angry certainty that it already had, Grandmama always acted as if we would manage.

We'd sit at the kitchen table so she could easily stand to stir something on the stove. The table was square, heavy planks of local maple milled by one of the two- or three-man operations that survived on the leavings from Weyerhauser, the giant corporation that owns half of Washington state and turns Douglas fir into money.

The table was the first thing she made her new husband buy after they came back together from the war. Before the bed. Grandmama smiled when she told me this.

"He was not happy, but I told him, 'A table is the center of a kitchen, a kitchen is the center of a home, a home is the center of a family.' " The table had straight-back chairs with thick, overstuffed sheepskin cushions. We picked herbs from her garden and hung them from threads she tied to cupboard handles. Fruits or vegetables, depending on the season, filled bowls on the counter.

She argued with the butcher at our supermarket about cuts of meat, which were never thick enough and had too much of the fat trimmed away. "Don't cut it off. Leave it!"

"But you're paying for something that just cooks away!"

"If I am willing to pay, give me what I ask," she said with a shrug I'm sure was taken as dismissive. She relished the fat of a T-bone, saying that's what gave it flavor, and my grandmother is the only person I've ever known to think the skin of a fresh-caught salmon is the best part.

Discussions with the produce manager often ended with her giving a quick shake of her head and a sigh, walking out with nothing. "Better to do without."

She bought at the farmers' market when she could. She disdained corn, saying it was fit only to feed animals, but she loved Washington apples that crunched with crisp sweetness. She cut locally grown zucchini, still with nettle-like spines, into long slices to mix on the stove with onion, and tomatoes so plump they seemed about to explode. She browned tiny red potatoes, rolled in olive oil and rosemary, until they were wrinkled and crisp.

Sitting at that table on afternoons dark and heavy with rain, Grandmama taught me to play backgammon. She explained there are special places on the backgammon board, which ones to occupy, and which to avoid at various stages of play.

"Don't be in a hurry, Jessi," she'd say if I failed to build a defense before I tried to attack. "It is better to let the opportunity come to you."

Later she taught me by simply asking, "Are you sure?" when I would make a bad move, which then turned to a look over the top of her glasses, asking with her eyes. Eventually, she would just smile and pounce whenever I made a mistake.

She taught me to use the doubling cube to take advantage of apparent weakness — my own or my opponent's.

"Fear has twice the power of hope. They must always know there is more to lose," she taught me.

Grandmama didn't ask — ever — if I'd done my homework, or tell me what time to be home from a date.

But I always did my homework, helped in the kitchen when she would let me, and came home at a decent hour because I knew she'd be waiting up when I walked through the door.

It was later that summer, probably around August, when I ran into Sam standing in line waiting to order lunch at Bob's Burgers. He was on leave from the Army and looked great with a lot of muscle, taller, straight shoulders, every inch a man.

I walked up to him — honestly glad to see him, but yes, I was flirting.

"Hi, Sam," I said.

He looked at me, startled, then stepped back. "What do you want?" he said to me.

"I was just saying 'hi …' " I said, surprised by his response. He looked around like demons were about to crash through the door.

"They catch me talking to you, I go to jail," he said.

"What are you talking about?"

He said my lies — about my age and that he'd forced me to have sex — changed his life.

"But I didn't say you 'forced' me. I said you talked me into it!"

"Same thing, and that wasn't true, either," he said.

"I know, but everyone at the police station was asking why it happened, making me feel it was wrong, giving reasons why it wasn't my fault. It just seemed to be what I had to say!"

He pointed, not to a booth where we could sit, but to a corner where it would appear we'd bumped into each other coming out of the bathrooms.

I quickly learned my little lie had done a lot of damage. Sam described the hell he'd been through since we were caught. Interviews with psychologists. Restraining orders. Threats from my family that I knew nothing about. The college scholarship he'd lost.

He ended up in the military, "... which isn't a bad thing, all things considered," he concluded.

My heart sank. "Oh Sam, I didn't know!" I told him. "We can fix it! I'll tell everyone how it really was!" He just shook his head, looked at me like I was dog shit, and walked around me and out the door.

I cried most of that night from feelings of loss and shame, though I didn't know then what I'd lost. It wasn't just his respect. It was my self-respect, too. It felt like I'd been standing on concrete and something fragile and important slipped from my hands, the feeling between knowing it's going to break but before it actually shatters.

When I was a little girl, my grandmother was showing me a cup she brought over from France. Yes, that cup. She handed it to me, but I wasn't expecting something so delicate to be so heavy. I dropped it, and it crashed to the floor.

I remember looking up and into her face to see if I was in trouble. What I saw there was far more devastating. It was a look of pure pain, pure loss. I burst into tears.

"It's not your fault," she whispered, reaching for the broom. When I tried to help, she shooed me away. The pain in her face already replaced by grim determination.

When I asked for forgiveness — what I really wanted was relief from that awful feeling — she just kept sweeping and said in her heavy French accent, her lovely mouth set firm against the possibility of tears, "*Tout passe, tout lasse, tout casse*."

"I don't understand!" I cried.

"Everything passes, everything wears out, everything breaks."

That phrase, especially, shaped who I would become. Six months after I last saw Sam, I tripped and fell into a backwater of shame and self-absorption chilled by consequence that could not be unfrozen.

Chapter 3

Guilt grows out of accusation by others and is often destructive; shame flows from betrayal of self, and can be transformative.

"Oh, no."

I was sitting at the table in Grandmama's kitchen reading in *Port Vicente News* that a local man, a soldier, died while entering a village outside Kandahar in Afghanistan. Sam! He was a medic whose team was there to support the soldiers, but he had stopped to look at infections on the leg stump of a boy who had stepped on a mine left by the Soviet occupation. A sniper's bullet found the gap between Sam's helmet and his body armor.

Services were scheduled.

"Yes? What do you read?" my grandmother asked from where she stood at the huge porcelain farm sink in "our" kitchen.

"Sam, the boy I was with when … the boy when the police …" I just put my finger on the page as I sank into myself as if I were melting. I went slowly up the stairs to my room.

I didn't rise from the cocoon of bed the first day, the second day only to pee and drink a glass of water. Grandmama was in the kitchen, and she opened her arms to me. Though I was taller, she held me as if I were a child and she let me experience grief with ugly raw crying that went on until I was empty.

On the third day, my grandmother came into my room and sat on the edge of my bed.

"Jessi, today is the service for Sam. We will go."

"I can't go!" I was surprised she would even suggest it. I was the reason Sam died. I was the one everyone blamed for Sam being in Afghanistan in the first place. I had no business at a service that wouldn't have been necessary if I had not raised an umbrella of lies.

"I think you must go," Grandmama said.

"Why?" I snorted. "So people can think his memorial is no place for the slut who sent Sam into the Army? So people can think I'm so shallow, I see myself as Sam's bereaved lover?"

"Are these things true?" Grandmama asked.

"It's what they will think."

She sat there on the edge of my bed for a minute, looking down at her hands, which she turned over to look at her palms, as if she were holding a hymnal.

"It is time for you to wake up, Jessi, and not be so selfish," she said at last.

"Selfish!?" I was shocked at what she said. How could she possibly mistake my pain for the loss of Sam as selfishness?

"Sam is dead. I did not tell the truth about what happened between him and me, and because of that he is dead. How can you call me selfish?!" It was the only time I remember ever raising my voice to Grandmama.

"Jessi, sometimes I do not use English very well. Perhaps I used the wrong word. But selfish is the only word I know that describes what I am trying to say."

"What do you mean?!"

"Did you build the bullet that killed that boy? Did you shoot the gun? These are the reasons he died, not you. Did you send him to that country? Did you put him in the Army? No, you did not do these things, but these are the reason he died, not you. You made love to a boy. This did not kill him."

"I lied that it was his fault. It was MY idea!"

"Yes, that lie was not right. But you were still only part woman and part child, and that lie came from those who knew more about life than you could know. It was this town, this America, that made making love to that boy a crime, not you."

"I told the lie!" I didn't know why I was clinging so hard to my pain.

"Jessi!" my grandmother said, more sharply. "You are a drop of water, not the river! Taking responsibility for bad things that happen outside your power is the same as taking credit for good things you did not do. That's why I say selfish. We go to the service. You and me."

She left the room then, and came back with a long black dress that she put on the bed. "I think you can wear this with your black sweater to cover that it does not fit as well as it could. Please take shower, you do not smell as good as you want to in public."

She extended her hand to the side of my face. She did that at times when she was trying to let me know how much she loved me. I held that hand to my cheek. Some of the intense pain of the last three days left me.

"I stink, huh?"

She gave that small French shrug, with a half smile.

We could walk from my grandmother's house to the simple, white Church of God building one block off the harbor where the smell of the fish processing warehouse could still be detected. I'd been there to services before, when fishermen or loggers, friends of my parents, had died, usually in the line of work.

The dress was too small for me, but Grandmama razored the seams and pinned fabric into the gaps, and all that was covered by my sweater. It was certainly long enough, made for a different era.

At the door of the church was an easel with a collage of smaller photos that surrounded one of Sam in uniform. Photos of him as a little boy, in high school wearing a football uniform, but of course none of high school graduation. I felt his goodness in those photos, and a tear rolled down my cheek. Grandmama wiped it away as we sat in a pew about half-way down, next to the wall on the left as we faced the altar.

Most of the people who came in did not recognize me, but the few who did were not pleased. I wanted to crawl under the bench or flee out the side door. The wait, while the church filled, was long and excruciating. But nobody came up and asked me to leave, which is what I half expected.

Eventually the service started. There were lots of words about God's will, Sam's honor, that he had received awards in the Army, that he was a good man who often sacrificed for others. Then they handed a microphone around the room, and people shared stories. I wanted to run and yet wanted to listen because there were many things I had not known, even though we had talked a lot in the months we were together before we were "caught."

The hand-held microphone was making its way from the back of the church to the front. Those who had not wanted to speak just handed it on. The person in the pew behind me stuck it over my shoulder. I started to hand it to Grandmama. She smiled gently at me, and ever so slightly, gave one shake of her head. I started to hand it to her again. Her smile did not change, and she gave a small shake, again.

The church was utterly silent, I didn't know if it was outrage or morbid curiosity. I did not know what to say to those looking at me.

But I stood.

"Sam should not have been in Afghanistan. He should have been studying biology at the University of Washington. He wanted to be a doctor. I guess that's why he became a medic. He wanted to make the world a better place. Everyone needs to know that Sam was so good, so kind, so funny, so honest, so dedicated, that he glowed inside.

"Sam was sent to war because we were young and loved each other, I think, but also because of a lie. I was part of that lie. I will live with that forever, but if there is a heaven, Sam is there. If there is a God, I hope He'll forgive me."

I sat down amid murmurs and frowns, and handed the microphone to Grandmama, who squeezed my hand. I was crying, but not sobbing, I'd left all that on my pillow at home.

Grandmama handed the microphone to the woman next to her, who handed it on, who handed it on to someone who told a funny story about crabbing with Sam in the bay, and what Sam had found in dockside garbage cans to use as bait, and how they debated whether they would want to eat a crab that would eat that kind of garbage.

Eventually it was over and we left.

Outside, parked in front of a black minivan the church used as a hearse, were two police cars, there to stop cross-traffic as the procession made its way to the cemetery on the hill south of town. As Grandmama and I walked past, one of the officers stepped away from the car.

"Jessica, why are you here?" asked Officer Riddle.

I was prepared for that question coming to the church but not afterwards, and it startled me.

"I came … I came to say good-bye, I guess."

"After what he did to you?"

"What he did to me? Look at what I did to him!" I hissed.

"He took advantage. He got what he deserved," she hissed back, so quietly I don't think even my grandmother heard it.

"No." I said that word, and doing so changed something in me. What had been helplessness, mixed with pain, was now a hardened resolve. "Sam did nothing wrong, and neither did I What *you* did to him, and to me, was wrong. It was wrong and ugly and I can't even imagine what you must be like on the inside."

Grandmama took me by the arm. Oddly, she had a slight smile.

"Come, Jessica. It is time for us to go," she said.

Chapter 4

We rarely think of the little streams that braid themselves into a river, until after rivulets become creeks become tributaries become floods large enough impede us, or carry us away.

The "B" in Honors English kept me from being valedictorian. I was a little too opinionated about "Giants in the Earth," which I said celebrated weakness, not romance. It turned out to be my teacher's favorite book — Ms. Murty was not married. Otherwise, I earned straight "A's" in high school.

When a good university in another state offered a partial scholarship, I was ready to put my childhood behind me. Life in a college town where there was more sun than rain was so different from where I grew up.

More than anything else, I didn't feel so much like an outsider. My jeans and sweaters and hiking boots seemed to fit right in. I could have conversations that seemed to be about something. There were people with all sorts of hair and different skin colors. I didn't stand out because everyone was different.

Between studying, working in the admissions office, and picking up shifts as a waitress to earn money for clothes, books, mac & cheese and ramen, it wasn't like I had a lot of time for a huge social life. Once in my freshman year I went to an off-campus party with some of the girls from the dorm. It was a little wild. At some point, a girl I didn't know climbed up on the table and danced to a song I don't remember. She was gorgeous, and seemed to laugh as if nothing made sense but was somehow funny.

After the first song ended, someone said, "Take off your sweater!" She did.

After the second song, someone suggested she take off her jeans. She did.

After the third, someone suggested that since she was nearly naked, she might as well be completely naked. So she did.

Then it was time to step off the table. She hadn't taken off her platform shoes. Stepping down, she rolled her ankle and started to fall. Fortunately, there were plenty of hands to catch her.

Lots and lots of hands. Everywhere. All over her. She laughed some more and didn't complain, so the hands carried her into a back bedroom and continued to touch her. They touched her all over, gently, moving her legs apart, exploring. She let them, then one of the boys took his clothes off, too.

The room was full of young men and women, and we were all looking. I pushed to the front just as she pulled the boy on top of her. He made love to her slowly while holding her wrists over her head. At first she was smiling while looking into his eyes and down to where their bodies merged. Then she closed her eyes and wasn't smiling, but her face had a soft serious look as if she had become someone else or was connecting to a more significant world. She moved her hips to pull him deeper. He gave a soft growling cry when he came, and I liked that, too.

I thought about that a lot over the next several weeks, sometimes touching myself. What had happened didn't seem right but it was so arousing. Every time I remembered all those hands caressing her naked body, strangers touching her, an electric shock shot from between my thighs to the top of my head and down again, and my breathing changed.

It was confusing, wanting something so badly that I wasn't supposed to want, wondering what that meant, whether I was perverted, even though the girl actually involved seemed comfortable with what happened.

On my visit home that first Christmas, I asked my grandmother, without really asking.

"Why do so many people think sex is immoral? Why do they say we 'lose' our virginity? Aren't we really gaining something?"

It was one of the few times I'd ever seen her laugh out loud.

"They invent unnatural law to control the natural, so we can live in villages without fighting. Look at the world through your eyes, not theirs."

My eyes kept seeing all those hands, everywhere on that girl's body.

Although I didn't have a lot of free time in college, I did on occasion smoke pot, which made me self-conscious in ways I didn't like. I drank beer, which just made me feel full. Tequila gave me a rotten hangover. Champagne tasted sour unless it was expensive. Cocaine was fun, but it borrowed all that fun from the next day.

Generally I didn't like to drink; it took too much of the edge off.

There was an irony there, for men who thought we had to smoke something or drink something before sex. A man using drugs to be spontaneous and sensual is not the same as a man who is just … spontaneous and sensual. If the man was right, I'd go to bed with him and would rather be sober, if being under the influence of erotic arousal is sobriety.

I don't think it is, but I'll leave that discussion to experts.

As to guys using alcohol to "loosen up," that was rarely successful and often risked miscalculated dosage. More than once, with barely a pause between stages, a man went from being wound way too tight, to loose and funny, to drunk and aggressive, to vomiting in a toilet if not in the cab.

Not once did that increase either his libido or my interest.

As to plying me with drugs (alcohol among them), reducing a woman's control over her own actions can be coercive and ugly. I want to remember the night with a smile.

My major was psychology. It was either that or English. I liked the fact that psychology seemed to be useful, but didn't like it enough to earn an advanced degree, and had no interest in being a therapist. I'm sure there is great value in therapy, and those in the field do excellent work. For me, it's too much self-absorption. Grandmama used to say, "What matters is what you decide to do, not what you did long ago or what other people did to you." Biology, psychology, or happenstance: deal with it.

It was spring of my junior year. None of the guys I'd been hanging around with were love interests. The cute ones were gay, a couple of others were fun but not sexually appealing. Most boys wanted to own my time almost as much as they wanted my body. I didn't have that time, and the arguments weren't worth what the guys brought to the relationship.

So I was single and had been. Which meant I was also, shall we say, in the mood on a Friday afternoon when Becky, one of several short-term roommates who drifted through my three-bedroom house off-campus, told me she'd been invited to a fraternity party by a guy she "sorta kinda" knew.

"You want to go?" she asked me while I was boiling water for noodles, with olive oil and cheese.

"God, I am so tired," I said.

"Please? I really hate going alone. We don't have to stay long. There are some really great guys there. It's a pretty laid-back place."

"A laid-back fraternity party?" I was skeptical. Still, it was only a short walk from our house, it was a nice evening, I had the night off from work and completed everything for school. Tired as I was, I was also ready for a little R&R.

"Yeah, okay."

The party was the standard go-around; loud music, kegs of beer, a "bar" set up in one room, a tank of something for filling up balloons, joints, blow, anything and everything. After a while, things turned a little heavy, making out on the couches becoming a grope-fest and nobody much caring.

I had two large cups of whatever it was that filled the punchbowl. Somebody pushed a mirror under my nose with fat lines of coke and a straw, and I didn't say no. I was pretending to be interested talking to a boy who often came into the restaurant where I waited tables, but honestly, some of the sexuality around was beginning to turn me on.

Then one of the most beautiful men I'd ever seen joined us. He was tall, muscular, with thick dark hair, long eyelashes above gentle eyes.

"Hey, Jeremy," he said.

"Hey, Kent," said Jeremy. "Great party, yeah? You ready for the game next week?"

"Yeah, I *think* so," said Kent, with not-quite-ironic seriousness. Then he turned to me.

"Hi," he said with no further interest in Jeremy.

"Hi. Are you on the football team?" I asked, guessing from the width of his shoulders and the fact that a football game was being talked about on campus.

"Rugby," he said. "Football without helmets. Amazing we can spell our own name. Good thing mine only has three letters. I'm Kent." He held out his hand, into which mine disappeared.

"Nice to meet you, Ken," I said.

"No, Kent."

"Doesn't 'Kent' have four letters?"

"See what I mean? What's yours, by the way?"

"Jessica."

"Beautiful," he said. "My favorite. I especially like how it can be soft and flowing, or shortened to the tomboyish 'Jessi,' or be cropped to a professional minimum: 'Jess.' "

That was about when I decided I wanted him. That night, preferably, within the next ten minutes, if possible, and then the ten minutes after that, and the ten after that, and then we'd see if another hour would do.

We chatted for a few minutes about nothing in particular, waiting for Jeremy to realize his chances with me had gone from nearly non-existent to less than zero.

"What's your major?" Kent asked.

"Psychology. But I'm just a senior, so there's still plenty of time to change to astrophysics if I decide to." Surprising how many boys took me seriously when I said that. Maybe they didn't really hear what I was saying. Kent laughed.

"What's yours?" I asked.

"History and economics, but I'm really prelaw. I come from a family of lawyers, so might as well take advantage of the golden fleece."

I tried to pay attention, I really did. And I think I did okay, but while he was talking I kept imagining sliding my tongue into his mouth, and wondering what his cock would feel like in my hand. When he started asking me polite questions about where I lived, where I grew up, I asked if he had a room where we could talk more quietly. He flashed a bright smile.

"I thought I'd be the one to ask you," he said and led me upstairs to his room, tucked into a corner with windows that looked out on the street and had a small balcony.

"Do you have a roommate?" I asked, not really caring about the answer.

"Yes, but he's at a cross-country meet in Sacramento for the weekend," Kent said.

We sat on his bed. It wasn't long before he had my shirt unbuttoned, and I unbuttoned his. We kissed. His tongue felt just as wonderful as I'd fantasized downstairs. Pheromones, or his aftershave, ratcheted my heat to a fever.

Mother Nature puts a pretty high reward on sex. Sex and heroin addiction have similar brain chemistry. We are designed to want it whether freezing or sweltering, whether starving or just after finishing off a woolly mammoth.

Biology pushes women to desire men like Kent. What better way to perpetuate our own chromosomes than by hooking them up with a specimen like him?

They say an Olympic Village is a hotbed of sex. Can you imagine being among the best bodies in the world, swimmers and gymnasts and runners and weight-lifters in peak physical condition, coupled with the passion it takes to be in the Olympics in the first place, and not wanting to have sex with them?

Kent had that kind of body, and that kind of emotional drive. My God, he was beautiful. Men talk about the curves of women, but men have some fantastic curves as well.

After he had my shirt and bra off, it wasn't long before he had my pants off too. I was hoping my panties would slide off with my jeans to cut the wait, but no, he played me by sliding his finger under the hem, brushing me ever so slightly until my hips rose involuntarily to catch his hand every time it slid by.

I wanted him so badly I wrapped my legs around one of his giant thighs just to bring myself some relief. His hand in the middle of my back pressed me to him while he kissed my throat, and I was able to push myself against him in ways that triggered almost every nerve in my body.

I don't know when I noticed the door of his room was open. I don't remember it being closed. But I didn't much care, not then and not even when the room began to fill with other young men and women.

When I opened my eyes, they were standing close to the bed. Kent's mouth was on me and I had my fingers knotted in his luxurious dark hair. I saw both girls and boys filled with lust and envy. One couple touched each other while watching us. A girl next to them had one hand on the front of the jeans of the boy standing next to her and the other fondling her own breast.

The delicious blend of intimacy and anonymity is almost pure eroticism when you have sex with a stranger. It's heightened when other strangers are watching. It's a deeper wanting than exhibitionism, but related. That feeling washed over me like a wave and caused a complete surrender of mind to body.

Eventually the room emptied, Kent had emptied more than once, and I was as fulfilled as I had been filled.

We lay there long enough for parting not to be awkward, then we peeled ourselves apart, dressed. He said he'd call, I said please do, and neither of us gave the other our number.

Chapter 5

Adversity is fertilizer. It can be shitty when fresh but advances growth when the sun shines.

I was in the kitchen of our house having a cup of tea and reading for a class when Becky rolled in the next afternoon. I'd seen her drinking hard at the party house and huffing whatever it was from the balloons. No one knew where she was after Kent and I said goodnight, so after a while I gave up looking and came on home.

"Hey!" I said when she came in.

She looked worse for wear. Since I hadn't had that much to drink, I felt great.

"Hey," she said, making a beeline for the fridge. "Is there any milk?"

"I don't know. I don't drink it," I said.

"What's this?"

"Chicken Alfredo. I made it night before last. You're welcome to some, but leave me enough for lunch, okay?"

Becky threw a glance at me out of the corner of her eye, took about half of the Alfredo and plopped it on a plate.

"You'll want to heat it up. About two minutes should work."

"You always cook the weirdest things," she said, putting the plate into the microwave.

"You don't have to eat it. But put a paper towel over it so it doesn't spatter all over, okay?" It took her a few seconds of looking around to focus and find the paper towels that were about eight inches from her left hand.

"Everything you make is always really good, but it's not like things I normally eat," she said.

"I've never made peanut butter, but I'm willing to give it a try," I said. I wasn't trying to be snotty, I was just kidding around. We did that all the time.

While she was waiting for the Alfredo to heat, Becky busied herself around the kitchen. She even washed a fork. I doubted she'd wash the plate when she was done, but after great sex and a pretty good night's sleep, I wasn't going to make an issue of it.

"So, did you have a good time last night?" she asked me when she sat down across from me.

"I did. That was fun. Thanks for making me go," I wasn't going to indulge whatever quest she was on for details.

"That was quite a show you put on," she said.

"Really? Were you there too?" I knew she could have been, but I didn't remember seeing her.

"For part of it." Her tongue fondled the spoon and now she was making eye contact, but her eyes were not friendly.

"Glad you enjoyed it," I said.

"I saw the rest this morning."

"Excuse me?"

"Yeah, that guy you were fucking had a camera set up over the window, pointed right at the bed. You were probably too busy to notice."

She took another bite, still looking at me. I didn't say anything, so she went on.

"You look like a porn star in the video. God, you can see every detail, from your toenail polish to the color of your eyes. It's pretty amazing."

"Are you serious?" I asked, finally. My breathing had become shallow. I'd never questioned why Kent hadn't turned off the lights, and now realized why the reading light had seemed brighter than ones in the standard college frat house den.

"Yeah. He was talking of selling the film on the Internet," she said, now looking down for a minute at the meal I'd made and given to her.

"Cool. Maybe I'll be famous. Clean your dish when you're done." I grabbed my book and my tea, and went upstairs to my room.

That was pure brass. Inside, I was starting to implode.

The violation seared me like sunlight through a magnifying glass. My morning's satisfied fulfillment flashed out of existence. Memories of luxuriating with Kent's beautiful body crisped to sooty ash. Heavenly sensuality was scorched, blackened, and bitter.

After an hour — because if I didn't do something I would have gone back downstairs and bludgeoned Becky just for breathing — I called Grandmama. I hoped and prayed this would be one of the times she heard the phone and would decide to answer.

"Hello?" came the voice in the accent I knew and loved.

"Hi, Grandmama. It's Jessica."

"Yes, of course, sweet Jessi. Who else would it be?"

"Grandmama, someone is trying to hurt me. I don't know what to do."

"How long have you known this someone?" she asked. "They are close to you?"

"No, I don't really know him. I just met him."

"Did he hit you? Or he was not gentle?"

"No, it wasn't anything like that. It was more emotional."

"How can your emotions be hurt by someone you do not know?" Her question had an edge.

"It's a little complicated," I said, and she knew, as she always did, that I didn't want to go into details.

"If you don't know him, then he doesn't know you?" she asked.

"No, he doesn't know me, either."

"Then it is not really you he is trying to hurt. It is something inside of himself that is wrong."

"But it will hurt me," I said.

"Then you must put 'you' into what he is doing, into what he thinks, into what he feels. Or perhaps, like in backgammon, is it time to double the consequences?"

It took a bit for that to sink in, and we both let it. Then I said, "I love you, Grandmama."

"In this minute, you love that I give a paddle for your boat when the water does not smell so good, I think," she said. "But I love you, Jessica. This is enough."

She could be dismissive at times, but she was right. She had given me not just a paddle, but built the boat, too.

When I showed up at the frat house, there were about a dozen boys watching a football game where the bar had been set up the night before. It still reeked of booze and pizza.

The boys who hadn't suffered blackouts were glad to see me. I laughed and joked and went right to Kent's room, as if invited for an encore.

I told Kent I thought he was scum, and I wanted the original file and any copies.

"You know Jess, I don't think I can do that," he said with a smirk I'd not seen on his face the night before. "It's my property. It was taken in my room, and it might have some value."

"I didn't know you were making a video."

"You knew there were people in the room, that we were "in public," as it were. That's sufficient to show you had no expectation of privacy. Implied consent. You knew others were watching, and you knew they had cameras."

"That's different."

"Not so different that I couldn't use it in court."

"You set me up right from the beginning, didn't you?"

"Actually, I didn't know it would be you. I hoped it would be somebody, and you were the prettiest girl here last night."

"So you intended to film whoever you could seduce, and then sell it?" He nodded, and gave a little shrug, as if to say "so it goes."

"You are such an asshole."

"We all have our faults. I think I have a few of yours on tape," he smirked. "If you're nice, I won't include your real name in the credits."

"Where I live, loggers beat up on fishermen and fishermen beat up on loggers, just for fun. Every one of them is a friend of mine and they'd enjoy nothing more than beating on you."

"Oh? You've got a posse, do you?" He was enjoying this.

"These guys haul crab pots and set chokers for a living. None of them are as pretty as you and would love nothing more than to mess up that face."

"No, Jess. No logger or fisherman is going to come here and thump on me because a local girl decided to fuck for the camera. I'd just hand them a copy of the tape to take home and jack off to."

"Please give me the tape."

"No. And I have stuff to do. Anything else?"

I walked down the stairs furious, as much by my helplessness as anything to do with "honor." It wasn't that I would be seen fucking, it was that I was being used. By the time I hit the bottom step, I knew I had to do something or I'd carry this forever.

I didn't go outside. Instead, I walked over and stood in front of the TV and unplugged the power.

"Hey!" said at least three guys, but an advertisement for chips they'd seen time after time was playing, so the protest was mild.

"Is it hot in here, or just me?" I asked, and unbuttoned the top three buttons of my shirt. I figured that would buy me at least five minutes from brains that evolved to dump all available blood from cortex to penis at the promise of seeing a female breast.

"How many of you were here last night?" I asked. All the hands, except one, went up.

"How many of you watched Kent have sex with me upstairs?" Not everyone, but it a clear majority. A couple of boys looked confused, then disappointed when brought up to speed by the one sitting next to them.

"I'm a freshman. I'm sixteen. So every one of you who just raised your hand is guilty of statutory rape."

I let my lie sink in for a minute.

"You're no freshman," said one guy, sitting on the floor at my feet.

"Tell you what," I said, reaching into my jeans pocket for my ID. "I'll show you my driver's license if you'll show me yours, so I can tell the cops who was here." I held out my license with my thumb over the front so he couldn't see anything.

"That's okay," he said waving a hand. My willingness shook him up a little.

Jeremy, the boy I'd been talking to when Kent showed up last night, stood and left the room.

"How many years in jail do you think you'll spend for rape and abuse and furnishing alcohol to a minor?" I asked. Nobody offered an answer.

"Most of you know what happens in these kinds of situations. Nobody comes out ahead."

A couple of guys walked in through the front door. When they saw me in my half-buttoned shirt, they found a place on the floor.

And it was about then that Jeremy and Kent came downstairs and into the room.

"Wonderful! Here we have the perpetrator who organized the rape, and got all of you into a lot of trouble. Everyone knows Kent, the rugby star, I assume? Thank you, Jeremy."

"What rape? There was no rape," Kent said.

"How many of you remember Kent pinning me down, holding my hands over my head with one hand while he touched me with the other?"

One boy started to raise his hand until an elbow caught him in the side.

"You liked that!" Kent said.

"How do you know that, Kent? Did you ask?"

"It was obvious."

"Did everyone just hear Kent say he did not ask if I liked being restrained while he molested me?"

"That's not what I said."

"Really? That's what I heard. Isn't that what you heard?" I asked the boy who would not show me his license. He scooted back just a bit.

"You consented to everything. It was your idea to go upstairs."

"Kent, I don't think what a drunk sixteen-year-old likes or doesn't like is really relevant," I said.

"You're not sixteen," he said. "You're a senior."

"That's what I said so you would talk to me, but I didn't know you would get me mindlessly drunk — or drugged — and lure me upstairs."

"You weren't that drunk when we went upstairs!"

"Did everyone just hear Kent admit he took a sixteen year-old upstairs for sex?" I asked, looking around the room.

"How many of you saw the tape this morning?" Nobody raised a hand. "It doesn't matter. Becky is at my house and she'll tell the cops who was here. Then, how will you deny being guilty of enjoying child pornography on the day after a rape, if not of assisting in the rape by furnishing alcohol, and participating in the production, sale and/or distribution of child pornography?"

Boys were starting to look a little sick now that fear and guilt were piled on their hangovers.

"That isn't what happened!" Kent said.

"It's going to look so good on your application to law school, Kent. By the way, I don't know how much money you hope you'll receive from the video, but I don't remember signing a modeling contract. Can a sixteen-year-old even sign a contract? I don't *think* you got one from my legal guardian, though we can ask." I pulled out my phone as if to make a call.

"What do you want?" asked Jeremy, who hadn't left the doorway where he'd stopped after coming downstairs. Though he looked about 14, Jeremy probably had more functioning brain cells than any two of the rest of them. Except for Kent. He had the I.Q. and the smarts that come from playing mind games against sophisticated, successful adults who live the lives of an upper class.

"I want the tape. I want you to delete images of me that are on your phones."

"You won't take it to the police? Or the school?" asked another boy sitting close to my feet.

"This ends here if you want it to end here. Though if a single image of me shows up on the Internet, all bets are off. You'll all be giving interviews to the police and press and collecting your things from the college within a day."

"Give her the tape," said the same boy. Kent looked around, and he could see others nodding at him. Still, it took him a minute.

"Okay. Come on up. I'll give you the tape," he said at last.

"No. You bring it down, with the camera, so I can see that it's real. I'm afraid to be alone with you."

"C'mon, don't be stupid."

"How many of you heard me say that I was afraid of Kent?" I asked the room. They were actually looking at him, this time, and not me. Several nodded their heads.

"They heard me say it. Please don't force me upstairs. Please. Not again."

The doubling cube Grandmama taught me to use in backgammon was causing Kent's potential loss to climb much faster than the possibility that he might win this game.

He was back down in a minute, camera in hand. I put both in my pocket after watching enough to convince myself that the tape was the one from last night.

"Hey! Not the camera! That's mine!"

"I'm walking down the street with it, Kent. Please call the police if you'd like. I'll hand it over to them as soon as they arrest me. I'm sure you can have the camera back after the trial, but the tape will be needed as evidence and probably held pending additional charges."

"Let her have the camera!" said another boy I recognized from last night.

Kent curled his lip at me, but he nodded, slowly. Then, he actually smiled.

"Jesus Christ," he said. "I don't think you should waste your time with astrophysics. You're just like the bastards at my father's firm. You'd make one hell of a lawyer."

I wandered down the running path next to the creek that ambled through campus toward town. Once on the main avenue, I stopped at Melissa's Bakery and bought myself the largest cup of chamomile tea they had, one of Grandmama's favorites.

After drinking about half, I asked for a refill of hot water. And some salt. I added salt to the water, turned the camera on and submerged it in the cup. When it was dead, I put the lid back on and dumped the cup, with camera, into the garbage. It wasn't just an act of disposal. It was a declaration and recognition that a new future was opening up for me.

Kent said I would make a good lawyer. He would know. Why not, even if I'd never thought of it before? After three years of trying to decide between English and psychology, a single evening propelled me in an entirely new direction.

Talk about the value of a college education.

Chapter 6

Lawyering is not about rules, any more than football is about lines on the field. Law is about "story."

I had no illusions about saving the downtrodden or changing the world. I did not see myself as a savior, certainly not a martyr. But I loved solving puzzles, matching pieces to statute or case law, and finding those facts that established the story within each case. Or finding the story that both explained the facts and achieved my desired outcome.

In law school I also started to run again, which I hadn't had time for in college. The oxygen of a good run helped clear my brain after course work that was intense. I also enjoyed the solitude.

Boys becoming men were enjoyable, too; a lot of alphas in law school. But for all their brains and education, they weren't that different from boys in college or other men except the vocabulary was more sophisticated, the narcissists more charming if more abundant, and the sense of entitlement more acute — if better cloaked.

On more than one occasion, in language they could understand, I had to inform them that by planting their penis, they had not planted a flag. My sleeping with them once or twice, or even a half-dozen times, did not mean I had conveyed property rights. There was always some sort of trauma drama until I made it clear I was no longer interested.

My last was Prof. Ronaldo Angelotti, who asked me to drop by his office to "further discuss the question" I'd asked in class about real estate transactions. Yes, I knew on some level it was a setup. Yes, I knew on some level it would go someplace. Yes, that was the reason I asked the question in the first place. I thought he was hot, wicked smart, well-educated (Harvard Law) and funny.

Ronaldo was about as Italian as he could be, coming from the Boston area. He wasn't too tall, about six feet. He parted his dark hair on one side, but it fell heavily over his forehead. He wore jeans like most of the students, but with silk shirts. They fit him well, made it obvious he went to the gym but were not in bad taste. He wore loafers without socks. He was also 20 years older than me.

He asked if I could come by after his class at 2 p.m. on Friday. I asked if it could be later, like maybe 5 p.m. He immediately agreed, and we both had a pretty good idea where this would go.

"That was an excellent question," he said, after I sat down in the chair on the other side of his desk.

"Why? 'Appurtenant' was pretty obvious after you explained it. I felt pretty stupid."

"No!" he said. "I didn't make you feel stupid, did I?"

"It wasn't that hard to understand after you explained it. You did a better job than the book."

"It's just a matter of becoming familiar with new concepts. Do you have any other questions …?"

"I could probably think of some if I wasn't starving to death."

"Would you like to grab a bite to eat?"

"I'd really love some pasta."

"I know just the place."

We went to a nice Italian restaurant downtown. It was cliché: dark booths, red-checked table cloths, a wine-bottle candle holder dripping with wax, but the food was excellent. We had a nice bottle of Italian wine and talked about the law and a dozen other things.

Then we went to his house.

That man could do things with his tongue that seemed beyond humanly possible. He made my body do things that were beyond improbable.

But I gave as good as I got. I rolled him over to his back and kissed him hard on the mouth. I kissed him on the neck, then on his chest. Then I kissed his belly. I kept going with my kisses until he moaned, then threw one leg up and over him and pushed down and took him as deeply as I could. I leaned forward and kissed him on the mouth, then pulled back and upright and pushed down even harder still. Time stopped.

I could feel his heat inside me until I melted onto the pillows on one side and all we could do was lay there, exhausted, without saying a word.

Eventually, laughing and coughing sometime around 2 a.m., he said "You may have broken one of my ribs."

"That was amazing," I said.

"Will you spend the night?"

"I can't. I have an early class and need to pick up some things at my apartment. Is that okay?"

I don't know why I asked that.

"It is if I may see you again," he said, his dark eyes framed by thick long eyelashes.

"Maybe tomorrow I can come up with another question about contracts."

We played this game for two months. Things began to change near the end of the term. It always seemed that his priorities were "prior" to mine. He wanted to see me more and more often, and when it didn't work out, he wasn't happy.

"Hi Jessi. Come over later?"

"I can't, Ronnie. I have to study."

"You can study over here."

"You know how that turns out."

"I'll stay on my side of the room. I promise," he said, and I think he meant it.

"You promised last time, and we were fucking by 8:30. It was almost 11 before I opened a book."

"I wish you wouldn't talk like that," he said.

"You used to like my directness."

"That isn't direct, it's crass."

"It's me."

"It doesn't have to be."

"I have to go. Let's talk tomorrow."

"So that's a 'no,' you won't come over?"

"Geez, Ronnie. Please, I need to study!"

He was beginning to feel a little … confining. He was still funny, most of the time. He was still a great lover, all of the time. But he was making some assertions about how I spent my time that were not his to make. Somehow, things started becoming my fault.

Another afternoon he called when he knew I would be out of class. I'd not been answering his calls for a couple of days. I picked up because it came in as an "unknown number."

"Hi, Jessi."

"Oh. Hi, Ronnie."

"You don't sound pleased to hear from me."

"Just surprised. You must have cloaked your number."

"It's a new phone. I don't have everything figured out."

"Really? I didn't know they sold new phones with cloaked numbers."

"I have the same number, but I was pushing buttons trying to figure it out. Maybe I pushed the wrong one. How have you been?"

"Just studying. Busy time."

"You come to class late, and leave early."

"It seems like I'm always on the run. You know how it is."

"Or you're always about to go for a run …"

"You know running is important. I don't say that to put you off."

"Yeah. Want to come over this evening?"

"I really can't, Ronnie. I have so much studying to do. You know exams are coming up."

"You can study here as well as anywhere." His voice had an edge to it, as if he were winning an argument, and had proven my point of view was not valid.

"I don't think so. Can we reschedule?" I meant it, I really did. I just didn't want to see him that night, which I had already planned out with ramen noodles, green tea and law books.

"You're ducking me. What's going on? Is there somebody else? You can just tell me if there is."

"Shit, Ronnie. Guess what? It's not always about you, or somebody else and how that might affect you, or what you want me to do for you or to you, okay?"

"Hey, don't be that way! I made you dinner!" His voice became even sharper.

"You should have asked me before you went to all that work. I have to go."

"Why are you pushing me away?!"

"I'm not pushing you away. I'm studying for midterms. I have work to do. Goodbye."

After each of these episodes, he wouldn't call for a few days. If I called, he wouldn't answer the phone. When I did talk to him, he would tell me he hadn't charged his phone, or had to leave for a conference, or something. Eventually we'd reconnect, have a nice date, and the cycle would start all over again.

One night, before the end of the term, he talked me into coming over with an elaborate story that he had papers to grade and wouldn't have time to mess around. He would even let me use the office study in his house, and I could close the door, and he would let me work.

He did, too, after handing me a plate of lasagna when I walked into his house. But after I'd been working for about two hours, he knocked once on the study door and came in without waiting for me to reply.

"How much more work do you have to do?" he asked.

"About two hours. You going to bed?"

"Yes. Join me?"

"I can't."

"Why not?"

"What was it about 'two hours' you didn't understand?"

"That was rude."

"Yeah, it was. I'm sorry. I'm stressed. I've barely started on the stuff for your course, and I still have to review Environmental Law for Friday."

"Skip my stuff and go directly to Environmental."

"I can't. You've been introducing new case law every class!"

"Yeah, but you have an unrecognized understanding of the key concepts."

"Are you kidding? I grasp of about half of what you've presented. And your tests are not easy."

"Well, I can almost guarantee you'll receive a good grade if you just put your name on your paper."

"What?!"

He just stood there and smiled.

I didn't know what to say, at first. One of the things I'd admired most about Ronaldo was his sense of ethics. One of the reasons I'd been comfortable in the relationship, despite what was believed by some of the other students, was that we had a good boundary between who we were as lovers and who we were as professor and student.

I thought about arguing. But what was there to argue about? Was I supposed to tell my teacher that he was unethical, breaking our boundaries, becoming a creep? Was I supposed to go fuck him and lighten my work load, and never know if I had earned my law degree or bought it with his cock in my mouth?

"I have to go," is what I said.

"Oh, come on."

I opened my messenger bag and started to put my books away. He came over and started to take them out.

"Don't do that," I said, and snatched the bag away from him.

"C'mon, Jessi, I was kidding!"

"No, you weren't kidding. I can't believe you said that. I can't believe you think that. I can't believe you think that about me!"

For some reason, I was crying, but I didn't give a shit. He had demeaned me in a way that was hard to describe, and in a way that would certainly give him deniability if it came to that. I had no intention of letting it come to that.

"Give me my books."

"Jessi ..."

"Ronnie. It's been good fun, but I'm out of here. My books, please."

"Can we talk about this?"

"No. You've already said enough."

I reached over and took the books out of his hands, put them and my notes into the bag, put on my jacket.

"I'll give you a ride."

"No, Ronnie. I'm going to walk. I need fresh air. Thank you for dinner."

He stepped forward, as if to hug me.

"Don't touch me."

"This is bullshit. This isn't fair!" he said.

"You're right. It isn't fair. But I promise I'll forgive you, given enough time."

He spun out of the room and started throwing pots and pans into the sink in the kitchen. The racket was such that he could not possibly have heard me let myself out the front door.

I never went back to his class. I asked him, via an email copied to the department chairman, if I could take the final exam at another time than scheduled due to "unforeseen personal circumstances," under supervision of and graded by another prof, "since I know you are going on sabbatical and I do not want to inconvenience you."

He agreed, via an email to the department chairman and copied to me, suggesting two profs who had agreed to supervise and grade my final.

Several times I saw him at places he knew I liked to study: in "my corner" at the library, at a café just off campus. He knew when I liked to work out and run, and several times he was just in sight, watching me. He drove by my place several times, and there were a number of calls from an "unknown number" that I did not pick up.

The last time I saw him, he was parked outside my apartment on a lovely Saturday afternoon. He wasn't trying to hide. He drove a little Fiat roadster and the top was down. I came out for a run.

"Would you like a ride?"

I had decided to ignore him and just run on by. When he realized I wasn't going to stop, he stepped out of the car and said, "Jessi …"

I spun to face him, and cut off what he was about to say. Grandmama had taught me to pounce quickly in backgammon when using the doubling cube, and I wanted him to realize he had much, much more to lose.

"Ronnie, listen to me: This is stalking. If you *ever* park in front of my apartment again, the stink I put on you will never, *ever* go away. It will be part of your life *forever*. Do you understand?"

"Jessi, I …"

"That was a 'yes or no' question, Ronnie."

He'd started out looking at me with sadness, which became hopeful when I said his name, morphed into fear then anger as I watched. After my words sunk in, he walked back to his Fiat and drove off, without a backward glance. I proceeded to enjoy a run highlighted by brilliant foliage in crisp fall air.

Chapter 7

It's difficult to feed one sea gull. As soon as it pulls apart a few pieces of bread that *might* have been too moldy for peanut butter at home, the whole flock shows up and every one of them, except the largest and meanest, squabbles for little pieces.

There are a lot of hungry lawyers, even in Seattle.

I was staying with Christine and Marisa, roommates from college. Funds were low. The rejections were nicely worded: "Your application was quite impressive, but our firm is not currently hiring ..." They were still rejections.

I was a little desperate and thinking about picking up some shifts waiting tables at a local restaurant or working as a barista. I would not have been the first overeducated server in town.

So a little bit of the bright and cheery affect of fresh-faced job applicants had worn off by the time I met with Anthony Stevens of the firm "Stevens and Brown, PC." His assistant had brought me a cup of coffee as I sat down in one of two easy chairs in his office. My other interviews had been across tables in conference rooms.

"Call me 'Tony,' " he said after I addressed him as "Mr. Stevens" the second time. He asked a little about law school, but then about how I liked downtown Seattle.

"I like it here," I said.

"Why? It rains a lot." He asked this quickly.

"It feels 'real.' "

"What do you mean?"

"There are all sorts of people. There are suits and there are bums, bakers and bankers, hookers and high society. There's some great architecture, some bars with great music, and the water. It's real."

He smiled and asked about where I grew up, and seemed to appreciate my small-town, blue-collar background. No other firm seemed to care much about life before law school. Tony even asked questions about my grandmother.

"She never went back to France?"

"No. She won't even talk about it. I said I'd pay, but she just blew air out her lips, her way of dismissing ideas she thinks are foolish."

"How would you pay for that?" he asked.

"I'd find a way."

He smiled.

"What was her maiden name?"

That stopped me with a bit of surprise, actually. I had to think about it. "DuBois. Marie DuBois. But she was just Grandmama or Grandmere, to me."

Then Tony surprised me with a quick change of subject.

"Do you have a passion for criminal law?"

"Depends on whether I'd need one to land this job." The answer just popped out. That was his intent.

He laughed. "Let's have lunch today," he said.

"Sure." I'd planned to meet my roommates but quickly cancelled, and Tony and I went to lunch.

There's a nice little restaurant in the Pike Place Market, Place Pigale. You have to walk outside the market along a narrow catwalk toward the water, but if you can find a table, the food is wonderful and the view is spectacular. Tony ordered a martini.

"You want one?" he asked. I said no, thanks, and ordered a green tea.

"So when do I meet 'Mr. Brown?' " I asked while we waited.

"Who?"

"Brown, the other partner in Stevens and Brown."

"Mr. Brown is no longer with the firm."

He looked at me over the rim of his martini glass.

"There never was a Mr. Brown," I said flatly. It wasn't a question, though I can't say how I knew.

"No, there wasn't." Tony smiled broadly. "I needed to have something going besides being a new lawyer in a big city when I started out. So I became part of a 'firm.' Besides, whenever I'm asked to do somethingI really don't want to do, I just say 'I have to check with my partner.' He usually says no."

"So I shouldn't expect an interview with Mr. Brown?" I said, to go along with the subterfuge.

"He would like you very much. Let's order lunch." We ordered and made small talk while he drank half his martini. Eventually we talked about what I would do at Stevens and Brown, PC.

"I'm thinking about redeploying assets," Tony said. I waited for him to explain, but he didn't, so I played along. "What does that mean, exactly?" I said.

Later I learned Tony liked to make you ask. It's a thing with him.

"I think there's an under-appreciated opportunity in the criminal system. You might be just the right lawyer for that," he said.

His idea was that young women are sometimes arrested. Young women relate better to other young women than they do to old men, or young men, for that matter, who are either trying to control them or fuck them, he said.

"Women can sometimes get fucked over," I replied, partly to show I could handle the f-bomb.

"Most men are jerks. And the most dangerous jerks are the ones who say they are trying to help you, that they know what's best for you, that they will take care of you," he said.

"Even you?" I just couldn't resist, since we'd already started this relationship with a certain amount of candor.

"Especially me, since by acknowledging it I may seem different from the others."

Most importantly for Tony, though, was that young women often have people willing to pay their legal bills. He thought the combination of a law firm with a solid name and a bright young female lawyer (his words) working exclusively on behalf of women caught in "the system" could attract enough of those women, and their benefactors, to make a decent profit.

"Drugs and prostitution should be legal. But since they are illegal, there is opportunity."

"So we take advantage of those women, too?" Admittedly, I was feeling disappointment that this was where my law degree might take me.

"So they're all victims? Defending women against irrational laws isn't taking advantage, it's noble service."

"No, they're not all victims. But exchanging money for sex is degrading."

"Says who? If sex isn't the oldest profession, it's at least the oldest currency. Want to include marriage in this discussion?"

"It's not just about money. It's also about power. Pimps, violence, men taking advantage."

"Not our fault. You might as well say money takes advantage. If prostitution had support in the law, pimping might decrease. It's possible that violence against women would decrease if some men had easier access to sex."

"That's speculation."

"Of course it is," said Tony, starting to smile. "But women or men who accept payment, by choice or circumstance, can provide a wonderful service."

"You sound like you have firsthand knowledge," I said.

"I've had many relationships. Most of them involved a display of generosity, usually unstated, often overcomplicated, and with strings attached. An upfront transaction has many advantages."

"You'd rather be with a prostitute than have sex with someone you love?" I asked.

Tony smiled a little more broadly. "Sometimes."

I waited for the rest of the answer, but this was Tony, and he made me ask. Maybe even proving his point, if not about power, then about currency.

"Okay. Why?"

"First, there's less chance of coming away unsatisfied if you're dealing with a pro. Pardon the pun. Second, money makes sex simple. Love and sex together can be too complicated, both coming and going. Pardon the puns, again. If someone tells me they love me after sex, I can't be sure. If I pay someone, I know where their self-interest lies."

"Forget love. What if your partner just likes sex?"

"How do I know what she likes, and what she's just saying she likes? Or what she expects? Money clarifies the issues. Self-interest is the only thing you can trust when dealing with others."

It was months later when I realized this discussion was an essential part of the job interview. Tony was exploring not only my values, but also how I react when faced with opposition. I was starting to admire him in an odd way. When he asked if I'd come to work for him, I said yes. He offered a salary, not a huge amount but it would put me back on my feet. I said yes to that too, without bargaining, even after Tony put his hand on my arm a few too many times.

I had enough experience not to flinch. Some would say I might have missed an opportunity. Others, I'm sure, thought I took the opportunity. Tony looked a lot like Sam Elliott in a movie I'd seen, with the same twinkle and readiness to laugh, which he did often, if softly. He had long hair for these times, a subtle assertion that he was not "ordinary," or establishment, maybe a bit of an outlaw. He was quite a bit older than me. That can sometimes be a turn-on, but I didn't want to fuck this up, literally.

But he went a step too far when he suggested we go back to his place across from the office to "have coffee and work out the details."

The disappointment I'd felt earlier about how my law degree would be used, that had been relieved by our discussion about prostitution, returned with a vengeance and brought a whole gang of unpleasant friends. Anxiety that this job would disappear if I said no. Frustration that I had to worry about this now when all I wanted to do was work. Bitterness that a man would not be put in this situation. Anger that his invitation was likely to be repeated and I would always have to be on my guard or worried about the consequences. Fury that he dared place sex ahead of my worth as a lawyer, as a person, as a woman.

But Grandmere taught me that in backgammon, there is no point in showing anger at your opponent, or the dice, or the weather, but when a game seems hopeless it can be a good time for a bold move.

"I can't, Tony. Mr. Brown warned me you would ask, but said having a relationship at work was against the rules."

Tony laughed and nodded his head.

"Good. Then let's go back to the office and have my assistant pull some boilerplate out of the file and we can modify as we need to." He started to push back from the table, but I stayed seated.

"Can we talk for another couple of minutes?" I asked.

"Sure." He sat back down.

"I don't know if the invitation to go your place was a proposition or not. But I do know this: I can't work with uncertainty if I'm thought of as a piece of ass, if the job description includes blow jobs, if the semi-annual review is a tally of how often and how wide I spread my legs. That doesn't work for me on any level."

Tony sat there for a really long time, but he maintained eye contact. I could not read his emotions at all. After a few more seconds I reached for my messenger bag.

"Well, I guess I'm still looking for work," I said.

"No, you're not," he replied. "I'm extremely sorry I put you in the position of having to say what you just said, and want to assure you that you'll never again have those feelings, at least not as the result of working for me. The courage of your words confirms rather spectacularly that you are the person I need. And you need to know that had you said yes to coming to my place, you would not have been offered the job."

"You'd already offered me the job before I said no."

"And when my assistant calls about a minute from now to say I'm suddenly needed at the office, we would have parted ways today and the job offer would have been rescinded this afternoon due to 'an unforeseen change in circumstances.' If you'd fuck me to get this job, you'd fuck me over when a better one came along. It would have been a lie and I would not have been able to trust you."

His phone rang just as he said this. "No, actually, it's going quite well. Yes, really. Will you pull a standard services contract from the file and put it on my desk? Thank you." Tony clicked off his phone and looked at me with a small shrug, as if to say, "Your move."

"Okay," I said, after a minute of looking out at Puget Sound. "You know where I'm coming from. If you don't think I'm serious about this, there won't be any apologies when I walk."

Chapter 8

Quality is nearly impossible to define, but we know it when we see it.

Our offices were in the Seattle Tower, at the corner of Third and University, one of my favorite buildings in Seattle. The gilt entrance is small but nearly jewel-like in craftsmanship. The ornate architecture shows attention to detail, common to the finer buildings constructed just before the stock market crash of 1929, that no sixty-story, slick-glass bank tower built in the last fifty years can achieve.

I was impressed with Tony's sensibilities about the building, until he told me our firm was there because it was across the street from his apartment in The Cobb, an urban complex.

At first I thought criminal law would be romantic. Trust me, it's not. To begin with, your clients are usually criminals. Say what you will. Secondly, most criminals don't really have that much in the way of brains. Or they would not have been criminals. Or they would not have been caught. Again, say what you will.

But we were selective. The girl's source of funds for our fees was always the first consideration. Often the "source of funds" was surprising, and Tony could go to some amazing lengths to conceal who was paying the bill even as he tied the man paying the bill to a legal retainer.

Sometimes I wanted to take a case because "this girl really needs us." Tony always overruled me.

"We don't work for free," he said. "What we do is valuable. If a girl can't afford us, she can find somebody else."

"Sometimes doing the right thing can be the right thing to do," I said during the last discussion we had on the issue.

"Not if it doesn't pay."

The girls I defended were usually hauled in on drug charges or for prostitution. They were usually runaways from Port Angeles, or Aberdeen, or Everett, or Yakima, or Spokane, sometimes Portland, though some were from Seattle or Bellevue and were just rebelling from rich and preoccupied parents.

I would interview them, gather facts to show why what happened was not my client's fault, point out the sad situation and how they were seduced into bad decisions, they had no choice …

I would clean them up, dress them up if they were junkies, or dress them down if the rap was prostitution, make them look like homely, modest girls from some logging or fishing or manufacturing community, which they often were.

You'd be amazed at how often these girls would fight me on that, wanting to go into court in their brightest feathers, looking every inch the hooker they were accused of being.

I usually won the argument after pointing out that each hour they looked sexy in court could translate into a year in jail.

I would negotiate some sort of reduced sentence with the district attorney, often suspended if it was a first offense. It was a fun game, in a way. And at one level, I kind of liked it because I didn't really understand what all the fuss was about, why these girls should go to jail for selling what they had to sell, or buying what they wanted to buy, even if it was heroin.

Maybe Tony was rubbing off.

We soon built a nice little practice in my corner of the building. After a while, word was out that I was good at what I did and we hired office staff: two paralegals and one exceptionally good professional assistant.

The former were Sarah and Lily, two of the most white-bread young women you'd ever meet; they wrote a lot of the "stories" we created for our clients, in legalese. Claire, my assistant, was a black woman who was as real a human being as I'd ever met, except maybe my grandmother. Claire sat outside my office, expertly fielded questions thrown at her via the constantly ringing phone, had a wicked sense of humor, an incredible collection of dashiki dresses, and kept us organized.

When I had enough money saved up, I moved out of the apartment I shared with Christine and Marisa. Chris was always cleaning up and asking Marisa not to leave dishes in the sink, Marisa thought Chris wasn't contributing enough for dish soap and paid too much for toilet paper, and each wanted me to mediate.

I ate out of the same large bowl whenever I ate at home, drank out of the cup I kept in my room, and honestly didn't like the quality of toilet paper they would buy, not that my ass is that precious.

My new apartment was small but faced Elliott Bay. Aside from the train that rumbled, clanked, and screeched steel wheels against steel rails, I liked the place. I walked to work in ten minutes and wondered why anyone would ever commute an hour or more each way to live in a suburb. Seattle's traffic is horrific.

There was a gym midway between my office and my apartment. The apartment block actually had a gym, but the few pieces of equipment there were low quality and poorly maintained. The real gym I found was in an old warehouse that had been retrofitted with tons of nice equipment. I could stop by on my way to work or on my way home, depending on how I felt.

Seattle is a fascinating city. Maybe not New York or San Francisco, but it has history, architecture, culture and climate (rain, but damn little snow), the

University of Washington, and water. Not just Puget Sound, but lakes, mountain rivers, and the San Juan Islands stretching all the way into Canada.

There wasn't "a guy" in my life, but that was okay. My former roommates each had castoffs or leftovers or suggestions. Sarah and Lily knew about some handsome local lawyers or cute doctors. Claire always had an opinion of the men who came through the office.

Jim was a pilot who worked for Boeing. I met him at Angeline's, a bakery where I'd sit and read at lunch (with a bowl of soup). He was funny and handsome, and he asked me out for a drink. He came by the office to pick me up.

"Uh uh, honey," Claire said to me the next morning. "Not a good fit. You'll be bored in a month. Now don't get me wrong, it could be a good month and a month of good can be better than two months without, but you can do better."

"How do you know this?" I asked.

"While he was waiting for you, I asked if he'd like coffee or water or anything. He said 'no' nicely enough, but never looked me in the eye. Then he went over to look at the painting across from my desk. He didn't see the painting. All he saw was his reflection in the glass. You don't have any interest in those men," she said.

It took a while for me to trust her insight, but she was right, at least most of the time.

Chapter 9

Life-changing happenstance can be subtle. It can hide under layers of time. Days and weeks can pass, even years, between a moment that changes everything and realization of its significance.

Linda Williams was arrested downtown after a minor traffic accident. She wasn't driving, so it was odd that she was detained. However, when cops arrived she still hadn't put on any clothes and she wouldn't shut up when told to do so by the officer in charge.

It was her car, she said, and the "designated driver" was just doing her a favor by driving her home. But she was doing a favor for him, too, and told the cops the minor accident was the result of an absolutely incredible blowjob. Better, she said, than the cops had ever had. She offered herself as evidence. That's why she hadn't dressed; she thought it would validate "her friend's" defense.

"He's lucky he didn't lose his cock" said Lily, during our morning case review. Lily tended toward the pragmatic. "Or she didn't lose her tongue."

"It was a sideswipe," I said, seriously.

"Sounds like a 'head-on,' " said Claire.

"It's good she wasn't rear-ended," said Sarah.

"Was it a two-way street?" asked Lily.

"They were headed to a 'loads-only' zone," said Claire.

"We may have a 'prima facie' case," I offered.

Sarah laughed so hard she had to go to the bathroom.

Linda stood by her man. She stood there naked, extremely and loudly drunk, and generally full of attitude. So the cops arrested her for indecent exposure, public lewdness, and a couple of other pissant charges I was going to be able to make "go away."

But it became complicated. Drinking age in Washington state is 21. Linda, 19, whose father owned one of the larger log-export operations in Washington state, had used the best fake I.D. her substantial allowance could buy. The cops wanted to know where she acquired the fake driver's license. She wouldn't tell them. So the district attorney was not inclined to let this one go.

Because it could not possibly be his daughter's fault, and Daddy Williams had to blame someone besides himself or his daughter, he hired Tony to sue the nightclub where his darling baby girl, the prom queen who would be the eventual bearer of his legacy, had became so drunk and snotty. Tony passed to me the task of dealing with the legal charges against Linda.

The Seattle Area Social Association was a private club that catered to the more offbeat tastes of our fine city. Almost anything went at SASA, as long as it was consensual. As her blow-job defense to police proved, Ms. Williams was willing to consent to quite a lot. Linda not only used a fake driver's license to gain admittance into the club, she had been naked there, too, which she also told the cops and they entered into the record, I think just to be mean.

The club had been through legal hassles before and had a pretty good defense in Washington law. They were also represented by the top firm in the city. Tony and I were scheduled for "an informal conference to explore the potential for settlement" in a neutral law office on a floor below theirs in the Two Union Square building. I'd only been in the building once before, on an unbearably boring date at Sullivan's Steakhouse on the main floor.

I was with Linda to keep her from blurting something too honest, or to cover it up by saying that "what my client really meant to say was …" We were on time but the last to arrive.

When she and I walked into the conference room overlooking Puget Sound, on the opposite side of the table were Tony and Daddy Williams and two empty chairs for us. The other lawyers had their backs to us. I nodded to Tony and quickly guided Linda around the table to sit next to her father. I put my briefcase down and sat next to her.

On the other side of the table was the club owner, Chuck Simmons, who was just like you might imagine: a little too modern, or maybe a little too old for the too-scruffy style he was sporting.

To his left was probably the best-known lawyer in Seattle, as distinguished as his frequent photos in the *Seattle Times* social section made him out to be. Max Moore had dark mesmerizing eyes above an engaging smile of perfect white teeth, curly dark hair with just an accent of silver, a strong nose. With almost olive skin, he could have been Spanish or Italian. He wasn't that tall, maybe six feet, but athletic. He was so handsome it was distracting.

On Simmons' right sat a younger man, almost a younger version of Moore and no doubt one of the top young legal talents Moore had a reputation for cultivating, introduced as Mark Love.

After introductions were concluded and procedure described, Moore turned the conference over to Love.

"I'm sorry we have to be here today," Love began. "No one enjoys these types of proceedings, so perhaps we can make this one brief. Why are we here?" he asked Daddy Williams.

"That's not going to get us anywhere," Tony said to Moore before Williams began to sputter something in his outrage.

"Tony, we have a right to ask your client some questions," Moore said.

"You lured my daughter into your cesspool and got her drunk," said Daddy Williams.

"Daddy …" Linda Williams started to say, until I squeezed the hand I'd been holding — hoping it looked sisterly — for just this purpose. I'm sure I left a bruise. She did not finish her thought.

"It seems pretty clear from the police report, and the existence of fake identification, that your daughter went to the club of her own free will, expecting to be served alcohol, and broke the law to make that happen," said Mark Love. "What is it you allege my client has done wrong?"

"She would not have done any of that if he hadn't provided the opportunity. He created an attractive nuisance!" Daddy Williams said.

I cringed. Someone who knows nothing about the law telling lawyers how the law works is often embarrassing and rarely a successful strategy.

"Tony, have you had a chance to counsel with your client?" asked Max Moore in his deep, sonorous voice. That was code for, "Did your idiot really say that?"

"Some legal concepts are a little arcane," said Tony. That was code for "Yes, but he's my idiot."

"May I ask a question?" I asked.

"It's not …" Tony started to say.

"Of course," said Max Moore.

"How many underage drinkers have walked into your club?"

"He has done the best he can to be sure that everyone who enters is of legal age, certainly everything the law requires," said Mark Love.

"Really? He doesn't know that his club is popular among a certain clique of young adults? Some of whom are underage?"

"No, I don't know my club is popular with underage adults," Simmons said.

"Does the club have a Facebook account, Mr. Simmons?"

"Yes?" Simmons said, looking at his lawyers.

"I don't really see …" said Mark Love.

"The club is "liked" on Facebook by a number of people. Quite a few of them are under 21. Maybe it means something, maybe it means nothing. But it would not have been hard to check. It didn't take me more than 10 minutes."

"Checking a Facebook page is not serving drinks, nor is it required by law," said Mark Love.

In teaching me backgammon, my grandmother said the doubling cube could be used when either ahead or behind, but it was necessary to convince an opponent they had more to lose than gain if the game continued.

"Then let me draw a more direct line. How did your bartenders at SASA know that my client was of age? Or did they not check, as the law requires?"

"She had a fake identification."

"Really? Did she present it when she received a drink?" I turned to Linda. "Linda, were you carrying your I.D. when you went to the bar for a drink? Where did you carry it, if you weren't wearing any clothes?"

"No, people brought me drinks ... I think ...?"

"So, no one was asking you for identification? Okay."

"I ... I don't remember."

"That's right. You were too drunk to remember everything. So ..." I turned to Chuck Simmons. "Your bartenders possibly served a young, naked and obviously drunk woman more alcohol than she could tolerate. Probably good for business, but maybe not so good for the clientele. Possibly a violation of Washington State regulations. We can check with a phone call, I'm sure."

"That's not what we do. We have a policy against serving people who are too drunk."

"A policy unenforced does not exist. Does your establishment provide security for patrons?" I asked.

"Of course. It's policy to ensure the safety of our customers."

"So these are customers? Anyone may enter?"

"Our client misspoke, Ms. Jones," said Max Moore in that incredible voice. "The club has members, not customers."

"So we think Linda Williams was a long-time member? Perhaps since she was 18, or maybe 17? That could present problems all by itself. Or is 'private membership' a fiction to get around Washington State liquor laws that frown on obscenity?"

"Wait a minute ..." said Mark Love.

"I'm almost done," I interrupted him. "Your employees who were screening 'members' did not notice a young woman, two years too young to be there, so drunk that she is now incapable of recalling not only how much she had to drink but even whether she was asked for I.D., who could not have known whether anyone slipped her a drug that incapacitated her, whether everything that happened was consensual, whether she was assaulted ..."

"Ms. Jones, I think you've made your point," Max Moore broke in. "Obviously, everyone involved has some responsibility." He turned from looking at me to Tony.

"Tony, I think you and I might be able to expedite. Shall we let everyone go on about their day?"

"That might be productive," Tony said, still looking at me. Linda and her daddy left the high-rise together and after a quick good-bye, I walked back to our office through a fine Seattle rain, an intoxicating amount of adrenalin coursing through my system. I wished I could go to the gym, or go for a run.

I was still a little too wound up to concentrate on work, so I read through a copy of *Source of the Sound*, the local alternative newspaper. There was a story about the local homeless population that clustered around Pike Place Market.

Someone was feeding them. Local businessmen were outraged, since by feeding them "you just draw more ants to the picnic," said one, off the record of course. Politicians were outraged, because feeding the poor without going through proper channels and meeting certain standards "put the poor in danger." Gnawing hunger is not as dangerous, I suppose.

The *Source* wanted to blame someone, or congratulate them, or just be the publication to identify them, but no one knew where the food was coming from or who was paying for it. That mystery just added fodder for outrage.

Tony arrived back at the office an hour later.

"Where in hell did you learn that?" he asked me.

"Learn what?"

"What you did back there."

"What did I do?"

"Before today, I thought we'd lose this one. You used their arguments to validate our position. That was well done. They want to settle."

"I thought those were important questions to ask."

"Yeah, okay," Tony said as he walked away to make a phone call.

The next day, late afternoon, Claire buzzed me on the intercom.

"Ms. Jones, there's a Mark Love here, from the firm of Moore & Associates, to deliver some papers. Can you check them in?"

That was odd. Normally she'd just take the papers and drop them on my desk in order of intake.

When I came out, Mark Love was laughing with Claire. During the conference, I'd been preoccupied and hadn't realized how handsome he was. Today he wore a smile that flew around the room brightening everything it touched.

"That wasn't necessary, Claire. You didn't need to disturb Ms. Jones," he said, but then he turned to me.

"Moore & Associates was to provide transcripts of yesterday's conference. I thought I could save you some time by dropping them off on my way down to the Edgewater for a drink. Care to join me?"

"Thank you. That was very considerate," I said, trying not to be impressed. "Isn't the Edgewater too crowded at this time of day?"

"Our firm has a table reserved Monday through Friday," said Mark Love.

"I'll close up your office when I'm done, Ms. Jones," said Claire.

I almost snorted. She always called me Jessica, and I almost said "Who?"

"Thank you, Claire," I said, instead, then turned to Mark Love. "Let me grab my coat. I'll be right out."

Chapter 10

Sometimes men have a hard time discerning between being thoughtful and being pushy. I acknowledge it can be complicated, but much easier if they drop the assumption that women are the "weaker" sex.

"I can get us a ride," Mark said when we arrived at the lobby and saw it was misting outside.

"You know, I'd rather walk. I've been inside most of the day," I said, reaching into the messenger bag that served as my purse, briefcase, and gym bag to check that I had an umbrella. "A little damp won't matter."

"You sure?"

"Whether I want to walk or ride? That's not a tough one."

"Didn't know if you were just being polite," he said.

"No need to second guess. Generally I'm pretty easy to read, and if I say I'd rather walk, that's what I mean."

That came out sharper than I intended, but his asking if I was "sure" assumed either uncertainty on my part or that there was a need for him to "take care" of my emotions. I suppose I wanted to dismiss that assumption, or the thought that I was afraid of inconveniencing him. In any case, I didn't feel it necessary for me to reaffirm that I wanted to walk.

"If you'd like to get a car, just say so and we'll do that," I said, hoping to soften what may have seemed a little bitchy.

"No way. I never take cars. I always walk. Everywhere. I walked here from the East Coast to work in Seattle. Two days ago I walked to L.A. to deliver a summons. Then I walked back. Next week I'm walking to London for a conference on maritime law. They said I should swim, given the topic, but walking is what I do."

Okay, he made me laugh. That was good.

Seattle streets meander up and down and across the bluffs that form Puget Sound. As we headed down toward the water, they grew steeper. Wet gray concrete sidewalks sometimes reflect gray Seattle skies, but the city does not sit about and brood. Neon signs beckon from alleyways, First Street storefronts, taverns, and restaurants summon with warmth, and Pike Street Market flashes raucously with color and sound. It's fun.

"Maybe we should have taken the car?" Mark said as it started to rain even harder. "You're going to get wet."

"It's okay," I said, reaching into the messenger bag. I pulled out a telescoping umbrella I'd found at one of the tiny shops that sell unique and unusually expensive items. I popped it open and it would have been standard size, but another button unfolded it again to be easily large enough for two. I handed it to Mark.

"We can share," I said.

He laughed. "Never seen one of those. After yesterday, I should have known you'd be prepared."

"What do you mean?"

"That was impressive, what you did to me in that informal conference. I should thank you for the lesson on complacency. Obviously I didn't prepare as well as you did."

"You think if you had prepared better, the outcome would have been different?"

"Probably. But don't get me wrong. You did a great job."

"Why do you think the outcome would have been different?"

"Most of the time, the opposing side comes in looking to compromise, and they have a number in mind. I can usually flush that out with some pressure, and we start bargaining down from there, maybe even walking away paying nothing but a token to assuage feelings of honor. But I became complacent and forgot there are some really good lawyers in town, and you're obviously one of them."

"I don't know the outcome would have been different if you had prepared," I said nonchalantly as we turned the corner by the bronze pig at Pike Place Market. The scents from bakeries and coffee were inviting, but the rain was lifting other odors off the pavement at the market. Even they were more pleasant than those emanating from the tiny public park just beyond, now largely appropriated by street people and their dogs.

"Seriously? You don't think I would have been able to answer your arguments?"

"I'm just saying I don't know that it would have changed the outcome. And I don't know how relevant that is to your statement that you hadn't prepared."

There was a pause that lasted until we turned down the steep street that provided access under the Alaskan Way viaduct and across the railroad tracks to the waterfront. Someone, or someones, had cut an opening in the chain-link fence intended to keep street people from setting up camp in the dry dirt under the highway, above the dangerous tracks below, should someone tumble down the slope. I looked down the tracks, wondering if I could see my apartment building.

"Why don't you think my preparation would have made a difference?" asked Mark.

"Because I didn't prepare any arguments at all. I was just there to keep my client in line."

I turned my head in his direction, not so he could see me smile but to watch his reaction. He looked at me, started to say something, stopped, started to say something, and stopped again. When he looked down at his footing as we crossed the tracks, so did I.

The Edgewater is the name of the hotel. The bar and restaurant have a different name, but it's the giant, red neon cursive "E" that signals the location to the world. It's built on a pier over the waterfront.

As we approached the front doors, a large, dark silver car, nondescript if you didn't look too closely, sat closest to the valet station.

"Max is here. He offered to pick us up," Mark said, nodding at the car.

"What is that?"

"A Bentley Continental GT."

"It's beautiful. Next time, I'll accept the ride." I put my hand on his arm and made him look at me. I now knew why Mark asked twice if I really wanted to walk, but I doubted Max Moore, or his driver, waited too long for me to change my mind.

The log interior of the hotel recalls the time when lumber, not software, was Seattle's contribution to the world; when Weyerhaeuser was king, not Microsoft and Amazon. A table for eight was set along the window in the bar. It was the only one with a white linen table cloth. At the head sat Max Moore. Three other seats, backs to the window, were occupied.

Mark pulled out the chair next to Moore for me, and he sat on my other side.

"Welcome, Ms. Jones!" said Moore. "It's good to see you again. Under better circumstances, to be sure." He smiled that brilliant, engaging smile. I found it disarming.

Two men and a woman sat across from me. Moore made introductions, but since then I've forgotten their names, except the woman was "Mary." The waitress came up and asked what I'd like to drink.

"May I have a tonic with a squeeze of lime?"

"Oh, come on," said Mark. "They have a really great Long Island ice tea."

I ignored him.

"Tonic with lime," I repeated to the waitress.

"You don't drink?" Mark asked as she walked away.

"I ordered a drink."

He sighed.

"You don't drink alcohol?"

"I do when I feel like it." Yes, I was using elbows and knees in my interaction with him. I didn't know why at the time, though I may have a better idea now. Sometimes we fall into a role with certain people. It just seems to be how we communicate. I didn't feel like being particularly compliant with him.

"So, Ms. Jones, how long have you been practicing law?" asked Max Moore, to break the silence. "May I call you Jessica?"

"Please do. May I call you Max?"

"Of course," he laughed.

"I came to work for Tony out of law school. I've been there about 14 months."

"Really!?" said Max Moore. "That's all? Well, after watching you yesterday, I can say that I wish you had applied to our firm."

"I did, actually."

"You did? And we didn't hire you?"

"I received a nicely written letter back to my inquiry. It indicated that Moore & Associates was not hiring. I thought that was odd, since I'd just seen an invitation to apply sent to an entire class at Stanford Law School. A college friend down there sent it to me, knowing I was looking for work."

The table was very quiet. Max Moore seemed to look right into me then, still wearing an easy smile. He took a just moment too long to reply. I could not tell if I'd pissed him off, or if my directness impressed him.

"We need to review our procedures. You are someone we should not have overlooked," he said then, and looked down the table. The man farthest from him took out a tablet and wrote something down.

The waitress arrived with my tonic, and a backup bottle with the top already off. It was Canada Dry, the brand I preferred. That may have been a coincidence, though I was beginning to feel that coincidence was a relative term around Max Moore.

"Thank you for the drink," I said, nodding toward my glass.

We chatted about mostly nothing for 10 minutes or so, then Moore looked at his watch.

"I really am sorry we don't have more time, Jessica. You are extremely interesting. Unfortunately, I have a function this evening and I'm afraid with Seattle's traffic I'm already late. Perhaps next time, you'll let us give you a ride." Moore smiled that easy, approachable smile, but this time, it didn't have much warmth.

He pushed back in his chair. As he rose, everyone else at the table started to get up as well, so I did, too.

"No no no, please, everyone stay seated. Get something to eat, enjoy the evening. It's on the firm." Moore looked around, gave a direct nod to Mark who was settling back down to my right.

The remaining five of us sat around talking. The woman across from me, Mary, seemed to feel, since I was a woman, we had a special bond and that I wanted to talk about children and clothes. I actually wanted to listen to what Mark and the man directly across from me were saying about a case that involved an engineer alleging he couldn't get a better job because large tech firms were colluding against hiring each other's employees.

Finally, I decided that if I was going to work out, I'd better head to the gym. I laughed appropriately when Mary told me how her nanny had handled one of Mary's children who seemed to be always acting out. The boy had already driven three nannies away and he was only six years old, she said with a pride I didn't quite understand.

"This is so much fun," I said, looking around the table. "But, I have to go. Thank you all."

"Already?" asked Mark. "Let's have something to eat. You have to be starved. The food here is great."

"I know it is. I've eaten here before," I said, smiling at him. "But I can't eat before I go to the gym. It just sits in my stomach. May I have a rain check?" That was true. I had decided to go to the gym before Mark showed up at my office.

"I'll walk you back," said Mark, starting to stand.

"No, it's not far. I'd just as soon walk alone. Perhaps I'll find a shop along the way that has a blouse I just can't live without." I put my hand on Mark's shoulder and made a great show of pushing him back down into his chair. Everyone laughed. I was a woman, therefore, I was a "shopper."

Except. Not.

Outside the Edgewater, the rain had turned back into a fine, penetrating mist. I left the umbrella in my messenger bag and enjoyed the feel of cool wetness on my face. The barely hidden contrivance of the gathering still going on behind me was perplexing. More would be revealed, I thought, then I laughed.

"Moore will be revealed," I said out loud.

Chapter 11

Vulnerability and manipulation are hard to tell apart. Honesty is key, motivation a factor. What if a person who seems vulnerable doesn't understand their own motivation? What if the other has difficulty with trust? Biology, psychology, happenstance.

"I've had a hard time not thinking about you since the other evening," Mark said on the phone after inviting me to dinner.

Pause.

"Are you still on the phone?" he asked.

"Yes."

"Did you hear me?"

"That you had a hard time not thinking about me? Yes."

"Any response?"

"It was very interesting meeting all of you. It must be a very different environment than I have working here with Tony Stevens."

"That's it?"

"Thank you for inviting me?"

"Okay. Wow. Okay. So, are you … will you … would you … I was thinking about 6:30."

"Can we make it a bit later? I'd like to get in a workout. I've missed the last couple of days."

"Sure. As late as you'd like," he said. I don't know if I detected hopefulness in his voice, or a bit of suggestiveness. But there was something just a bit off and I can't really describe what I was feeling, or why I was feeling it. It had something to do with his saying he'd been thinking of me. It made me feel as if I had an obligation to respond.

We agreed to meet at a small restaurant called Taj Palace, not far from Pike Place Market. It was anything but a palace, but the food was excellent: spicy, varied, and the clientele a fascinating blend of East Indians and locals. A table of six huge men, possibly athletes judging by their size, were having a quiet but intense conversation several tables away.

Mark and I talked about law school, the Pacific Northwest, our hobbies, and jokingly disagreed about whether bicycle riding or running was more dangerous in Seattle traffic. A couple of hours went by easily.

"Hey, this has been fun, but it's time for me to head home," I finally said. I pulled my billfold out of my bag and put my credit card on the table.

"What are you doing?" Mark asked.

"Paying for my half of dinner. Should we tip 20 percent? The waiter was very good," I nodded toward the man standing near the kitchen.

"I invited you to dinner. You don't have to pay!" Mark said.

"I know. But I want to."

"There's no obligation for anything if I buy you dinner, Jessica."

"There's always an assumption."

"I don't have that assumption."

"Well, then it's my assumption, and I'll work on that."

When the waiter came, Mark got out his credit card and put it on top of mine.

"Separate checks?" the waiter asked, confused.

"Just split it in half," I said.

"Then you pay more than your share. I had two glasses of wine," Mark said.

"My treat," I said, but I was laughing, and by then he was laughing too. That felt good. He had a wonderful laugh.

But, outside, he tried to kiss me on the mouth. I turned my head, stepped back, reached out and took his hand.

"A handshake?" he said. "Seems a little cold."

"No, you have very warm hands," I said to his frown.

I didn't know if he'd call again, but he did. And he called after that, too. We didn't really "date." We just did things. We went out to dinner, deciding one month we'd work our cuisine from Viet Nam to Egypt. Seattle is a diverse city, but it was hard finding a Syrian restaurant.

We went to functions together. We went skiing. There were times when I spent the night at his apartment, especially when we had plans to go someplace early the next morning, or if we were joining friends (usually one of the lawyers in his firm) on a boat somewhere. His apartment was spectacular, near the top floor of one of the newly-created downtown "lofts" that weren't really lofts at all.

The first time, I asked for a blanket and a pillow, saying I'd sleep on the couch.

"No, you take the bed. I'll sleep on the couch," he said.

"I didn't come over to throw you out of your own bed. I can sleep anywhere if I'm tired."

"Please take the bed?"

"No, thank you. I'll take the couch. And if you try to take the couch with me, I *will* let you buy the cab ride home."

Adding sex to a relationship can complicate things. Most women know this instinctively. Most men learn it the hard way. Pun intended.

You can fuck on the first date, but that creates the expectation you will fuck on the second, even if circumstances, mood, anything or everything else is entirely different. You can fuck for the first time on the third date, and expectations might be different for the fourth, but probably not.

For some reason, I wasn't ready to go there with Mark. Part of the reason was he expected me to as soon has he had fulfilled the "proper obligations" so it would not seem he was just looking for a romp.

Once, he brought in some Turkish food: seasoned rice in grape leaves, lamb and baklava. After dinner and a bottle of wine, he asked a question that I knew he'd been wanting to ask.

"Are you gay?"

"I don't think so."

"You don't *think* so? You don't know?!"

"I've never been with a woman. That's the only way I could be sure, right?"

"Well, we could find out if you like being with a man …?"

"I already know I like that."

"So you're not a virgin?"

"Nope. Are you?"

"No! Why would you ask?"

"I thought you wanted to talk about our sexual histories."

"I just asked if you were a virgin!" His voice was rising, slightly.

"You also asked if I was gay."

"Well yeah, but that was first."

"Why wasn't it second? It would seem that asking if I was a virgin should have been first, then whether I was straight, or gay. Speaking of which, are you gay?"

"No!"

"Bi? Or something a little more adventurous, maybe unspeakable?" I was laughing by then, and so was he.

It felt good. Mark was so smart, quite nice to look at, and it was nice to see what I saw when he looked at me. We didn't always do everything together, though. I would not ride bikes with him.

"I don't know how you can be out there, fighting cars and trucks for space and wearing only a tiny helmet," I said on more than one occasion when he went on a two-hour bicycle ride. "Careening down wet streets where a single pebble can send you into the hospital, or the morgue … I've already decided, I will *not* come identify your body."

"It's the only time I get to wear spandex," he said. "I don't know how you can be out there, in the rain, pounding the concrete, chewing through the cartilage of your hips, knees and ankles, a target for every car full of punks who think a runner girl is exactly what they want for lunch."

"I carry mace and I don't smell good," I shot back.

"You smell pretty good to me."

One day he invited me to dinner in Port Townsend on the other side of Puget Sound. The invitation was garnished with the promise of bison which I'd never tried before. It was delicious. The waiter talked us into trying a wild blackberry crisp with locally made ice cream. We were still talking as the last ferry was already 100 yards gone from the dock when we got to the terminal.

"We've only got one room, the suite on the third floor," said the manager of The Palace, one of the vintage Victorian hotels in town.

"That will work," I said, before Mark could turn and look at me.

We walked up the long first flight of stairs, then up the second flight, without words. We turned to the left and Mark fumbled at the lock with the old-fashioned brass key.

"You can't get it in? That does not bode well," I said just as the door swung wide. He pushed it open, then I pushed him further into the room as I bumped the door closed with my hip. When he turned, I put both arms around his waist and pulled his pelvis toward mine. He looked down at me and I put my mouth on his.

I was relieved he was a good kisser. I'd been with men where there wasn't "kiss compatibility." It's not a prerequisite for good sex, but it's important for … a connection.

He stepped back after a while. Without bumbling, he stripped me. First he unbuttoned my shirt, every once in a while looking into my eyes as if to be sure. Just to let him know, when my shirt came off, I turned my back to him so he could unhook my bra. When it was loose, I turned back to face him and let him pull it forward off my arms.

I liked the way he inhaled when he saw my breasts.

When he reached for the button of my jeans, I said, "My turn." I intended to savor every second of this. I unbuttoned his soft flannel shirt, and pushed it off one of his shoulders, then the other. Then, to be either sweet or funny, it didn't matter to me, he turned his back to me so I could pull the shirt off his arms.

Instead, I pulled his shirt as far as his wrists, then twisted the shirt-tail around the rest so it made kind of a rope.

"Hey …" he said, then turned around.

"Hush." I unbuckled his belt and unzipped his jeans. Behind the light blue thin cotton of his shorts, his cock was hard. I kneeled in front of him and ran the back of my hand up and down the bulge. Mark made small sounds.

I liberated his cock from the fabric and ran my tongue from the base to the tip. I did it again. Mark's breathing changed. I had my arms around his butt while I did this, and was not letting go. Eventually I went down on him until he was as deep as I could stand it, then I stood, turned him back around to undo the spontaneous restraint I'd created and tossed his shirt aside.

We kissed. My breasts felt electric against his chest as his hands spread across my back pulling me against him, hands both gentle and firm.

Finally, I took his hand and led him to the side of the bed that was covered with a large, heavy sheepskin comforter. I pulled back the sheets, sat on the edge to wiggle out of my jeans, then slid in and pulled the sheets to my chin. By then Mark was naked and he snuggled in beside me.

He kissed me again as his hand cupped the bottom of my breast, then gently played with my nipple. When his hand went below my belly, my legs spread apart as if with their own desire. His hand pressed against the spot that turns me inside out. My hips pushed against his hand and his touch consumed me. Suddenly he rolled over on top of me, I wrapped my legs around his hips and pulled him inside until his cock found the very end of me and I gasped.

I pushed against him and until I was completely outside myself and could feel my orgasm building and approaching and building and approaching until it was there and all that there was and I shuddered, waves radiating outward, my back pushing my hips to consume him.

His breathing shifted and he buried himself deeper as he filled me, waves breaking on a shallow reef. Then he kissed me all about the neck and face, and so gently on the lips. I don't remember when I ended up on top of him, but woke with my head on his chest sometime long after midnight.

Chapter 12

Having sex with someone changes brain wiring. Much of what we think and feel is the result of genes seeking to replicate themselves.

This didn't seem to happen with Mark, maybe because we'd already established a routine, or a relationship. Or maybe I was fooling myself and didn't think it changed things because we didn't talk about it.

Sex just added a dimension to what we already had. A very nice one.

We still just did things, like exploring new restaurants. We accompanied each other to work functions. We went skiing. We went on boat trips. But now, these evenings more often ended at his apartment, where we would make love in the lights of the city below.

He cleaned out a drawer for me in his bathroom and a shelf in his closet where I put some underwear and comfies I often wore when we woke up on a Saturday or Sunday morning, and he bought a hair dryer for me and installed a lit make-up mirror by the bathroom sink. But for the most part, I would begin my work-week from my own place, and spent most weeknights there as well.

After a few months of life like this, one Sunday morning Mark asked if I would like to move in with him.

"No, I don't think so," I said.

"Why not?"

"I'm not exactly sure, but I like having my own place. A place to go and pull myself together."

"You seem together when you're here."

"I know. It feels good with you."

He'd gone down to the bakery while I was in the bathroom and brought back two croissants, and two muffins with fresh blueberries. We tended to eat these in little pieces. He tore a corner off a croissant and put it on my plate.

"Why not move in?"

"I'm just not sure if 'more' would feel more good."

"Why not give it a try?"

"I don't want to ruin what we have."

"What exactly do we have, Jessi? What are we?" he asked.

"What do you mean? We're 'us.' "

"Are we just dating, are we boyfriend/girlfriend, are we exclusive to each other, what?"

"Do you want to see other people?" I asked.

"That was unfair. I just asked you to move in with me."

"Okay, it was," I admitted.

Looking out at the city, I sipped my coffee. It had real coconut milk, something Mark stocked in his refrigerator as soon as he learned I liked it. Like eating croissants in little bites.

"I'm not interested in dating other people. I like being with you," I finally said. The relief that filled his eyes could be felt across the table. Outside the courtroom, Mark is really bad at hiding his emotions.

"Me either," he said, very quickly.

I got hit on all the time, whether at work, out for a drink with the girls, sometimes even when I was with Mark. Half the time, I wasn't aware of it, half the time I was, but whatever the time it didn't really matter. I had a pretty good life going with a man I adored and who adored me. There wasn't a lot to be gained from dating around.

Mark got hit on a lot, too. It didn't bother me much, unless the woman was indiscreet or disrespectful, or just stupid.

One summer evening at a restaurant built on piers over the water, a woman staggered over to our outside table.

"Hi honey," she said to me, "you know something? This guy's really hot." Then she sat right down. She was a decade or two older than we were, but still very beautiful. She had a thick mane of blond hair, and if it wasn't her natural color, she spent a lot of money on it. Her clothes were expensive too, and she said she was in town for a convention of medical prosthetic sales reps.

"Replacement parts," she said. "Everything from hips to knees to tits," she said, "but not mine." She grabbed Mark's hand and put it on her breast.

"See, real," she said while looking at me, as if to imply mine were not (they are) or inadequate (they're not).

She started to unbutton her blouse but the waiter talked her giggling friends into coming over and taking her away.

I think Mark was tempted, or maybe intrigued is the better word. A man's voice changes when his libido is engaged; he has a slight edge, a slight energy that can be felt more than heard or seen. I don't really know how to explain it, but most women can sense it. Maybe men can sense it in women, too.

I heard that slight edge of "the hunt" in Mark's voice after the woman was pulled away from our table. It made me a little jealous, more so than the sight of her exposed skin. Mark and I laughed about it later, but nobody knew how close that bitch had come to going for a swim with sea lions searching for scraps below our table.

But it went both ways. Once we were at a gathering in the top-floor bar of the building that housed his firm. As he and I were standing talking, every once in a while I caught Max Moore looking me over.

Mark left to get me a drink. I walked over to the window looking out over the Sound. It was one of those days Seattle offers up once in a while that makes everything breathtakingly beautiful. Huge freighters moved across the Sound to Tacoma, while others headed out to sea. Sunlight danced across the water as wakes folded back from each bow. From this height the waves were simple lines overlapping and moving through each other, seemingly unaffected by the interaction.

"It's a view, isn't it?" said a voice at my shoulder, soft, yet so deep it seemed to vibrate inside me.

I turned to see Max Moore standing what some would think was just a millimeter too close, his silver mane, a face that had seen time and weather but eyes so blue and laughing I caught my breath. A cascade of desire swept over me.

"Yes, it *is*," was all I could say, feeling like I was 13 years old, again. I was shocked at my physical reaction to this man. Though he was standing slightly too close to me, I wanted him to stand closer. I wanted those eyes to laugh for me and with me. I wanted to hear that voice again right now!

As we made small talk, there was an instant familiarity. Then I realized as he spoke, I was getting aroused, and he hadn't even put a finger on me. That's a good thing, too, because I probably would have put that finger in my mouth. He wore no obvious cologne that I could detect, but there were waves of some sort of scent from him that gave me images of being naked in front of a warm log fire someplace far, far away from this office building.

Mark got back with our drinks.

"Mark, I've been wanting to congratulate you on the Maersk case. Jessica and I were just talking about how quickly you analyze and get to the core issues," said Moore, looking at me and nodding, as if for assent.

That wasn't at all what we had been talking about, but I couldn't disagree right then. By making me complicit in the lie, Max had put me at a disadvantage. But I wanted to be there, owning a secret with this man!

"Hi, Max," said Mark. "I'm glad you two found each other. It's been a while since we all met at that informal conference."

"The conference on the Seattle Area Social Association … Max was so gracious when you took me to the Edgewater afterwards," I said.

"Ouch!" said Mark. "The conference where you spanked my client."

"Our client," corrected Max. "She caught us both a little flat-footed. Good lawyering … and Jessica, I remember you pointing out that we'd missed a chance to hire you," said Moore. He laughed with a self-deprecating shake of his head, leaning slightly toward me, as if he could not believe his own stupidity.

"That isn't what I said. Just that I'd applied to your firm." I was glad that Moore remembered me after such a brief encounter. "I would have loved to come work for you out of law school." At the moment, I thought I'd have done anything for him right out of law school.

I excused myself to the ladies room to gather my wits. Some older men can be erotic. Max Moore was one of those, exuding an aura of brains, confidence, and power that was sheer aphrodisiac, with eyes that seemed to be amused at a joke that only he and I shared.

"You okay?" Mark asked when I got back to his side. "You left in a hurry. Max had very nice things to say about you."

"I'm fine, I just had too much coffee today and didn't want to leave Max before you got back from the bar," I said. I did not ask what nice things Max Moore had to say, because I really wanted to know and knew that would show in my voice, just as "the hunt" had shown in Mark's voice for the blond.

But those were exceptional circumstances. I was happy with Mark, and he was happy with me. I can't tell you why having my own place was important when Mark asked me to move in with him, but it was. We were enjoying life, going places together, sometimes together for five days at a stretch when we could, off to see places we'd never seen.

Then one day, on a secluded beach in Panama, Mark presented me with a brilliant diamond about the size of a fat blueberry.

"Do you want to do this?" was his way of proposing.

"It won't ruin what we have?" was my way of saying yes.

We were a lot alike.

Chapter 13

It's odd how easily we fall back into old roles and reactions when returning "home" to spend time with those who surrounded us when we were growing up.

Maybe it was also odd my family had not met Mark before we drove down to give them the news, but we weren't that kind of family.

My parents seemed older, but they had a comfortable life with mom's pension from the city and my dad doing odd jobs as a carpenter. My sister Jordan had gained a lot of weight and was battling depression after getting married to a sweet guy we'd both known in high school who got drunk at their reception and cornered me to say he had always loved me and marrying my sister was second best.

I told him to never say that again, and he didn't.

Their two boys were five and seven and barely under control.

Grandmama did not seem to have changed much at all. She and I talked on the phone once a week, but always briefly, as if phone companies still charged by the minute.

"You are good, Jessi?" she would ask.

"I'm good Grandmama," I'd say. I'd tell her a little about what I was doing; dinners, work, and I told her I was seeing Mark, about what he and I did together.

"It is good you are happy, Jessi," she'd say when she was through with the conversation.

"I love you Grandmama," I always said in return.

"Yes, Jessi. I love you," she'd reply as if the words were hard for her to say and had to be pulled out of her. "But you always know this, yes?" She'd add, as if to tell me the words themselves were not that important.

On this trip to my parents' house, I sat next to Grandmama on the couch, her dark hair brushed back and held in a bun, my dark hair brushed back in a pony tail. We actually held hands for a while.

"You two ..." said my mother once when she walked by, with a small shake of her head.

Mark sat in the big chair where my mother sat when she and my father watched one of their favorite shows on TV. He protested he didn't want to take her chair, but she insisted.

"Mark, I have to be in the kitchen. Please, sit! May I bring you something to drink?" my mother said.

When everyone was in the same room, except my sister's husband who had taken his two sons outside to blow off sugar-induced energy, we made the announcement.

"We came down to tell you that Mark and I are going to be married. We'd like you to come to Seattle for the ceremony in a month," I said.

"Seattle? Why not here?" were the first words out of my father's mouth.

"We'd prefer Seattle," I said, even a little surprised at his obtuseness. "It's going to be a small wedding. Just family."

"It would be easier for the two of you to travel than the seven of us," said my father.

"This isn't about making it convenient for you," I said. "It's not that far."

"James," said my mother. "We can make the trip, and we can take Marie. Jordan and Bill can take their minivan with the kids. It's not that far."

"It will take a day of travel there, and a day back, that means two nights of hotels…" said my father.

"Mr. Jones?" Mark interjected. "I've already made arrangements for your family at the Edgewater Hotel in Seattle. It will cost you nothing. It's a wedding present from my firm. Please don't worry about that," he said.

That ended the discussion, though I was still a little chipped at my father for being such a jerk.

"Do you want some help organizing your wedding, dear?" my mom asked.

"No, mom, it's going to be easy. We don't want the hassle or drama of a big wedding. Besides, I could never compete with what you and Jordan put together."

I actually think she was relieved. My mother and my sister had created the wedding of "their" dreams, and it had been far more elaborate, and expensive, than anything I would ever want. I think that's why mother was so discreet with her question.

As the evening went on my father almost seemed to become proud of me, as he learned from Mark that his daughter the city lawyer was respected and sometimes referred to in a *Seattle Times* story.

But if I was almost the son my father had always wanted, Mark was certainly proving himself to be. He owned my mother, too. He told the story about how I would not move in with him, though he was quick to say that's not why he proposed. He told stories of our travels, and about his work. Not in a boastful way, just in passing. Entertaining.

"So Mark, will your parents be coming out to the wedding," my mother asked at dinner. "Do they like Jessica as much as we like you?"

"No, Mrs. Jones, my parents will be out of the country. They have sent their congratulations," Mark replied.

We never went to Mark's hometown, which was on the East Coast, to see his parents. He was estranged from his family, I don't know if that was his choice or theirs, he never explained. Something happened there Mark didn't talk about.

Whenever I brought up going to see them, he'd say he would think about it, but eventually he'd say no, that it wasn't going to happen. I finally quit bringing it up when he'd just look at me with a smile and wait silently for me to stop.

Mark bowled my family over with his laugh, his graciousness. At the dinner table, if Mark coughed with something in his throat, my mother and sister raced to the kitchen to get him a glass of water. If he just cleared his throat, everyone would stop talking to hear what he had to say.

I teased him about it later. Maybe I was jealous. Some of that adulation should have been mine, after all. I may have been making half what Mark made, but my income was still six figures. It was quite small of me, but … biology, psychology, happenstance.

Grandmama was quiet before, during and after dinner, not that she talked that much anyway. I asked her why, and she said something in French that I didn't understand about owl eyes being larger than owl mouths, and the source of wisdom.

I thought she might be embarrassed that her English wasn't any better than it was. She could never understand why her accent was still so strong, her phrasing not right. "Your accent is beautiful! I hope it never goes away!" I always told her. But she would just set her mouth into a grim line and give a quick shake of her head.

She got up to help my mother out in the kitchen, though from what I knew of each of them, Grandmama could have done the job much faster without my mother's help, even in my mother's own house.

Mark and I took Grandmama back to her house. She insisted on sitting in the back seat of Mark's Audi, not in the front. "You sit next to your husband," she said flatly, giving no room for disagreement. This made it hard for Mark or me to talk with her, and she offered no small talk. I thought at first she would bolt from the car when we got to her house, but she could not find the door handle of the modern car.

I got out and opened it from the outside, just beating Mark, who walked around from his side.

"Jessi, I will make your dress for this wedding," said my grandmother when she stood outside the car.

"Grandmama, I don't need a wedding dress. It's not like I'm a virgin in the 1700s."

"There are no virgins before marriage anymore. This is a good thing," said Grandmama. "But I will make your dress. Jessi…?" Grandmama never, ever asked for anything. This was a plea. I had no choice.

"Of course. I would like that," I said.

"*Merci. Merci beaucoup.*" Out of her handbag, she pulled a very old, soft and worn measuring tape. Right there beside the car, she took some quick measurements.

"You are stronger than in high school," she said to me, before putting the tape back in her purse. "But not much larger."

"I lift weights for exercise," I said.

But ignoring me, she turned to Mark.

"For the wedding, you will wear a suit? Something dark?"

"I certainly can," he said.

"Dark gray would be best," she said. Then she turned back to me, and held my face in her two hands. "My Jessi," she said, holding me there for a moment. Her eyes might have moistened, I could not be sure, before she let go and walked to her house, not turning around as she let herself in.

"I don't think your grandmother likes me," Mark said when we got back in his car.

"No, she's just hard to speak with at times. She's hard to read. She likes you," I said.

Chapter 14

On one hand, marriage is a contract with inadequate disclosures, poorly defined responsibilities, and little or no consideration given to termination. On another, it's a ceremony marking an event of deep meaning and great significance.

"Tony, you can do marriages, right?" I asked him after a conference on a case.

"I'm licensed. Why?"

"Want to marry me off?"

"Not particularly. I prefer thinking of you as single, and imagining our possibilities."

"Tony! That is SO wrong!" I said in mock outrage. We'd allowed a certain amount of sanitary innuendo into our working relationship, which may not have been a good idea but it didn't go much past his expressing interest and my expressing offense.

Tony just shrugged. "Who's the lucky young man?"

"Mark Love."

"Mark Love …?"

"He was the lawyer with Max Moore representing the Seattle Area Social Association."

"Ah yes. Fun case. Handsome young man. Well-connected. Good for you."

"No congratulations?"

"Jessi …" Tony started to say something, then he changed his mind. "Congratulations."

"That isn't what you started to say."

"No, it's not."

"What were you going to say?"

"If I wanted to say it, I would have said it. Congratulations is what I have to say." Tony reached over to put the papers in front of him into a folder, and then the folder into a leather briefcase so scuffed it looked almost like suede.

"I can't believe you haven't gotten a new briefcase. That one is really beginning to show its years," I said.

"We all are. Whatever."

"So, will you do the ceremony?"

"That depends. Will you be leaving me to work with your new husband?" Tony asked. All I could see over the top of the brief case were his eyes, and they were looking at me intently.

"Don't be silly. I love working in the Seattle Tower. At least IT has some class!" My answer was too flip, but I was a little disappointed at his lack of response to my news.

"You'd think some of it would have rubbed off on me," said Tony. "So?"

"No, Mark and I haven't talked about that, but I don't think it would work very well."

It was true. Odd as it may seem, Mark and I didn't talk about our careers very much. When together, we tended to avoid work discussions. It's not like we had an agreement or anything. It's just that we did law all day. We didn't want to do it all night, too.

"Yes, I'd be honored." Tony smiled as he closed the case, but it was half-hearted. "Tell me how you want the paperwork to read."

Even though "Jessica Love" sounded like the name of a porn star, I planned to take Mark's name. I never liked "Jessica Jones," and "Jessica Jones-Love" was only slightly better than Jessica Love-Jones," which sounded like an affliction.

We were married in a small chapel nestled among tall fir trees on Vicente Island, a mostly undeveloped and little known place in Puget Sound. To get there, we rented a small tour boat, and arranged to have an early dinner at Anthony's on the wharf after we got back.

Grandmama took me by the hand to walk through the chapel as soon as we landed. I don't think it was more than 25 feet wide and 50 feet long, built of rough-hewn timbers and white plaster. There was a small dais where Tony, Mark and I would stand for the ceremony.

"This will do," she pronounced.

"Do you remember the last time we were in church?" I asked her. She shook her head.

"The service for Sam. You made me go. I never thanked you for that."

"You are thanking me now, I think," she said, with a rare smile. Then she took me back to get dressed. The midnight blue gown, if you will, was long-sleeved but exposed most of my shoulders. It had a deep but not revealing cleavage. It was cut just above my knees in front but in back it draped in a suggestion of a train to my mid-calf.

"Grandmama, it's so beautiful! How did you do this?" I said when I put it on for the first time, a half-hour before the wedding.

"Jessi, I know you," she said.

"Yes, but …"

"And, I want you to wear this."

She opened a black velvet box. Inside was a blue stone, I assumed it was a sapphire. It was about the size and shape of a walnut, but cut with more facets than I could count. She fastened it around my neck on a thick silver chain, where it shimmered with light just at my breast bone.

"Grandmama, where did you get this?" I asked.

"That is not important. It goes with the dress," she said, in the voice she used to end conversations she did not want to have.

When Mark, wearing a dark gray suit, saw me, he said, "My god." He and I stood beside each other greeting everyone as they came into the church, he shook hands, I gave hugs, mostly. When everyone was seated, Tony said "Jessica? Mark?" from the opposite end of the building where he was waiting.

We turned and walked together, holding hands, down the aisle.

I did not ask my father to "give me away," nor do I think he was disappointed. There was no "Till death do you part," or similar language. In simple terms, Tony talked about love in ways I could not imagine coming from him, love as a giving and receiving, constantly changing, never perfect but an ocean between two shores, sometimes calm, sometimes with the occasional storm, but always the same ocean. It was lovely.

"You may kiss the bride," he said when he was done. Mark and I kissed.

"I may kiss the bride," Tony then said, and everyone laughed as I gently put my hand on his face and pushed him back. Then I gave him a hug.

We walked back down the aisle to light applause. Sarah, Lilly and Claire were sitting behind my family, and the two women with whom I lived when I first got to Seattle. That was pretty much it for friends and family on my side. Three couples Mark and I knew from his workplace, with whom we skied and boated, were on his side, but no family.

"Did you tell your family were getting married?" I asked him.

"Yes," he said after a pause. "Promise," he added with a smile.

"I thought Max Moore and his wife were coming."

"Max had a last-minute conflict, something that couldn't be postponed. He and Claudia sent their regrets."

"Really? What was the conflict?"

"He didn't say."

"It's a good thing we didn't ask him to officiate. Or was that why he didn't come?" I asked.

"He seemed perfectly okay when I told him you'd already asked Tony. I don't think that had anything to do with it. Something came up. Max has clients all over the world."

There was a break in the weather as we walked outside, though the entire island was rain forest often swathed in cloud. Everyone followed us out of the chapel and we all stood around talking. I watched for a while, then decided to rescue Tony from my mother who had pigeon-holed him as soon as he left the church.

"Thank you," I said. "That was beautiful."

"Well, it wasn't all mine," Tony said.

"He said he stole it from a Sufi magician," said my mother.

"A Sufi mystic," Tony corrected.

"What do you know of Sufi mystics?" I chortled.

"Just enough to know that I don't," was his cryptic reply.

"Well, thank you, and the Sufi too," Mark said.

"You're welcome. Is the bar open on the boat?"

He turned to my mother and said, "Thank you for your nice words. I absolutely have to wet my throat," and without giving her a chance to respond, he walked down the path to the dock where the tour boat waited to take us back to Seattle.

"Jessi, come, we need to change your clothes," said my grandmother. I hadn't realized she had walked up behind me.

"I thought we'd do it back on the boat?"

"No. The wedding is over. We'll do this now," she said. "We don't change clothes in a bathroom on a boat."

So we went back to the room reserved for the bride and I put on the skirt and jacket I'd worn out to the island. Grandmama carefully but loosely folded the dress she had made, then stood behind me to remove the gem around my throat.

"It is so beautiful. Where did you get it?" I asked her again.

"You will find out soon enough. Now is not the time for this story." She put the sapphire back in its velvet-lined box and the box back in her purse. "You have people waiting, your husband is waiting."

Saying that, she held my face in her two hands, her blue eyes looking into mine of the same shade. I saw hers were moist.

"*Ma chère*," she said. "*Ma petite* Jessi. Remember, please: *tout passe, tout lasse, tout casse*."

"But Grandmama, this is a time to be happy!"

"I am happy for you, *ma chère*. But is important to know that moments end, then you can fully experience them. This is beautiful, but it is beautiful for what it is now, not because it will be forever."

"Oh, Grandmama," I said, and taking her hands in mine, kissed the back of her fingers.

"You go now, to your husband. I will finish this."

She and I were the last to board the boat. When we were on deck, the horn blew a single long, vibrating bellow, then a minute later three shorter notes and the boat backed away from the dock.

Mark was weaving everyone together when I found him. He had my father and Jordan's husband talking to one of his friends from work who knew everything about old Dodge trucks like the one my father owned.

Claire was talking to my mother. They were both laughing loudly at something. Tony was talking to the two lawyers from Mark's firm, Sarah and Lily were talking to their dates, and my two friends from college were talking to the bartender. He was cute and going to get very lucky before the day was done.

Mark brought me a glass of champagne, which I downed, and asked for another when the steward walked by. I hadn't realized that I had been nervous, but did now that I was beginning to unwind. I wasn't particularly looking forward to dinner with all these people, but knew I had to go through it to get through it.

By the time dinner was finished, I'd had a few more glasses of champagne. Mark and I stood as the waiter came around to take orders for dessert.

"We have to go on our honeymoon!" Mark said. "I mean …" and he waved his hand around me as if anyone could understand what he chose not to say aloud. Everyone laughed as we waved our good-bye. Outside, a Bentley limo was purring at the curb, the driver holding the door open.

"What's this?" I asked.

"Max offered us a limo ride to the airport for our honeymoon, but we're not going straight there. Our plane leaves at six in the morning."

"Where are we going?"

"To the Coliseum Hotel."

"No, not now. Where are we going on our honeymoon!? He had asked me to let him handle all those arrangements. I snuggled next to him, and put my hand high on the inside of his thigh.

"Where would you like to go?" he said, responding by putting his hand on my thigh, finding warm skin. His touch made me open my legs just a little wider, which he welcomed by sliding his hand just a little higher.

"It's a big world. You told me to pack swimsuits and clothes for warm weather. Do you want me to guess?" I squirmed a little bit, then reached down and took his wrist and pulled his hand higher.

"Sir, did I hear you say the Coliseum Hotel?" said the driver over the intercom, on the other side of dark glass that separated his seat from ours. "My instructions were to go to the airport."

"The Coliseum …" Mark started to say.

"May we drive around for a while and enjoy the ride?" I interrupted him

"Certainly, ma'am," said the driver. "The car is yours for as long as you want it."

"Why don't you drive north. If we get to Canada, turn around and drive back to the Coliseum Hotel," I said. The champagne was having an effect.

"Yes, ma'am." The intercom clicked back off.

By the time the conversation had ended, I had unzipped Marks pants.

"Oh, God, Jessi," he said. "What if the driver can see?"

"Then he can see," I said. "But that glass is pretty dark." Mark tried to reciprocate, but was having trouble touching me the way I wanted, so I took my panties off and hiked the skirt up around my waist.

"Are you sure they can't see?" said Mark.

"No, but I am sure I don't care," I said. "I also doubt this is the first time anyone has ever had sex in this car, and it won't be the last."

I unbelted Mark's pants then, and pulled them down to his knees. I climbed on top of him and slid down the shaft that was sending a pulsing code of desire.

"Is this the champagne?" Mark asked.

"What do you care?" I responded.

"Hush," I added, when he actually started to answer.

His fingers soon found the buttons on my blouse, then the hooks on my bra. I grabbed one sleeve and then the other and pulled my hands free of the sleeves and straps. I unzipped my skirt. Fortunately, I was able to just pull it over my head.

"You're naked in this car with me. There is a man we don't know in the front seat and we don't know if they can see what's going on!" Mark whispered.

"Do you like that?" I asked, in the same whisper.

"Kinda," he said. I had his shirt unbuttoned then and leaned against him, my breasts against his chest, my mouth on his neck. I was still holding myself up with my thighs, but then relaxed a little to let myself down further.

He put his mouth on mine, and as the car swayed so slightly, we brought our breathing into and out of each other's mouth into sync.

"Ma'am, this would be a good place to turn around," said the driver from the front seat a while later.

"This will be fine. Take us back to Seattle, please," I said.

"Yes Ma'am."

"Driver, can we operate the windows from back here?" I said after a minute. It was a test.

"Yes ma'am. But we have climate control. Is it too warm?"

"So you CAN hear every word we say?"

"I can turn off the intercom."

"That's alright."

I put my finger to Mark's lips. I rolled down the two windows of our limo. It was not yet dark, but a rosy gray dusk that can fill northern Washington skies during summer evenings. A trucker honked twice in appreciation as we drove past.

"Jessi …" Mark said.

"Hush, baby," I said, and went back to kissing him while fresh cool air swirled around our bodies.

His arms around my waist pulled me closer.

"Oh, Jessi," he said softly, just as I gasped and said "Oh, Mark!" as an orgasm rolled over me.

We did not move for about five minutes, except when Mark rolled the windows back up.

"Driver, I spilled a bit of champagne. Is there a towel?" I said at last.

"Yes, ma'am, in the compartment behind the front passenger seat. There's also a bottle of warm, carbonated water, just water and unsweetened, in the cabinet behind my seat, if you'd like some over ice."

I appreciated his delicacy.

I took a towel, spritzed it with soda, cleaned Mark and myself, and we got dressed. I folded into his arms and was almost asleep by the time we got to the Coliseum Hotel. Mark got me to the room where we both went to sleep until a wake-up call came six hours later, so we did not miss our plane to Greece.

Chapter 15

Leaving a home where life has changed us can feel quite melancholy. Even when the future has wonderful promise, there's a feeling of roots being pulled from the soil. Such is "place."

I would not let Mark help me move out of the funky little apartment by the railroad tracks below Pike Place Market and into his much nicer townhouse loft. I spent a Saturday morning moving my things and had no idea why the apartment had such a hold on me.

Mark's townhouse looked out on Lake Union, but was not a work-day walk from the office. We usually drove together and parked in a space provided by Mark's firm in the basement of their building. From there, rain or shine I enjoyed the five-block morning walk through the city to my own office in the elegant Art Deco Seattle Tower, once the tallest in the West.

I think Mark was a little jealous that I liked my offices so much.

"It was built in 1928 before real earthquake standards of construction, the elevators are slow, the offices small …"

"My office is closer to the water," I'd retort when I was feeling feisty, knowing that ruffled a feather.

"Yes, but from my office, you can actually see the water," was his standard reply, poking fun at the fact that while architecturally amazing, the 28-floor "tower" was now buried in the shadows of buildings twice as tall.

From his office in the US Bank Centre at 6th & Union, he could see Puget Sound on a clear day. Moore & Associates had a complete floor, as befitting a firm made up of the most-aggressive, best-educated, and well-supported lawyers in Seattle. Some of the lawyers at Mark's firm had staff who had staff to do research.

Lawyers there had offices on the perimeter with windows, while the staff "bull-pen" was open and in the center. The four partners had corner offices, and the senior lawyers, or those generating more income for the firm, had a view of the sound or Mt. Rainer. Competition within the firm was scored by whose office was where.

"They moved my office today!" Mark said once after work. "I have a view of the Sound!"

"Why? What? …" I asked.

"I think it's for my work on the Shell Oil case. Max said something about that last week. The fees were substantial."

"They just move your office in the night?"

"Yeah. I came in and Lori, our morning receptionist, said, 'Congratulations. Your name is on a new door.' She pointed toward the west side so I walked down the line found my office about four doors down from Max. They even put my photos back on the desk exactly where they were."

"Who was in that office before?"

"William Olsen. He handles trusts and wills, mostly. That's not where our revenue growth has come from."

"Does he have your old office?"

"I don't know. I didn't check," Mark said.

My boss, Tony, had an office on the floor above mine. There was no integration, except by phone. I had my staff, Tony had a couple of assistants and Joanie, a woman with a silver bun held together with what looked like a chopstick who was probably 20 years older than he was, had worked for him for decades and who put up with exactly zero bullshit.

Tony lived across from our building. He said "Not my responsibility" whenever asked about providing parking for employees. In fact, Tony seemed to regard cars as a nuisance. He walked where he needed to go in downtown Seattle, and didn't go far from there. Most of the time it was from his apartment to Sami's Café where he ate breakfast, then to work in our building, then to a different restaurant for dinner.

Even for a parking space, I wouldn't trade my office for a corner suite in the tallest building in Seattle. It's hard to describe why the old brick building with a gilt-and-black marble interior felt so much like home to me, but it did. Such is "place."

My little team was busy. Not many of our cases went to court, but sometimes I wasn't able to negotiate a plea acceptable to both my client and the DA's office, especially if it was a drug case we had to argue under federal jurisdiction.

Federal cases were tougher, and we didn't win them all. There was the case of Sheri, who was twenty-five and originally from Bellingham. She had been living in Seattle since she dropped out of college her junior year. She thought she was a singer who had no reason to waste any more time in school.

She did pretty well in gigs with well-known local bands. But a "friend" suggested if she really wanted her career to take off, she would have to cut a demo record and take her band to Los Angeles and put it in front of some studio executives. It would be expensive, but he could "help her out."

All she had to do was bring a backpack from Canada to the US. Ferries come and go between Victoria, British Columbia and Anacortes in Washington. But passengers on those ferries have to go through Customs. Not everybody is searched, but honestly, if there's a profile for stupid drug mule, she was it. They went through her backpack and found heroin and hashish.

What they didn't find was any credibility in her story that she had picked up the wrong pack when getting off the ferry. It didn't help that she had grown up in Bellingham, her father's company built aluminum boats, and she had been back and forth across that border like some people go to the beach for a weekend.

Deborah Riddle, the police woman who "helped me" when I was in high school, was on the list of witnesses. She was now working for the feds. I thought for only a moment about objecting because of our personal background, but I doubted Riddle would remember me and didn't particularly want to open that can of worms.

As trial approached, Lily kept combing the facts for a plausible story that would generate sympathy, which Lily did better than any of us. Sarah investigated the behavior of border agents to see if one of them might have stumbled in a way we could get some or all of the charges tossed. I dug through the laws of both countries, looking for an opening.

I told Sheri and her father that the odds were stacked against them. They insisted she was innocent, it was a mix-up. The federal attorney was willing to bargain down to two years, with time served, less than half of what she faced if found guilty on all counts.

Sheri and I stood together in the courtroom when the verdict came back. She fell toward me when found guilty on every charge, and fainted when Judge Burns gave her five years in prison. She had to be helped from the courtroom to where she would be prepped for prison.

On the way out of the courtroom, Deborah Riddle was waiting for me in the hallway.

"You did a good job but she got exactly what she deserved," Riddle said.

"You told me that once before, and you were wrong then, too."

"We've met?"

"It was about 15 years ago. My name was Jessica Jones, then."

"Ohhh …" she said, and I saw her retrieve the memory. She started to say something else, but I wasn't much interested in reestablishing the connection and just walked away. I was also feeling disappointment in the verdicts even though I'd anticipated that outcome.

But most of the time, we were pretty successful. We developed a reputation as the firm to hire if the client was female and money was no object. I didn't do the billing, just kept track of my hours — but I know that not one phone call, sheet of copy paper or paper clip was unaccounted for. Tony made sure of that.

One day he told me he was taking me to lunch.

"Tony, I can't. I've got to keep after a case that's going to trial on Monday. Lily is bringing lunch back to the office."

"Yes, you can. We're going to lunch."

We left when Tony was ready, even though I wasn't. He was usually easy-going, but he seemed tense, if not grim. We wandered down to Pike Place Market, where he always ate — sometimes at Place Pigale, sometimes at Pike Place Chinese Cuisine, sometimes at the Soup & Salad MFG. Company. Sometimes from a vendor on the corner. But always Pike Place Market.

"Tony, why do you always come here to eat? You basically live in a six-block area of Seattle," I asked.

"It's comfortable," he said, preoccupied.

"Is it because you like watching all these people?" I asked, as a man without a shirt walked a pit bull past us, accompanied by a woman twice his size with bright purple hair and pushing a baby carriage with another dog inside.

Tony stopped, forcing me to stop as well.

"See that truck?" he asked. There was a produce truck parked in the middle of the street near a giant bronze pig. The back-end was open and the driver was muscling a handcart piled with boxes onto the lift gate, which he lowered to the ground, then pirouetted around to push the load into the maw of the market.

"Yes. So?"

"That was my job for seven years. Through college. While I went to law school. Every day, or night, depending on my class schedule. Hauling what needed to be hauled to this market. Loading, unloading, trying not to run over people who had fallen down drunk at 3 a.m. Getting up to go to class. Doing it over again.

"So I don't come down here to watch all these people, as you say. I come down here because these people *are* my people," Tony said.

As if to make the point, a man in rags walked by and said, "Hiya, Tony!"

"Hey, Leo. How's it going?"

"Eh ..." Leo mumbled, as if that said it all.

"Yeah, I know," Tony said, as if there had been an actual exchange.

Tony led me into the concrete caverns of the market to Sami's Café. We got a table right away, even though the place was crowded. The waitress brought a beer to the table along with our silverware and water glasses.

"Thank you, Sami," Tony said.

"You bet. Usual?" she asked.

"Yeah."

She turned to me. "How about you, hon?"

"I haven't looked yet," I said, motioning to a menu in Sami's hand.

"She'll have the same," Tony said.

Sami must have known that, because she still hadn't even put the menus down on the table. "To drink?"

"Green tea?" I asked, which received a grunt and a nod.

"What am I having?" I asked Tony after she left.

"Sheep brains in a light broth," Tony said.

"Uh, Tony ..."

"Relax. Fish. Something good, something fresh. Catch of the day. I don't know how it will be prepared, but it'll be good."

Sami brought my tea in what seemed to be an instant. Tony sipped his beer and looked out over the water.

"You're going to get a larger percentage of the fees you are generating," he said after a bit.

"What do you mean?"

"I'm making you a partner, of sorts. You will get a higher percentage of what's left over after the bills are paid."

"Why are you doing this, Tony?" I asked.

"Because I'm a good guy, and you deserve it," he said.

"Tony, I don't trust anyone who doesn't act out of self-interest." That was his pet phrase.

Tony laughed loud and long.

"Good for you, Jessi," he said at last. "And my self-interest is this: If I don't up the ante, someone is going to take you away from me. Then I'll have nothing."

He never called me Jessi if we were around anyone else. The first time he did it, I thought he was being condescending or making an overture, because I never referred to myself as Jessi. The only ones who ever had before Tony were Mark and Grandmama, at least since college.

But at some point, I realized that when Tony did it, it was not a subtle put-down as much as a "tell." When he thought of me as Jessi, he was not on his perpetual guard.

He was right, too. I'd received a couple of feelers from other firms. But I didn't know he knew.

"Somebody leak? Or ask you for my references?"

"Remember when I was late back to the office after the Daddy Williams case?"

"You were negotiating with Max Moore."

"Not really. Moore wanted to talk about a merger of firms, under his letterhead but I would come in as full partner," Tony said. "He has repeated the offer."

My heart sank. That would mean I would be at the same firm as Mark. And I knew that would create problems, even if I didn't yet know how. The thought of Max Moore disquieted me, too.

"What did you tell him?" I asked, tensing.

"That I was honored, that I would think about it," Tony said.

"And?"

"I'm offering you a greater percentage of what you generate," he said. He drained his beer just as Sami put a fresh one on the table and cleared the empty in a single motion, as if this were a well-practiced routine.

"I don't get the connection," I said.

"For a while I couldn't figure it out, either. Moore doesn't need my book of business. Yes, I do pretty well, but merging would cost Moore as much or more than he could get training another pack of his own dogs. I didn't see his self-interest, and Moore doesn't make stupid mistakes."

"So what did you conclude?" Sometimes I just hated this game of Tony's, making you ask for the next piece of information, the connections between dots he so reluctantly doled out.

"Max Moore doesn't want me. He wants you. He wants the business you've created, the reputation you've made in the community."

Tony's eyes hovered over the beer at his lips, but those eyes were locked onto mine. I was being read, and Tony could read anybody.

"Really," I said. I relaxed. As soon as I did, Tony did too. Nonverbal communication is bred into us by millennia of social evolution, and often contains more information than words.

"What?" Tony asked.

My turn, Tony, I thought. I was going to make him wait. Finally he smiled, knowing exactly what I was doing.

"Okay," he said, "What?" with just enough plea in his voice.

"I don't want to work at Moore & Associates. My husband works there. I would be lost in his shadow. I would be lost among all those lawyers, all of whom have more prestigious degrees than I do, fancier names, bigger egos. I like what I'm doing, and I like where I'm doing it."

"I'll let Max know that as much as we appreciate his offer, we're not interested," Tony said, with a wide smile. He knew I meant what I said, and he knew with the additional money he just put on the table I'd be very happy to stay right where I was.

Such is "place."

Chapter 16

Finding freshness in life is like a rhythmic caress that finds fresh skin, the discreet thrill of a massage that moves from back to front, hitting the raisin in an oatmeal cookie.

A beautiful brick house on Queen Anne Hill, on Highland Drive and not a stone's throw from Kerry Park, came on the market. It looked out over the bay and included a view of the Space Needle which served as an exclamation point, a beacon, reminding us always of where we were.

With my increase in income and Mark's new status within his firm, we were earning real money and had discussed if we wouldn't be better off building some equity rather than paying rent. Even then we struggled to come up with a down-payment, but with a little help from Max Moore, we bought the place just before a full-price offer came in from one of the new tech millionaires who planned to tear it down and build something ugly and four times too big for the neighborhood.

The house was rough from age, which is why we could afford it, but Mark had worked as a carpenter in summers during college and I knew how to muscle a wheelbarrow and could certainly use a crowbar.

We even moved in before the house was finished to save on rent money. On more than one occasion, Claire would brush sheetrock dust off my suit when I got to work in the morning, or before I headed off to court. But she always did so with a smile and a nod of her head. I think she knew, in her wise way, that this was the best time of life.

For six months, Mark and I spent four hours after work every day and all of every weekend stripping walls back to the lathe, running new wire, tiling, painting. With engineer approval, we removed two walls to join the living room, family room, and the kitchen into one large space with a wall of tall windows looking out over the city and Puget Sound, during the day marked by the commerce of huge ships and at night by the sparkle of brilliant lights spread below.

Everybody drew a breath when they walked into that room, even Mark and me. Every time.

Then Mark and I bought a small place, a cabin really, on Orcas Island in the San Juans. That one we did not touch, we only used it one summer while we kayaked around looking for orca, talking about having kids.

We kept arriving at the same place in that discussion.

"Jessi, I understand if your clock is ticking, and you really want children. But I've never heard you say you wanted to be 'Mom.' Why would we trade this for diapers full of baby shit?" We agreed that just seemed like too big a sacrifice. I think we were both too selfish for kids. Mark and I went where we wanted, when our schedules coincided. That could end up anywhere. We also both loved the gym. We had a pretty nice routine of work and play.

"You won't miss playing catch with your son? Teaching him to drive?"

"I have other ways of occupying my time," he'd say, and move to distract me, as he always could, with a touch that promised a satisfying romp wherever we were. We seemed to have a perfect physical fit. I don't know what that is: some combination of relative size, location of erotic trigger zones, the color and taste of each other's skin. Chemistry. Pheromones. I often wondered how I could be so satisfied spending hours lazing my fingers over his skin.

We were pretty happy, so it's hard to say why what happened next happened. I don't mean "how" it happened. I really mean "why." The ultimate cause, not just what we lawyers call the proximate cause, or how one thing leads to another. I don't know if we were bored, if we fell under the influence of something stronger than we were, or if we just became who we really were. Biology, psychology, or happenstance. But, one thing did lead to another. It always does.

It was late summer, a Thursday. Mark and I had gone out to dinner, which we did far more often than we ate at home. Both of us could cook, but neither liked to do dishes. We had been talking about taking Friday off, which is the reason I remember that it was a Thursday.

Hell, I have lots of reasons to remember that day. It was a Thursday.

Somewhere between standard Seattle cuisine of organically grown romaine lettuce and a Dungeness crab-stuffed Copper River salmon, Mark looked out over the water and asked, in the most unbelievably nonchalant voice I have ever heard him use, "Would you like to go to that SASA place after dinner?"

"You bored with me, sweetie?" I asked, and was only half-kidding.

Mark and I never talked about our sex life, especially our pasts. I'd not told him of my previous experiences, and he hadn't offered to discuss his. We were both healthy young adults with history. I guess we each assumed that if there were anything to say, it would be said.

Yes, I had my fantasies, and I assume he had his. But that's just normal. Talking about them would make it seem less normal.

Our sex was still wonderful. By that point in our relationship, we could anticipate what the other would do next. Most often we looked forward to that next thing, too. But routine is routine. I think we probably took the same amount of time, more or less, each night we made love. Often that's good, but it's still routine.

"Of course not," he said, tracing the vein on the back of my hand with the tip of his index finger. "I was just curious. I saw an article about the place the other day in the *Sound* and it reminded me. Just thought I'd ask."

Source of the Sound, the local alternative newspaper. Leftist, proud if not arrogant, often full of anger about other people's money. But it was a fun read, especially when it took on Seattle's elite, and the classifieds were a hoot. A bald, one-legged, subterranean goat-wrangler with halitosis could find a date in the classifieds of *The Sound*. She wouldn't even have to spell "goat." You could pick up a copy anywhere in the city and one of us often brought a copy home.

We'd even argued light-heartedly over the editorial point of view. He thought *The Sound's* series on the "Secret Samaritan of Pike Place," was over-done and disagreed with the paper that whoever was providing food to local homeless was doing a community service.

"It's harming an important landmark," Mark said.

"Even the poor have a right to be in public places when they want to be," I countered.

Source of the Sound also had articles about the Seattle "scene," straight, gay, alternative, weird. So I wasn't surprised there would be an article about SASA.

But it was unlike Mark to be tentative like that, which made me curious about what he was thinking. The truth was, I'd been curious about SASA too, ever since I'd first heard about it from Linda Williams while trying to put together her defense. And for the other, obvious urges that I'd pretty much buried since college.

To put Mark at ease, and give my own curiosity a little cover, I said, "Sure. Sounds like fun. But I want another glass of wine first."

SASA was in an industrial part of town, not too far from the water and under one of the overpasses for the freeway. The sign was nearly invisible. That seemed creepy right on the face of it, but we had made our decision and neither one of us wanted to be the one to chicken out.

We pulled open the steel door and walked into a tiny alcove surrounded by black velvet curtains. There was a small desk with a huge man sitting at a computer. The music from the other side of the curtain was loud and pounding.

"ID?" said the man.

"We didn't bring ID," said Mark, who thought it would be better if we left all our valuables locked in the car. Plus, we didn't really want to be leaving a fat, wide paper trail of our attendance.

"Well, I can't let you in without ID," said the man, not really frustrated but not entirely patient.

Mark and I went back to the car to get our ID. When he opened the trunk where we had stashed my purse, he asked, "You still want to do this?"

"Sure. I don't know. Do you?" I gave back the non-answer as I pulled out my driver's license.

"I don't know. I guess. We're here," was his nearly equally noncommittal reply. He took his license out of his wallet that he'd left in the door of my

Porsche, the car we had taken to dinner because it was more fun to drive than his Audi.

Back at the alcove, the large man looked at my ID, then at Mark's, and typed into his computer.

"You're members, right? You aren't coming up on the list."

I'd forgotten that SASA was a members-only club. "Can we join now?" I asked.

He sighed in a way that made it clear that what would follow was an oft-repeated conversation. He picked up a cordless phone and hit a button. "Hey. Got Newbies." Pause. "Yeah."

"Wait here," he said.

"That's okay, we can …" Mark started to say.

"Just wait," said the man. He still had our IDs so we couldn't bolt, as I think we were both ready to do.

Just then the outer door opened and a couple about our age came in. There was just barely room for all four of us in the alcove. I was somewhat reassured by their quality clothes, and they were nice looking. I was less reassured by the handcuffs hanging from the strap of her purse, and how she looked at Mark who was at least a head taller than her date.

Her date looked at me with a smile that seemed either overly friendly, or ravenous, I couldn't say at the time. He was somewhat handsome, but not really my type.

The large man behind the desk said, "ID?" to them, and they gave him their licenses, which he typed into the computer, then he said, "$100." The man gave him his credit card, signed the tab and they slipped through the curtain. I tried to get a peek inside but all I got was a flash of color.

Less than 30 seconds later a heavy-set, pretty woman came through the curtain where the couple had disappeared.

"Welcome! My name is Elizabeth. You've never been to SASA before?" she said in the warmest, "would you like some cookies?" voice I have ever heard. Our nervousness dropped by half.

We both shook our head. "Well, let's take five minutes to get to know each other, I'll give you a quick tour, and you can decide if you want to join!"

"They still need an orientation," said the man behind the desk.

"Yes, Mike, I know the rules," said Elizabeth, in a tone clearly indicating who made the decisions. "Come with me," she said to Mark and me.

We walked through the first curtain into a "hallway," defined by more heavy curtains. Elizabeth stopped after a few steps and turned to us. "Mike's a volunteer. He's very dedicated but sometimes he gets a little officious," she said. I don't know why, but I was surprised to hear her use the word "officious."

"Are you members of any other club? Do you have any experience with the lifestyle?" she asked.

Mark and I shook our heads. I was confused by what she meant by "the lifestyle."

"You ARE newbies!" Elizabeth said with a big smile. "Come on, then."

Chapter 17

The erotic has deep roots in our psyche. It's not layered on, like how to hold a fork, or being respectful of authority. Eroticism expresses biological imperatives derived from propagation of the species.

The man and woman who had entered the club while we were in the vestibule were ordering drinks at the bar. Warming trays on tables along the wall glowed with small flames but were still empty of food; a half-barrel was filled with bottled water and ice; comfortable chairs surrounded tables like any lounge. There was a small stage and several doors leading out of the room and a few couples sat on couches talking.

"Where is everybody?" asked Mark.

"Oh, honey, it's pretty early," said Elizabeth. She glanced at a huge watch with a white band on her large wrist. "It will fill up in about 45 minutes."

"This is the couples area," she said, leading us through a door opposite the bar. Inside the large room were alcoves, not unlike the little cabanas you see around swimming pools at fancy hotels. Each was not much bigger than the double bed it contained, gauze curtains separating one from the next.

"Single men aren't allowed in here," said Elizabeth, "but you can bring another man in with you if you like. Or you can join another couple."

Mark looked around the room. "Does it ever fill up?" he asked.

"Oh hon, on weekends it's standing-room-only. You'd be amazed at how many bodies you can get on one of those beds."

"And if we want to be on one of those beds, just the two of us?" Mark asked.

"No one can join without an invitation. That's Rule #2. No touching without asking."

"What's the first rule?" I asked.

"No means Nooo," she said with a smile.

"And if someone breaks that rule?" asked Mark.

"They don't. Oh, it's happened and will surely happen again. But it's rare, and when it does, that person is invited to leave and never come back. Most don't want to lose the privilege."

Elizabeth took us back to the bar and then into the next large room.

"This is for those who have more … intense tastes." She flashed another smile.

In the middle of the room hung a swing made of nylon straps. Hand cuffs and ankle cuffs hung from a ten-by-ten foot section of chain-link fencing fastened on the opposite wall. A giant X-shaped frame with rings fastened to the arms sat in one corner. A chrome wheel to be used in ways I couldn't imagine rested on the floor. Workout benches with chains hanging off them were scattered about.

"Wow," I said.

"It can get a little noisy in here," Elizabeth said with her perpetual smile.

"What happens if someone wants to stop? I assume saying 'no' or 'stop' can be part of the game. But what if something goes too far and the other really wants it to be over?"

"We have what we call 'safe words,' and everybody acknowledges the safe word before play begins. It has to be something that would not be said in the context of the game. A particular color, for instance, or just an obscure word."

The last room was just a small movie theater for about thirty people. An erotic movie of two women with artful tongues was playing on the screen.

"Some people come in here to watch, some like to share," said Elizabeth. "Come on to the office. We'll have the official talk, I will comp you tonight's visit, and you can decide if you want to join." She took us into her office on the far side of the dance floor from the bar. Inside, a large one-way mirror looked out into the main area.

One wall had a row of monitors that featured every conceivable angle of the rooms we had just been through.

"Marketing materials?" asked Mark.

"To keep you safe," Elizabeth shot back. "We take safety, and privacy, very seriously."

"The talk" included the basic rules of SASA permission, and other strong recommendations such as to use the clean sheets and towels that were stacked everywhere and the condoms that filled large fishbowls on every flat surface. She also filled us in on the very few sex practices that were banned "in the interest of essential cleanliness."

Use of cameras and cell phones was forbidden. "That's what gets most people in trouble," she said, "and even then it's usually because someone got a call or a text and didn't use the head on their shoulders."

While we were in her office, SASA began to fill up. Many of the people seemed to know each other, and there were many hugs exchanged, and a lot of laughter. Some people stood at the bar after ordering their drinks, others made their way to the food and were eating at one of the tables in the dining area.

"Would you like to stay?" Elizabeth asked. "It's fine if all you want to do is watch."

I looked at Mark; he looked at me. I think we both shrugged and nodded at the same time.

I hoped my act was convincing. I was afraid they could hear my libido standing on a chair in my brain screaming, "Hell YES we'd like to stay! Bring it ON!"

Elizabeth took us back out to the front alcove. When there was a break in the stream of people now coming in, she pushed back through the curtain to the first chamber by the front door.

"Go ahead and let Mike enter your information," she said to us.

"Mike, log them in as out-of-town guests under my name," she said to him.

"But they live here in Seattle," he said.

"Mike, I know where they live," she said. Without another word, Mike took Mark's license and then mine, typed notes into the computer and gave them back.

"Enjoy," Elizabeth said. "If you have any questions, ask anyone with a SASA shirt on," and pointed at the bartender who was wearing a black shirt with SASA embroidered in red.

We wandered over to the bar.

"What can I get you?" asked the bartender. Mark ordered a brandy. I asked for a White Russian just to have something to sip.

"What do you think?" Mark asked, again in that nonchalant voice that indicated he was being guarded.

"I think it's going to be an interesting evening," I replied, my voice every bit as noncommittal as his, but with desire not as hidden as I intended.

"What if we get seen by someone we know?" he asked.

"Well, my guess is that they are here for the same reason we are, and not likely to talk it up all over town," I replied. Even I wasn't totally convinced by my answer, but it sufficed given everything else I was feeling at that moment.

People began to dance after a while, just like any other bar in the city. Except sometimes women danced with women a little more suggestively, sometimes kissing deeply. Men danced behind women, hands cupping breasts, sliding necklines down to expose breasts, or sliding up thighs and dragging a skirt with them until panties were completely exposed, if panties were worn.

We'd moved from a table to one of the couches where we could see over to a corner of the room where a woman had begun to dance with a brass stripper pole, surrounded by couches where men and a few couples sat. She earned applause after every dance, and every time another piece of clothing came off.

Finally her beautiful body was naked, and after that song she kneeled on a couch facing two men, a knee between the legs of each so that she was open. She reached down and unzipped the trousers of both and took each hard cock in her hands. She kissed one full on the mouth while the other explored between her thighs.

Mark had been gently fondling my shoulder, and then I felt his hand at the zipper at the back of my neck. I didn't move while he unzipped my dress to my waist. I did nothing except feel my body throb with excitement. He slid his hands under the straps of my dress and played with my shoulders. I wasn't wearing a bra.

He and I both knew what was going to happen as the fabric slowly moved down my arms.

When the straps fell to my elbows, I could feel his body stiffen. I didn't move. I had my right hand on his leg, my left around my small drink, which I set on a nearby table. I pulled my left hand free of the fabric, then my right, and the dress fell to my waist.

Looking around the room I saw others watching and felt the thrill of being half-naked with people all around us. Then I leaned back, closed my eyes and put my mouth on Mark's. His right hand came around to cup my breast, then caressed my throat, then down between my legs.

"What's our safe word?" Mark asked, his voice heavy, husky.

"Backgammon," I said, the first word that came to mind not likely to be used in conversation, not there and then, at any rate.

"May I touch?" came a voice seemingly from the back of my neck. I turned and opened my eyes and a man stood behind us. Before I could say anything, Mark said, "We're not ready, but thank you." I was relieved and disappointed in the same instant.

"C'mon," said Mark, taking my drink in one hand, my hand in his other. With my free hand I held my dress around my waist as he walked me into the couples area over to the last open alcove and sat me down on the edge of the bed.

"Lift your hips," he said, and pulled the dress down over my knees and off my feet, leaving my shoes. "Scoot back," he said, and I slid back to lean up against the pillows facing the room. A few more couples had followed us in and stood around the bed as Mark got undressed.

When he lay down beside me, he touched me just like he did in our own bed at home. He kissed me on the mouth, his right hand playing with my breasts. Then his lips played around their soft roundness, and he gently teased my nipples with his tongue. He pulled my panties over my upraised hips as as he kissed his way down my belly. At the end of the bed stood about fifteen people.

One man leaned in to ask Mark if he and his wife could play.

"We'd like to just be with each other for now, but thank you," Mark said, turning back to me.

A man and a woman standing closest to the bed were touching each other while she watched Mark between my legs. I locked eyes with her date. His eyes were dark and soft and quite beautiful. His face was so full of desire that it was nearly like making love to him as Mark made love to me. It wasn't long before waves of pleasure made me arch my back and cry out as the longest orgasm I'd had in years swept over me. Years.

I pulled Mark up to my face, and he put his mouth on mine as I guided him into me. I opened my eyes again as he kissed my throat. I saw the woman had gone to her knees in front of the soft-eyed man, taking him deep into her throat as he stared at us.

I could tell Mark was about to come, and I was nearly ready to come again. When the man at the foot of the bed exploded into the mouth of the woman in front of him, Mark came hard into me and my body gave itself up to another wrenching orgasm. We lay limp together as the crowd drifted away.

"My God," I said at last.

"Yeah," was all Mark said.

Eventually we got dressed, walked out of the club and into a remarkably soft Seattle night. We didn't talk on the way home. I kept a hand between his legs, and he kept a hand between mine. When he needed to shift, he let go of the wheel for a moment and shifted with his left hand. I'd never felt so close to him.

At home we made love again before we fell asleep. It was anything but routine.

Chapter 18

Happenstance causes situations we'd never intentionally embrace. A new boss with control issues is hired, we go on a bad date with someone who then won't leave us alone, someone runs a red light when we've just entered the intersection. Good intentions are not insurance. On the other hand, if every boss is controlling, every date ends with a stalker, or we're always getting in accidents, maybe something else is at work.

Claire thought it would be a good idea for our entire team to meet every morning to keep us all on the same page. She'd have a round of coffees and muffins or bagels delivered. She would hand out spreadsheets with cases, filing dates and scheduled court appearances. We'd discuss who was where and doing what while Claire took notes for our meeting the next day.

Scheduling was interspersed with Claire talking about her sons or occasionally teasing me about not having children, or Sarah talking about her partner Sally whose possessiveness seemed to cause Sarah more exasperation than joy. Lily, always the quietest of the group, didn't participate much in that back-and-forth. We didn't think about it much, but one morning we found out why.

We'd ended the meeting and gone back to our desks. I'd closed my door to concentrate on a brief when I heard voices raised.

Then I heard Claire use a voice I'd never heard.

"Listen, mother-fucker, you get back in that elevator and on the street right fucking now or your ass is gonna be in jail in fifteen fucking minutes, do you hear me?"

I opened the door and saw her standing about eight inches away from a stocky man in work clothes. He was about her height, but his round face was blotchy red while facing hers of beautiful café au lait. When I came out he turned toward me, and Claire moved again right in front of him.

"Where's Lily?" the man asked over the top of Claire's head.

"Why? Who are you?" I said.

"I've got this, Jessica," said Claire. "Did you hear me?" She said again to the man. "The elevator is that way. You get on it and leave this office. Now."

"I'm Lily's fiancé. We have to talk," he said.

"You are NOT my fiancé," came a voice from the other side of him. Lily had come out of the door of the office she shared with Sarah. Sarah was right behind her. The man turned to face Lily.

"Aw, shit," said Claire, as she moved around again, this time to put herself between him and Lily.

"We're getting married in a month!" he said.

"No, Roger! I broke it off!" Lily said.

"You said yes! We need to talk!" he said.

"No, you need to leave. Now!" said Claire.

"There's nothing to talk about!" cried Lily, in tears.

Just then, Tony came around the corner from the hallway. I'd forgotten I agreed to meet him to go over the meeting I'd had with my team.

"Hey. What's up?" he asked in a very reasonable voice.

"Who are you?!" said the man, looking for a fight.

"I own this firm," said Tony. "And who are you?"

"I'm Lily's fiancé. She won't answer the phone, she won't answer the door. I need to talk with her," said the man.

"We are NOT engaged!" said Lily.

"You just want to talk with her? That's not too hard," said Tony. Claire started to say something, but Tony locked his eyes on hers and with a shake of his head, said, "Claire, will you make sure a conference room is available for me and Mr…?"

"Hall. Roger Hall," the man said, starting to calm down.

"Mr. Hall and I will go into my office and I will get his side of the story. Lily, you go with Jessica, and she will get your side. Then we'll all get together, and if you two need some private time, I'm sure that can be arranged.

"Will that work for you, Mr. Hall?" Roger nodded. As he was leading him away, Tony said, "Claire, will you make sure conference room 911 is available?"

Tony took Roger Hall down to his office. As soon as they turned the corner, I took Lily into my office and locked the door. Claire was calling "conference room" 911 as soon as they were out of sight.

Lily told me a disjointed and tear-filled story about a three-year off-and-on relationship with Roger. He wasn't a bad man, she said, but "I don't want to have his children!" she kept saying. She'd filed a restraining order, but Roger kept lying his way out of being charged with violating the restrictions.

I'd learned over the years sometimes cops don't put a priority on those kinds of offenses, but it's not always their fault. Often victims don't cooperate, there's always a web of lies, and it's rarely rewarding work.

Within five minutes, I heard the elevator open, then the stairwell door. I heard a murmur of male voices and opened my door. Uniformed officers filled the room, guns drawn.

Claire was talking to the cop in charge. They all went down the hall, where Claire tapped on Tony's door and said, "The conference room is ready, Mr. Stevens, Mr. Hall."

Roger Hall was the first through the door.

"That's him!" Claire said. In seconds Hall was on the floor, his arms tied behind him, before he could start to scream "Lily! Lily! Don't let them do this!"

He was out of the building and in a car on his way to jail before the coffee on my desk had cooled. Lily and Sarah went into their office. "I'll take care of her," Sarah said.

"How did you get them here so quickly?" I asked Claire.

"Honey, you don't think I know what to say to police to get their attention?" was all she said. "You don't need to know. It's better if you don't."

Tony looked at Claire and smiled. He walked over to her and they gave each other a small fist bump.

I realized then there was an awful lot I didn't understand about how the world worked.

"That was really dangerous. What if he'd had a gun?" Mark said that night. "I can't believe your firm doesn't have a policy. Max Moore has a full contingency plan for security. People don't even get to our floor without being vetted, reviewed, and escorted. We're discussing installation of a metal detector for particularly contentious cases, like divorces."

That kind of deflated me. I thought what Tony and Claire had done was nearly heroic, and Mark was picking it apart. Not just the idea of it, but the people. His reaction made me cringe, but I didn't know why. And I was tired of hearing "Max Moore" this, and "Max Moore" that.

Max Moore had apparently taken my Mark under his wing. They worked on cases together, Mark doing fieldwork while Max did strategy. Not unlike what I had with Sarah and Lily, but Max and Mark had a full platoon of Sarahs and Lilies, too..

Mark was being schooled with an education no law school could provide. I may have been a little jealous, but there was something else. A week before Roger Hall bulldozed into our office and was taken to jail, this time for real, Claire had buzzed me on the intercom.

"There's a guy with a three-ball voice on line one asking for you," she said. "He won't give me a name."

"A what?"

"A three-ball voice. He's got at least one extra, or the two he's got are the size of lemons," she said.

"I'll take it," I said, curious.

"This is Jessica Love," I said into the phone.

There was no doubt who the voice belonged to as soon as I heard, "Good afternoon, Ms. Love. Would you consider having a drink with me after work? To discuss some business, of course."

God, Max Moore didn't even have to announce his name; he knew that voice of his was enough of an introduction.

"I really can't, Mr. Moore. Mark and I have some plans. Would tomorrow work?"

"Not as well," said Max Moore, "and I think Mark may need to change the plans you had for this evening. He and I are on a deadline, and he's going to have to stay a little late. I'm sure he'll let you know as soon as he has a chance."

As if on cue, my cell phone beeped and Mark's picture appeared on the screen. Mark's text confirmed that he would be working late, and maybe he and I could catch a bite downtown after he was done. I silently cursed the confidence of Max Moore while texting Mark back to give me a call or text when he was done. XO.

"What would you like to discuss?" I asked Moore.

"Can you meet me at The Edgewater, say at 5:30? I'd rather go over it in person."

Moore was already at "his" table in the bar at The Edgewater looking out at the water when I arrived. He stood when I arrived and made pleasantries until the cocktail waitress took my order for a vodka rocks.

"Not a martini?" he asked.

"I really don't care for vermouth," I said. But then I wanted a martini.

Despite telling myself on the walk from my office to The Edgewater that I would be immune to the man's effect on me, it was amazing how his presence seemed to have an intimate conversation with every sexual organ in my body. Then there were his eyes that seemed to laugh, smile, comfort and seduce all at the same time.

I knew my Mark was as straight a male as exists, but I could see why the sheer presence of this man in Mark's life was intoxicating. He could be the ideal role model, father figure, and best friend all rolled into one.

For each of us, Max Moore was the essence of dominant male.

Eventually he looked at his watch.

"I know you're curious about why I asked to meet with you," he said. "I would like you to consider joining my firm. Mark has said wonderful things about you, and so have others in and around the community."

"Which community?" I asked.

"The legal community," he said.

All of a sudden I got a sense of falling. An intense version of the feeling I'd gotten when Tony told me that Max Moore wanted to merge firms. That my little operation would disappear in that colossus. That somehow, I'd lose my identity, be subject to the will of people I didn't know and who didn't know me, that I would be known as Mark's wife.

"I don't think so," I said.

"You haven't heard the terms," he said.

"I've got pretty good terms with Tony," I said.

"Tony is not known for being overly generous," said Moore. "Maybe this will change your mind."

He pulled a gold Cross pen from his pocket and wrote a number on the corner of the beverage napkin under his drink. He picked up his glass and turned the napkin around so I could read it. I was thankful it wasn't too much more than I was currently making. When I looked up again, the glass came down and condensation obliterated the number, including the dollar sign.

"Well, I'm glad to know Tony appreciates my worth," I said, which caused Moore to raise his eyebrows. "I have to thank you for the opportunity, but I must say no. Tony has been good to me."

"You're sure?"

"I'm sure in this moment," I said.

Max Moore tore the corner off the napkin and rolled it into a tiny ball as he nodded and changed the subject to the Seahawks or the economy or something else completely innocuous.

"Well, I should let you go," he said at last.

"Does Mark know you were going to make me this offer?"

"No."

"Should I tell him?" I asked.

"I have no plans to do so. There could be repercussions difficult to anticipate."

Moore smiled and put a $50 bill on the table to pay for our two drinks. "The rest is for her," he nodded toward the cocktail waitress. He nodded to me and walked to the front door where the valet had kept his Bentley.

When Mark texted me a few minutes later, again as if on cue, I texted him back that I would meet him for dinner at The Edgewater. I left the bar and got a table in the restaurant where I sat looking out over the waters of Puget Sound thinking about Max Moore, about Mark, and about Tony.

Chapter 19

Happenstance isn't all bad. It also provides unexpected opportunities. Of course, we don't always know what will turn out well and what will take us down.

An oil transfer ship ran too close to sharp rocks not far from the refinery at Anacortes, Washington. The ship did not sink and its double hull mitigated the damage, but the spill that did occur killed crab and seabirds. Mark represented the company against sanctions by the federal and state governments and against lawsuits by fishermen, environmentalists, and Native Americans, who for once were all on the same side.

Mark won by convincing judges and juries that the accident was not the result of negligence but an act of nature that could not be avoided, and by promising that the company would immediately take measures to prevent the same thing from happening in the future.

In essence, he argued that the company would stop doing what it hadn't been doing and would start doing what it already was. Legal fees were nearly equal to the damages paid. Mark earned kudos, a bonus, and a week at Max Moore's house in Aspen, Colorado.

"Want to go skiing?" Mark asked.

"Colorado? I think we can do that," I replied, knowing I could take a couple days off.

It was a wonderful few days. Weather and snow were nearly perfect, once we acclimated to the altitude. We also planned a nighttime layover in Denver on the way back to Seattle.

We'd added "clubbing," as we called it, to our life. Not every weekend, or even every month, but we'd go sometimes after dinner, or if there were special functions at SASA. We had two rules: no touching by others, and either of us could say "enough" and we'd leave, no discussion or argument. Neither of us had yet found a reason to say "enough."

Out of town, we'd find clubs wherever we were; San Francisco; Vancouver; Portland. It was really surprising how often we could find some place to play.

The Palace in Denver was unmarked except by a number on the building. We paid for a seven-day membership — that was the minimum, even though we were flying out the next morning — as well as the $100 couple's entry fee. Single women paid $20, but single men had to pay $200. The prices helped manage the mix of the clientele, and no doubt reflected something about biology.

Denver has a very different feel than Seattle, and this extended to The Palace. It's hard to define, but maybe it was a bit more upscale than SASA. An athletic and quite handsome man on one couch looked like a well-known baseball player. He wore a finely tailored suit. The two women who sat with him, a blonde and a brunette, could have stepped right out of a Victoria's Secret catalog. They leaned around him to kiss and fondle each other.

"Look at those three," I whispered. "They're just incredible."

"Those women are no more beautiful than you," Mark said, a lovely lie I chose to believe. We each had a couple of drinks, then got up to dance. Others were dancing, too. Women had their hands all over the front of their partner's pants, men were caressing and fondling more than moving to the music, and more than one pair of breasts were exposed.

Mark and I found ourselves back against the wall, in a bubble of space of our own. The wall had straps for other kinds of play on special nights. As we danced, I touched Mark and pulled his zipper down. I loved the feel of his hard cock even inside the fabric of his shorts.

He turned me around and unzipped the back of my dress. It was not tight fitting, and as soon as I rolled my shoulders forward, it fell from my arms to my waist and then to the floor. I kicked it to the wall, feeling much better in my bra and thong. Mark took off his shirt, and he was magnificent. Couples around us gave us a bit more room.

The DJ didn't let any dead air between songs. Mark pressed me back against the wall, facing the room, and I put my hands up to take the straps hanging on the wall. I wrapped them around my wrists in faux bondage as his hands played all over me.

We were the only ones on the dance floor, now. I looked out on the room, feeling how vulnerable I was and could see how the men in the room moved when I pushed my hips out and down. When Mark found exactly the right spot it was a good thing I had the straps in hand, because my legs would not have supported me.

We stayed there for several minutes. Finally Mark asked if I wanted a drink.

"I'd love a bottle of water," I told him. We gathered our clothes and found a couch. Mark got up, dressed, then walked downstairs to the bar while I put on my panties and bra, then slipped back into my dress.

A tall, thin man stopped Mark on his way back, nodding in my direction. Mark smiled and said something, but I could tell he was edging away, trying to get back to me.

"What did that man say?" I asked as he sat down, twisting the top off a water bottle he'd pulled from the bin of ice downstairs.

"He thanked me for our sharing," Mark said. We sat and drank our water, watching other couples make love on beds that surrounded the space.

"Would you like a massage?" he asked after a while, and motioned to the massage table along one wall of the room. It wasn't in an alcove and there were no curtains, of course.

"That would be quite nice," I said. "I'm a little sore from skiing." I knew I was going to be naked again and I liked that, but was in no hurry.

We wandered over to the table. I took off my dress and bra while Mark spread out a thick fresh white towel; then I lay face down. Mark started to work my shoulders. I jumped from the cold when the hand which had been holding his drink touched my skin.

"Sorry," he said, and rubbed his hands together to fight the chill.

The tall, thin man walked over, accompanied by a brunette nearly as tall as he was, also thin and with beautiful proportions. The man, I think, wore cologne that was very subtle: light and smooth but present by its fragrance, not by quantity. Expensive, I thought.

"There's some product in the basket," he said and pointed at a small shelf under the table, next to the towel basket. Mark found an oil, warmed it in his hands, and started to massage my legs, then my back.

When he got to my butt, my thong came off. I so wanted to be touched, once in a while my hips raised involuntarily, as if to capture his hand. Eventually, they were successful.

"You might want to try this," said the man, standing so close the fabric of his slacks brushed my hips. He reached down and looked into my eyes as he pulled something from the basket and handed it to Mark. When Mark's hands came back to me, whatever he had been handed was like liquid warmth and incredibly slick. Wherever he touched me, warmth spread, inside and out.

"Why don't you turn over?" Mark asked at last.

I did. The thin man and brunette were standing there, and others had begun to gather. On my back, I was naked and being oiled, in a city I didn't know, surrounded by men and women watching Mark put his hands on me. He knew my body so well, and I moaned a little whenever he brushed a nipple, but soon his fingers were inside me, and my hips were moving against his hand, trying to consume his touch.

Just before I was about to orgasm, he stopped, reached down and brought up a towel and placed it gently over my eyes.

"Mark …" I said, but he put his lips on mine, then he pulled back a little and said, "Shhh, it's fine." He stood at my side and touched me, bringing me back in rhythm. Suddenly I felt hands under my neck, massaging the base of my skull, in addition to Mark's hands at my hips.

"Mark?"

"Enjoy this," he replied, and kissed my lips, then let his lips wander down to my nipples, then down to my hips. He ever-so-gently pulled my knees a bit farther apart, then a bit farther still.

The hands at my neck massaged my jawline while Mark's tongue explored. I felt his hands on my breasts, then, circling my nipples with his fingers. But then at the same time, I felt his hands on the inside of my thighs, pressing them gently farther apart. I had six hands on me, now, and I was lost in the sensation.

A fourth pair of hands started massaging my feet. Every once in a while they would move my heels out just another inch on the table. Mark's fingers had found my G-spot.

"Mark, I want to see," I whispered to him, as I was getting closer and closer to an epic orgasm.

"Do you?" he asked.

"Yes," I whispered. I wanted to see him touching me, all these people.

Slowly the towel came away from my eyes, and Mark's hands went back to where they had been massaging my face and my neck. The hands at my breasts belonged to the tall brunette, and the tongue at my vagina belonged to her tall, handsome partner.

The two women, the models who had been on the couch, were each on either side of the table, massaging my feet and holding my legs apart so that I could be completely and thoroughly entered.

"Mark?" I asked again, but he bent over the table and silenced me this time with the softest kiss I could imagine. He barely pulled away before I cried out in the painful pleasure of total orgasm, my hips coming off the table, my hands grabbing the wrists of the brunette as if they were handholds, before I reached down and pushed away the tongue that was tickling my now incredibly sensitive clitoris.

We stayed for another couple of hours, playing just with each other, having drinks, eating, and taking a shower just before it was time to leave. I collapsed against Mark in the taxi on the way back to our hotel. We didn't have sex again that night. Neither of us was capable.

But the next morning, each of us wanted "just one more." We missed our 7 a.m. plane back to Seattle and the next available flight didn't depart until almost 13 hours later, at 7:55 p.m. Mark's office handled all the details. They had someone on staff whose full-time job was to get lawyers and clients to and from Seattle. We checked our bags and caught a cab back to Denver.

Some people believe there's no such thing as coincidence, that everything is preordained. I don't know if that's true, and don't think they know, either. But I do know that lives hinge on seemingly inconsequential events. Happenstance.

Chapter 20

Temporary chemistry often, if not always, dictates how we view the world. Sometimes we're wearing rose-colored glasses, sometimes shit-covered lenses. Trouble lurks when we ignore our own state of mind when thinking we are being "objective."

Mark and I walked through Denver's historic district, Lower Downtown or LoDo as it's affectionately known by locals, a nice collection of renovated buildings. We gawked at the architecture while holding hands, still in a state of endorphin bliss. I caught the smell of snow; my senses were heightened and I was especially aware of scents.

"I love you," Mark said at one point. He did not often say that. It meant something.

"I love you," I said, and that meant something, too. How incredibly lucky I felt in that moment, walking and holding hands with this man of high intelligence, so handsome he turned heads in whatever shop we entered, a man so confident he could be gentle, a husband who had achieved so much so young that together we were building a lifestyle of financial freedom, and finally, a partner with whom I could explore sensuality to its fullest, without fear.

We ducked into the Tattered Cover, a huge bookstore in an old building with solid wood walls that gave me the feeling of belonging, kindled by a sense of quality and the warm patina of time. There was an aroma of paper, perfumes from magazines, a lemony polish from fine-grained wood, scents from fresh baked goods and coffee. It was nearly overwhelming.

We were hungry, there was a café inside where we could get coffee and a roll and check our email through their wifi. But for a long time we just sat close, Mark's hand on my thigh.

"Last night was amazing," I said at one point, remembering the massage.

"It was," Mark said. "So was this morning."

I didn't say anything while lingering on the soft yet intense lovemaking that caused us to miss our plane.

"We did break our rules," I said. That wasn't just idle conversation: I wanted clarification about how Mark was feeling. The warmth between us was strong and possibly all the information I should need, but we were treading new ground.

"The 'no-touching-by-others' rule?"

"That's the one."

"It seemed like you enjoyed it," he said with a smile.

"You're not hearing me complain," I said. "Maybe we should have talked about it first, though? It was a little scary for a minute."

"I'm sorry," he said.

"You don't need to apologize. It was just a surprise. As you said, I enjoyed it. It was the most erotic experience of my life."

"Mine, too. I didn't plan it. The tall guy and his wife came up and showed me where the lotions were. He asked if his wife could help with the massage. When I started to ask you, she shook her head, put her fingers on her lips and just put her hands on your back. I was going to stop her but by then you obviously knew it wasn't just me and you seemed to like it. It just went on from there."

"It's okay. I liked it. A lot. But does that change the rules?"

"I don't know. What do you think?"

"It seems like it does, but I think we need to be carful about communication. I'm not immune to jealousy, and neither are you, I suspect."

He just smiled and shook his head, by doing so he said no, he wasn't immune either.

I don't know what jealousy is, or where it comes from. I suspect it's a biological mental circuit we're born with so we're not always last to the teat as babies, then Mother Nature uses it again when we have our own babies to give our genes the best chance of survival. Biology, psychology, happenstance. Like that time the blond came over to our table in Seattle and unbuttoned her blouse.

But here Mark and I were, holding hands after an experience Mark initiated that could have made him insanely jealous, but instead seemed to draw us together as close as we'd ever been. Some things are more complicated than I have the ability to figure out.

Mark pulled out his laptop and cleared a secure connection to his office. I wandered around the bookstore, and bought a few magazines I always enjoyed but rarely had time to read. I called my office.

"Well, hello there!" said Claire. "Long time no hear! Having fun?"

"It hasn't been that long. Four days," I said. "And yes, we're having fun."

"That's a long time for you, missy," Claire said with a laugh. "And I'm glad you are actually taking time away. You'll have plenty of work to do when you get back, though."

"No emergencies?"

"If there were, I would let you know. Nothing that won't hold till Monday."

"Thank you, Claire."

"You might give Tony a call. He's been looking for you."

"He leave a message?"

"Tony? Oh yeah. Took me five minutes to write it down." Claire said this with such obvious sarcasm we both laughed. Tony loved hoarding information. If he wanted to talk to me, he would talk to me only and not bother telling anyone else what the subject might be.

"Hey, Tony," I said, when he picked up the phone.

"Where are you?"

"Denver. Skiing with Mark."

"When you getting back?"

"Seattle tonight, office on Monday. What's up?"

"Come see me Monday?"

"Sure. What's up?" I asked again.

"See you on Monday. Have fun in Denver. Great town." He hung up.

I loved Tony, but at the same time I so often wanted to just slap him around for being more who he was than anyone I knew.

We were in cattle country, so Mark and I had steaks for an early dinner. Being from Seattle, we didn't even look at the salmon or halibut. The smell of fire-seared beef and chopped romaine salad was a full invitation. We made it to the airport in plenty of time to make our departure for the three-plus-hour flight. We were the first to board, since our seats were at the very back of the plane, but we were lucky to have two together.

I let Mark have the one by the window, on my right, so he could rest against the fuselage. He pulled up the arm rest between his seat and mine and stashed it between the seats so I could fold into him.

As the plane filled, the seat to my left on the aisle was taken by a fellow who wore blue jeans, a canvas vest and the name of a tractor company on his green ball cap. He smelled like fresh laundry detergent.

I pushed my elbow into Mark's ribs as the plane began to fill. He looked at me and then down the aisle. The tall thin man from last night at the club was coming down. He saw us at about the same time Mark looked up and saw him. He gave us a smile, then put his bag up in the overhead compartment by his seat five rows ahead of ours. Instead of sitting down, he came back to where we were sitting.

"Small world," he said. "I want to thank you for last night, if this isn't a violation of protocol."

"Not at all," said Mark. I shook my head in agreement that it was not.

"You have an aisle seat?" asked the man sitting beside me.

"I do," said the tall man.

"Let's switch so you can be by your friends," he said, and stood before any of us could answer, pulled a backpack out from under the seat in front of him and moved up the aisle. He looked back once, pointed at the seat below where the tall man had put his bag, then sat when he got a confirming nod.

The first thing I noticed when the thin man sat down was the same cologne, or after-shave, or shaving cream, I'd noticed the evening before. It had the scent of wood-smoke without any of the char, just the warmth. Full. It lit off every nerve-ending in my lap..

"Michael," he said, extending a hand first to me, then to Mark. We gave back our first names.

"Seattle?" Mark asked. We were all on thin ice, not wanting to offer too much information, already knowing as much as we did about each other.

"Sandy — you met her last night — and I are moving to Seattle next month. She stayed in Denver to wrap some things up, and I came up to get a handle on my new job."

"What does Sandy do?" I asked, avoiding anything more specific.

"She works for Social Security. We're lucky they have a policy that allows spouses to relocate in exceptional circumstances. When I was hired by Amazon, she put in for the transfer and it was approved. How about you?"

"Lawyers," Mark said.

"Both of you?" Michael smiled.

"Not at the same firm. We'd never survive," I said. Michael laughed.

Small-talk continued while the plane filled, and when Michael leaned over to hear something Mark said, or vice versa, I could feel the pressure of their shoulders on mine. I was pinned between them, their faces close to me, and Michael's scent mingled with Mark's. I felt my breathing change before we even left the ground. Their conversation continued and I let my mind wander to erotic places.

"This is really arousing, you and him being so close," I whispered to Mark as we approached cruising altitude.

"Really?" Mark said with a smile. "Would you like to get closer?"

"Yes."

He reached across me, pulled up the arm rest between my seat and Michael's. Michal looked at me, then at Mark, and back at me, and smiled.

Mark reached into our travel bag and got out the oversize fleece we carried on planes. He offered one end to Michael, who draped it across his lap, and from there it crossed mine and Mark tucked it in on his other side. I was wearing tights under a long bulky sweater that went half-way to my knees.

I put my hands on the inside of each man's thigh. In moments each man had a hand on the inside of my thighs. I pulled their closest knee toward me, then draped my legs over each of theirs. We explored what we could through fabric, until the seat-belt light went off and I unbuckled each of their seat-belts, then — awkwardly — the belts of their pants and found a hard cock with each hand.

We played like that for a while until I could stand it no longer. I lifted my hips to shed my tights and triangles of thong that came off with them, all happening under the blanket. Michael's hand found me first. Mark pulled my right leg further back over his, then he took over my pelvic massage, and then they alternated touching me.

The two flight attendants selling drinks had pushed their cart far up the aisle; they were busy and blocking access.

"I'm going to cum," I heard Michael say. I leaned over pushed my butt hard against Mark and took Michael with my mouth. A minute after I'd straightened back up, Mark said "Oh, god..." and I pushed my butt against Michael. Mark came just as my lips enclosed him.

They continued to touch me until I leaned over and pressed my forehead into Mark's shoulder as I came, and I honestly don't know whose hand had done the honors.

A while later, I pulled my tights back up while each man put himself away. Mark rolled our blanket back up and stuffed it into the bag at his feet.

"Anything to drink?" asked the flight attendant when she wheeled the cart to our row. Michael asked for a beer, Mark ordered a Scotch and water. I asked for a full can of ginger ale.

Chapter 21

Everybody operates on assumptions, but those can change for those not afraid to admit it when they're wrong.

Some people found Tony cold. I liked that he didn't waste time pretending he cared about small talk. But his being so taciturn could be difficult.

"Hey, Tony," I said when I walked into his office on Monday.

"Hey, Jessi," he said. "Colorado was good?"

"Yeah. Had fun."

That was sufficient for Tony, who just nodded his head and waited for me to initiate the real conversation.

"You wanted to talk?"

"There's a case coming your way. Claire has a meeting scheduled."

"Yeeaaah ...?"

"It could be significant. Will you listen to what they have to say?"

"I usually do," I said.

"They might be difficult."

"How?"

"You'll see."

"So why is it important?"

"I'd rather not say," said Tony.

"That's it?"

"Yep," was all he said.

When the women came into my office an hour later, it was obvious they were mother and daughter. They were both over six feet tall with high cheekbones, almond eyes, thick blond hair. They were stunning. They could have been fashion models. Maybe they were, or had been. I couldn't help myself and looked down to see if they were wearing high heels. They were, but not extreme.

Walking around my desk, I held out my hand to the mother. She ignored my hand and looked me over head-to-toe. I don't remember what I was wearing. If it was black, then my earrings might have been, too. If it was warm, then I'm sure my top was sleeveless unless I was going to court. My arms are more than a bit cut with muscle, and I don't mind showing them off. My skirt may have been short or I may have been wearing slacks, depending on how I felt that morning.

I don't know what caused the mother's reaction to me, but I do know I didn't much care for her as I offered my still-outstretched hand to the daughter. She shook it without smiling. Then I turned back with my hand still out and stood without saying anything until the older version of cold beauty reluctantly took it. We might as well establish some ground rules.

"I'm Claudia Moore," she said, "and this is my daughter, Ashley." She paused for effect, but I didn't respond. Two can play that game. I motioned to the chairs as I went around and sat behind my desk and waited, like Tony would do.

"Ashley needs some legal services, and we've been told you are good at this sort of thing," Claudia said at last.

Ashley had brought in some cocaine from Canada. A fair amount. She got popped when the ferry landed in Anacortes and Customs asked her to open her bag. Instead of the clothes of a rich girl coming home from holiday, there was a sizable stash of party drugs. She insisted there was a mix-up of bags on the ferry. That's such a lousy alibi, I'm always surprised anyone uses it anymore.

"Ashley, you're going to have to do better than that," I said.

"What do you mean?" she asked in a voice that was at once entitled and dismissive. She glanced at her mother.

"Please don't speak to my daughter that way," said Claudia Moore.

"What I mean, *Ashley*," I emphasized her name and pointedly ignored the elder Mrs. Moore, "is the excuse you just gave me won't hold up. You had a bag in your possession. That bag had drugs in it. Saying it's not yours won't get us very far."

"But that's what I was told to …" she started to answer, and again looked at her mother who had already started to interrupt.

"That's your job, Ms. Love. We were told you are good at what you do. If that is incorrect, we'll find someone else."

The intensity of my dislike for Claudia Moore jumped tenfold. I may not like being bullied, but I really hate being manipulated in such a stupid way.

"That's entirely up to you," I said. "But I have set aside a half-hour for this meeting, and I'd like to be sure you get your money's worth."

After a pause, Claudia Moore said, "Do you really not know who I am?" Then, as an afterthought, "Who we are?"

"I do. But why should that matter?" I asked. That was not necessary, but she'd pissed me off.

"Because I'm married to Max Moore. Your husband's boss. And you're Mark Love's wife? Such a surprise."

The statement could have meant she was surprised that Mark found such a gem, but her tone said she was surprised he would marry so low. I had to make a choice in that moment to either fold up my attitude and let her walk all over me, or let her walk out the door, or act like none of that mattered. I was tempted to have Claire show them out right then.

But Grandmama had taught me over backgammon that strategy is superior to emotion.

"Why isn't Moore & Associates handling the case?" I asked.

"Really?" Asked Claudia. I had to hand it to her. She used scorn like a bulldozer. I used silence, eye contact, and a slight smile as a ravine.

"There would be obvious conflicts for the firm to represent the daughter of its founder. Questions would be asked. It's far simpler to go outside for counsel. Besides, we really have researched our options. You are generally regarded as the best for this kind of case. Even Max has been impressed."

I may have become a bit cynical, but I'm not immune to being highly regarded by the most accomplished lawyer in Seattle. So I gave a small smile and relaxed about one millimeter.

"Ashley, we are probably looking at some sort of plea agreement. It's your first offense, right? Were there any special circumstances that caused you to bring those drugs into the U.S.?"

"But they told me ..." she started to say, looking at her mother.

"That isn't the line of defense we're pursuing," said Claudia. "Ashley is not guilty. That wasn't her bag. It's not something she would carry."

"How do you know, Mrs. Moore?"

"Excuse me?"

"How do you know that wasn't Ashley's bag. Have you seen it since Ashley's arrest?"

"No, but ..."

"Were you with Ashley in Victoria? Do you know she didn't buy another bag while there?"

"No, but ..."

"So your opinion is based on ...?"

"I know Ashley. I believe what she tells me."

"Yes, but the judge doesn't know Ashley, and neither does the jury. We have to have more to go on than your trust of your daughter."

"I think..." Claudia Moore started to say.

"Let's save you some time. I will go over the arrest, and the evidence. I'll review the case and decide if it's one we want to take. Ashley, it should not take me more than four or five days. How about I call you in a week, next Monday?"

"You can call me," said Mrs. Moore.

"How old are you, Ashley?" I asked the younger version.

"I turned twenty-three in January," Ashley said.

"Since your daughter is of age, if I am her lawyer my communications should be with her."

"Please don't instruct me in the law," said Claudia Moore, with the tone of queen to handmaiden. I ignored her and turned to Ashley and started to ask her for contact information.

"Please communicate to me through my mother," said Ashley. She was obedient, if not overly bright.

"And assume my communication back to you is from my daughter," added Claudia Moore. The girl looked at me and nodded.

They had just added to a long list of reasons why I did not think I would take the case of Ms. Ashley Moore, but I still wanted to think about it when I wasn't reacting to the attitude. She was the wife of Mark's boss. Besides, I'd promised Tony I'd consider what they had to say.

As I was showing them out, Tony came around the corner.

"Hello, Claudia," he said.

"Tony!" She opened her arms and walked quickly to him. He opened his arms, too.

Sometimes you can just feel energy between two people, even when they aren't saying a thing. What flowed between those two in that moment would have stressed transmission lines for Seattle Power & Light.

Not one word was spoken. They held each other two moments too long.

"You look good," said Tony, pushing away at last.

"And you are obviously well," said Claudia, studying his face.

And with that, she gathered up her daughter like an extra piece of luggage and walked out to the elevator.

"You know each other?" I went fishing for the backstory by stating the obvious.

"We did," was all he said and walked away down the hall.

A half-hour later I knocked on his door, entered when he said, "Come in."

"I'm taking a pass on the Ashley Moore case," I said.

"No, you're not," Tony replied.

"Excuse me?"

Not once had Tony ever overruled me when I didn't want to represent someone. Once in a while he would say I couldn't represent someone, if he thought the case would be bad for the firm or not pay well, but he never made me handle one I thought smelled bad.

"You're taking the case," he said.

"But Tony …" I started, then he held up a hand.

"Jessi, the case is yours. Tell yourself whatever you need to tell yourself to be good with it. That you are doing me a favor. That it's good for the firm. That I'm occasionally an asshole. All of those may be true. But you are taking the case. Okay?"

I respected Tony too much to let him down when he was making a plea in such honest terms.

Chapter 22

Not everything, or anything, is preordained in any way that we can understand. We evolved to find patterns in cause and effect. When we see a pattern but not the cause, we call that coincidence.

Mark and I ran into Michael and Sandy at SASA about two months after we got back from Denver. There aren't that many places, even in Seattle, where couples of our tastes can play.

Mark and I had each gotten a drink and were sitting on a couch where we could see the dance floor, bar, and entrance. Mark was watching an erotic movie on one wall, I was watching people.

"Look," I said when Michael and Sandy walked in through the curtains with Elizabeth, the woman who had given us the tour on our first visit that seemed so long ago.

The couple was striking in their height, as well as the grace with which they moved. I watched people who were watching them.

We stood and Mark said "Hey," as they got to us. Michael looked at Mark and then me, and said "Hey," in about the same voice.

Sandy flashed a wonderful smile. I hadn't seen that in Denver, as I was a bit … preoccupied. Nor had I realized how pretty she was, how fine were her features in addition to the length of her legs and torso.

"Hi!" she said, holding out her hand to me. "It's nice to see you again. Michael told me he'd flown back with you two. Made me jealous. I would have loved to have been on *that* flight!" she said.

"You all know each other? Wonderful!" said Elizabeth. "In that case, would you mind showing Michael and Sandy the club? They're not newbies, as I can tell you know, so maybe you can show them the rooms and where we keep things? I have to tend to Mike at the front door."

"Happy to, Elizabeth," I said.

Mark bought them each a drink and we wandered through SASA. Most clubs are similar, and it didn't take long. We ended up on the couch where we started.

We made small talk. Sandy asked me questions about the law and she told me things about working for Social Security. I didn't really pay much attention to what Mark and Michael were talking about until Mark said my name.

"Jessi, what do you think?"

"What do I think about what?"

"Would you like to show Michael and Sandy the view from our place, have a nightcap? The club is pretty slow, and this is not my favorite DJ."

"I think that would be wonderful." I didn't hesitate before I said that. I didn't really think about it. They were nice people, and the conversation was fun.

"Can you give me the address?" asked Michael. "I need to get gas. I'll just plug it in to my GPS and we'll be there as soon as we can." I texted Michael the address and we all headed out past Big Mike in the foyer. He was wearing a green and blue 12th Man shirt to show his support for our Seahawks.

"Night," he said, in a cheery voice that indicated the team must be winning.

When we got home, Mark set out glasses and a bottle of nice cognac while I freshened up a bit.

"OH MY GOD!" Sandy said as she walked into the main room and to the windows where the city spread out below like gemstones on a black velvet cloth.

"That's the Space Needle. Look at the ferry coming in!" she said. "This is the most amazing view I've ever seen!"

Mark poured four glasses of Cognac and we stood at the windows.

"What is this?" asked Michael, holding up his glass.

"Louis Royer X.O.," said Mark.

"It's very good!"

We gave them a tour of the house. Uncharacteristically, when we walked past the bar, Mark refilled everyone's glass. None of us objected.

"Let's sit down," I said at last. I sat on the couch facing to the northwest. I was surprised when Michael sat next to me and Sandy sat on the other couch. Mark looked at the tableau and sat next to Sandy.

It did not surprise me when Sandy put a hand on Mark's thigh. He quickly looked up and over at me, and I gave him a smile of assurance. I saw his legs relax and spread slightly, allowing his left thigh to rest along Sandy's right and allowing Sandy's hand just a little more room.

At some point Michael draped an arm across my shoulders. The conversation continued just as if everything were completely normal, as if it were Mark's arm around me, or my hand on Mark's thigh.

Michael unbuttoned my blouse while Sandy talked about something I can't remember. What I can remember is the feel of the fabric coming away from my breasts, and then his long fingers toying with a nipple.

At some point I moved my hand from his thigh to the hardness beneath his slacks. By then, Sandy had Mark's belt undone and her hand wrapped around his erection.

"I think we'd be more comfortable upstairs," I said.

"That's a great idea," said Mark. "Let's get a refill and head on up."

"I'm good," said Michael, holding up his half-full glass. Sandy allowed a little to be splashed into hers.

"I'm not ready," I said. "Maybe in a bit."

Mark poured some for himself, and we all headed to the master bedroom.

Sandy slowly removed Mark's shirt, finished undoing his slacks. After he sat and had kicked off his shoes, she pushed Mark backwards onto the bed and took him in her mouth. It was the slowest, most sensual blow job of his life, at least his life with me. I was learning something.

I was still standing, watching. I could feel Michael behind me. He slowly pulled my blouse back and off my shoulders, then kissed the back of my neck, one of my erogenous zones. I reached up and put my hand to the back of his neck. It did not take long for Michael to have me naked, and himself, too. He pushed me down onto the other side of the bed, and put his mouth on me.

"Oh, oh," I heard my Mark say in a minute, and I watched his back stiffen. Sandy never removed her mouth. A bit later Sandy was naked and started kissing my breasts, my throat, then she put her mouth on mine. I could taste Mark mixed with the Cognac and it was intoxicating.

I was starting to climb the wall when I felt Michael's cock slip into me. Sandy stopped kissing me and slid down to where her head was on my belly and her right hand played just above where Michael's shaft sank to the back of me. I opened my eyes and saw Michael's face with the dreamiest expression, then he looked down and deep into my eyes.

The feeling of connection was incredible.

I heard Mark get up and go into the bathroom.

Michael's eyes closed as I let out a small sound. My hips lifted on their own and pushed against him. I heard Michael exhale as he came hard into me, as I lifted my hips even higher to receive him.

I heard water in the sink in the bathroom, then it shut off. I had no concept of time. Michael pulled out of me just as Mark came into the bedroom.

"Sweetheart, would you bring me a towel?" I asked him as I had asked him a hundred times before. Michael was lying on my left side, Sandy on my right, his hand rested on my abdomen.

"A towel?" Then, as the realization came home, his face changed and he walked to the bed and looked down where my legs were still open and Michal was dripping out of me.

"That wasn't supposed to happen!" Mark said.

"Sweetheart, it'll be fine if you can just get me a towel," I replied, looking at the bed and completely clueless to what he was thinking.

"Oh, fuck! You let him cum inside you!" Mark said to me.

The tone of his voice made me no longer care what dripped on the bedspread, or the carpet. I sat up, swung my legs for momentum and stood on the floor in front of Mark.

"What's going on?" I asked him.

"He just came in you!" Mark said.

"Yes…?"

"Mark, I'm clean, no STD's" said Michael.

"That's not what this is about!" said Mark.

"Honey, what *is* this about?" I asked.

"What do you mean? He just came inside you. You wanted him to!"

"Yes. And you just came with Sandy. That's why we came upstairs, right?" I was honestly confused.

"It's not the same! That was just a blow-job! He made love to you. You made love to him!"

"Just a blow-job?" said Sandy.

"Sandy, this is between them," Michael said.

"Then we should probably get dressed," said Sandy.

"Yes, you should," said Mark. "And you should probably clean yourself up," he said to me, with a nod to the bathroom.

Mark grabbed his clothes and walked out the bedroom door.

For a moment, I just stood there, stunned.

"I don't know what happened," I said to Michael and Sandy as they put on their clothes.

"It's okay," said Michael. "It happens."

"Jealousy is a biological force," said Sandy, "though sometimes we say 'bio-illogical.'"

"I'm so sorry," I said. "I had no idea."

"Neither did he, probably," said Michael. "It's the 30-second syndrome."

"What's that?"

"Everything's great while everyone is under the influence of endorphins, but 30 seconds later, other emotions rise to the top. Sometimes it's not pretty."

"How did you you two deal with it?" I asked. "Was it hard on your marriage?"

Michael laughed, and so did Sandy.

"Oh, we're not married," Sandy said.

"She's my sister," Michael said.

"Ohhh," I said, air escaping my lungs.

"We'll let ourselves out. Good luck," said Sandy.

They walked down the stairs while I went into the bathroom and took a long, hot shower, letting the heat and hot vapor permeate my skin.

When I got out, I brushed my teeth and put on my robe. In the bedroom, Mark was already under the sheets but was facing away from my side of the bed.

Though his breathing did not sound like he was sleeping when I crawled under the covers and leaned over to give him a kiss, he did not move or respond in any way.

Chapter 23

The next morning Mark said "I had too much to drink last night."

"We all did," I said, thinking it was the right thing to do at the time. Looking back, I don't.

That was it. We were busy over the next few months. The Ashley Moore case was consuming. Because of who she was, the news media were all over it. Because of who she was, Claudia Moore would not accept any strategy that had Ashley pleading guilty to anything. We argued about it right up until the trial.

"Ashley says it's not her bag, so it's not her bag. Make them prove it's hers."

"She was holding the bag," I said, not intending to be cute but smiling at the reality of the cliché.

"Inappropriate," Claudia said. "Make them show that the drugs were in her bag, and prove it's her bag."

Arguing was futile.

Claudia insisted again, out in the hallway before we went into the courtroom.

"Have them open the bag," she'd said.

"Giving the jurors a look at the evidence makes it more concrete for them that a crime was committed. If we leave it conceptual, we may have a better chance for reasonable doubt."

"It would be better if you showed some confidence in Ashley's innocence. Have them open the bag," she said.

It pissed me off that Claudia wanted to direct the defense, but there were other factors that went into my decision to do what she said. Sometimes it's better to seem unafraid of the evidence, to show faith in the outcome even when it seems hopeless. A jury often responds to confidence. It was a strategy not unlike what my Grandmama taught me about backgammon.

In court, I asked Agent Robert Miller, who had conducted the search, to list the drugs he found in Ashley's bag when she got off the ferry.

He read out the short list: Pot, ecstasy, coke.

"Is this the bag Ashely was carrying?" I pointed to the bag on the evidence table.

"We'd have to compare evidence tags to be sure," said Agent Miller.

We confirmed the evidence tags.

"Will you show the jury what you found in the bag?" I asked him.

Agent Miller put on rubber gloves. At least I could show the jury that it was odd there were no fingerprints on the packaging materials, slick bags and wrappings that could have easily captured a print. Of course, the prosecution would just argue that the bags were wiped and carefully placed, but I hoped to sow reasonable doubt that someone who wiped fingerprints off contraband was unlikely to carry that contraband through customs.

Miller opened the bag.

The bag contained clothes that would fit a tall, stylish young woman.

Nothing else.

Agent Miller was flabbergasted. The prosecutor was outraged. The judge was not amused.

There was a recess. Another bag was found that had the same identification number. That one contained drugs. But now there were two bags, nearly identical, with two indistinguishable tags and both apparently in uninterrupted possession of the Feds.

I had no idea how that happened.

"Do you know anything about this? Anything at all?" Judge Burns asked me at the bench.

"No, sir. I'm stunned," I said. He looked at me for a long minute, and then I guess he decided he believed me. He gave the prosecution 48 hours to sort it out, but he told them that without a clear, simple explanation, he was going to dismiss.

I won't call it coincidence, but it's amazing how certain people seem to appear, disappear, and then reappear in your life. Deborah Riddle, the cop who interviewed me after having sex with Sam when I was fifteen years old, was the supervisor called in to explain. She hadn't handled any of the evidence, but there were embarrassing moments for her on the stand.

According to her testimony, the bag with the drugs was in federal custody. A second bag was also in federal custody. She could not prove which bag was the original. I could park a truck in the middle of that reasonable doubt and two days later, Judge Burns dismissed the charges. I thought that would be the end of it.

As I walked past Agent Riddle in the courthouse, I looked at her and said, "She got exactly what she deserved."

"How dare you," she snarled back at me.

A week or so later I was at one of my favorite lunch spots. I may have been reading a brief, or the *Source of the Sound* with its continued obsession over who was feeding the homeless at Pike Place Market. I don't remember.

"That was out of bounds," said a voice at my shoulder. I turned to the florid face of Agent Deborah Riddle.

"What was out of bounds?" I asked.

"Planting evidence. Breaking the law in how many ways God only knows to get that bag planted in our custody. Damaging the career of Agent Miller."

"I have no idea what you're talking about. I had nothing to do with anything like that," I said. "Your team had the bag, and apparently more than one bag. Reasonable doubt."

"Bullshit. The only reason you would have had Miller open that bag is because you knew the bags had been switched. You knew what would happen in that courtroom."

"So, you're an expert on what I know? On what I think?" I shot back.

"I remember you from the first time we met, and when we talked after that disgusting party," she said. "We were different, but I respected you in a way. You were true to who you were. But what you did this week was out of bounds. And it painted a target on your back for every cop and prosecutor in this city."

"Is that a threat, Agent Riddle?" I asked.

"Consider it a warning," she said. "You'll get what you deserve. Everyone does." And with that, she walked away.

Her warning bothered me on a couple of levels. First was the obvious. Nobody wants to be a target for anything.

But more importantly, I hadn't really given enough thought to the fact that there was a lot wrong in the Ashley Moore "win." At first I hadn't much questioned the screw-up in the Feds' handling of the evidence because I had not created it. I just used it. I just did my job. And I was pleased with the victory, not only because I liked to win but because that win was a validation, of sorts, especially after the similar case I had lost.

So, even though at some level I knew there was a stink in there someplace, I tried to push it out of my mind. Agent Riddle's accusations brought it back. Where had that second bag come from?

Claudia Moore had insisted that I have Agent Miller display the contents of the bag in court. So I called her and asked if we could meet.

"My schedule is really quite full," she said on the phone.

"It won't take long. I'm happy to come to your home." I started to say.

"No. My secretary just gave me a note. I can meet for lunch at 1:00 p.m. this afternoon."

She chose a café in Bellevue, L'Escargot. It had been established in a grand old house on a hillside, set back and up from the corner of a busy intersection, with tables that spread from the sidewalk to ivy-draped gardens in back shaded by huge, old-growth fir trees. The wait-staff was young, dressed all in black and quite attractive, which no doubt enhanced the flavors of a $35 salad.

I was shown to a table outside on the sidewalk. A few minutes after my iced tea arrived, a very large, black Mercedes stopped on the street right in front of me. Cars behind slammed to a halt, one honked its horn. The back door opened and Claudia Moore stepped out onto the sidewalk.

"Half-hour," she said to whomever was driving behind darkened windows. The car whispered off.

"Have you ordered?" she asked as she sat down. No pleasantries offered.

"No, I thought I'd wait for you," I said.

"I made the reservation. They know me here, and they know what I like."

As soon as she said this, a tall glass was brought to her with ice and what looked like a mint leaf. Before the server could turn away, Claudia Moore looked at me and said, "May I order for you? I know the menu so well." Before I could answer, she turned to the server and said, "She'll have my usual."

My grandmother had often told me, "Respect yourself and others will respect you. To demand their respect gives them reason not to." It was a way of saying, "Choose your battles." I chose to have the same lunch as Claudia.

To lower the barriers, I made a comment about the car.

"So, is that Max's Mercedes, or are all your cars monogrammed?"

"Excuse me?" Claudia said. She seemed confused.

"Behind the back passenger window. There is an 'M' inside an 'M.' A monogram for 'Max Moore,' right? Or is Claudia your middle name?"

"Um, no," she said with a smile and much too slowly, as if to give herself time to figure out how to explain without making it obvious that I was an idiot.

"Actually, that's the model of the car. It's a Mercedes Maybach. But I can certainly see how you jumped to that conclusion. There are not a lot of them around, even in Bellevue."

"And I doubt one has ever rolled through the lumber and fishing town where I grew up. Very nice," I said, unhappy that she'd put me at a disadvantage, like the rich so frequently do to those who've not experienced their privilege.

"But you didn't want to talk to me about cars, I'm sure," Claudia said.

"No. I wanted to ask you a question that's been bothering me since the trial." I took a sip of my iced tea.

I waited for a moment, and was rewarded when she finally asked, "What's that?"

"You pressed me during the trial for the bag to be opened. Normally, displaying the drugs would not have been a good idea. But you seemed to know that there were no drugs in the bag. How did you know that?"

Normally so quick, so superior, and so dismissive, she should have fired a comment right back at me. She didn't. The first thing she did was glance right and then left, as if to see who was close enough to hear our conversation.

Then she said, "I wonder where lunch is?"

As if on cue, a server appear with two large bowls of romaine lettuce topped with a thickly grated cheese and finger-long lengths of beautifully grilled salmon. I could not identify the dressing. I took a bite.

"I believed in my daughter. Apparently you did not," she said at last.

"There were two bags, Claudia. With the same tag number. Someone tampered with the evidence. Do you know who? How did you know this would happen?"

"I believed in my daughter. What else can I say? My daughter was found not guilty thanks to your excellent legal representation. You should be very proud of winning such a high-profile case for an important client. I'm sure this will bring you cases for a number of years."

"Claudia ..."

"Do you like the salad? I developed it in concert with the chef. It took a few tries, but he has such a marvelous touch. Oh! Excuse me." She reached into her bag for her cell phone, looked at the screen, pushed a couple of buttons. I had not heard it ring.

"It was nothing important," she said immediately after slipping the phone back in her bag.

"Claudia ..."

"Is it possible to be tried twice for the same crime in this country? Once you're found innocent, aren't you're innocent?" she asked.

"If the crime violates both federal and state law ..." I started to explain.

"I just don't think we should rehash this. We're all so busy. That's in the past, and we all should move on now, don't you think?"

"Claudia ..." I was willing to be patient, to wait out her feints. But she had the last move, and I should have seen it coming given the size of the rare Mercedes Maybach that just then pulled to the curb.

"Oh! I have to go! Please, just one more token of gratitude, may I buy your lunch? They'll put it on my tab."

She stood and looked down at me for a moment too long, then flashed the brightest smile, but it had no warmth. When truly beautiful women are cold and calculating it's like a brilliant white cloud on the horizon that hides violent lightning within. Claudia walked to the curb, opened her own door to the back seat of the huge sedan and disappeared behind its darkened glass.

I finished my salmon and romaine salad. Claudia knew I would not find answers to my questions, and I decided there wasn't much benefit in pursuing it as I fended off servers who were entirely too attentive.

Chapter 24

On the rare mornings before work when we had an extra few minutes, Mark and I would sit at the table and share our view of the city over coffee. One of us would scootch a chair over near the other to be close and sometimes we talked about what to do after work, about who might get what groceries, about what errands most needed attention. We almost never talked about work, and sometimes we didn't say much at all and just enjoyed sharing air.

A couple of weeks after the visit by Michael and Sandy, when I moved my chair over to be close to him, Mark stood up to pour himself more coffee. I waited for him to come back, but he wouldn't meet my eyes and just gazed out over the bay.

"What's up?" I asked at last.

"Nothing. What do you mean?"

"Mark…?" I asked. It took too long for him to answer but finally he did.

"What was it like for you with Michael and Sandy?"

"You were there. No mystery, right?"

"Was it special? Extra, I mean?" Mark asked.

"It was good."

"I don't ever remember you having an orgasm like that."

"I'm sure I have," I said.

That was not as bad as saying "You're right, Mark, that orgasm with Michael rocked my world and set a new standard." Which was not true in any case. But the words "I'm sure I have," were bad enough, with the implication that I couldn't think of a better orgasm in that moment.

I should have remembered an experience exclusive to just Mark and me that was better than the evening with Michael and Sandy. If I couldn't remember such a moment then I should have made something up. Instead, I gave his insecurity the fast lane on a very congested highway.

"I don't think you've ever had an orgasm like that with me," Mark said.

"Babe, you were there. You were part of that one." Again, not exactly the best choice of words.

Then it was time to go, Mark didn't say anything more and I let it drop as we drove down to work and talked about, who knows, the weather I suppose.

It amazes me still how fucking clueless I was, or maybe I was in vicious denial. That evening it all fell into place.

We had eaten at home. I was rinsing the plates before putting them in the dishwasher, which always drove Mark crazy.

"If we have a dishwasher, why do you have to wash the dishes?" he always asked. That evening he said nothing.

"You've been awfully quiet," I said.

"Oh, I'm just a little preoccupied with some things at work. No big deal," he mumbled toward the floor.

Mark can make nearly anyone believe nearly anything in the courtroom. There, he's building his "story" of the case. Part of his success is an ability to create a possibility so detailed, so real, that even he can get lost. But it's still a story.

Outside the courtroom, when faced with a personal conflict, he looks down and he mumbles like a six-year-old with his hand in the cookie jar. And he looked like a cookie-thief right then.

"What's up?" I asked, again.

"I'm having trouble with the other night."

"Which night?"

"Michael and Sandy."

My heart sank. Not because I didn't see it coming, but because then I saw it coming like a speeding bus, straight at me and I didn't have a clue how to avoid it. I sat on a chair at the table. Suddenly I was six years old again, too, and had just dropped my grandmother's teacup. Sometimes there are no take-backs.

"Which part?"

"The way you reacted, watching him touch you, how you responded."

"That bothers you?"

"Yeah."

"Why? It was your idea."

"That doesn't make it better, for some reason. I don't know why, but it's bothering me a little," Mark said.

"A little, or a lot?"

"A lot."

"Yeah," I said, "I can tell. You want to talk about it?"

"No, I don't think so. I just have to process it a bit more."

"You want to process it with me?" I asked, trying to open the door again even as I knew he wouldn't walk through.

"I don't think it works like that," he said.

"I don't think it can work any other way." My words came out calm, but I was feeling overwhelmed.

"It's not your fault," Grandmama had whispered to me long ago when I dropped her teacup. I flashed on the horror I felt even before the cup inevitably shattered on the floor. I heard her voice now, as I searched the past and then the present for something to say that would make the feeling of awful anticipation go away.

"I'm sorry, it's just been eating at me," said Mark.

"*Tout passe, tout lasse, tout casse,*" I said.

"What's that mean?" he asked.

"Everything passes, everything wears out, everything breaks," I said.

"What does that mean?" he asked.

"That it's not your fault," I replied. Not because I didn't want things to be different, but because there was nothing I could do to make them different, and just like my grandmother, if I gave in to wanting it to be different, I would come apart.

Everything passes, everything wears out, everything breaks.

"I just need to process it a bit," he said.

"Yeah. Well, you let me know," I said with what I imagine was the same expression of grim determination my grandmother had as she swept up fragments of her beloved teacup, her youth in France, her heritage.

A week later Mark moved out to a small furnished apartment not far from Pike Place Market "to get his head together."

"You know this isn't fair," I said as he was packing clothes into two large suitcases sitting on the bed in our room.

"I know. I can't help it."

"You were the one who broke our rules in Denver," I said.

"I know. I just didn't think I'd feel like this. I thought it would be contained."

"What do you mean?"

"Somehow it's different. Somehow it diminishes me."

"How can it diminish you!? It was your idea!" I said.

"I know." He just left that there, as if it didn't matter that it was his idea, and that started to piss me off, too.

"This whole fucking thing was your idea," I said.

"I know." Again he just left it as if that didn't matter, and looked again like that cookie-stealing six-year-old.

In that moment, I despised him: for looking like a child, for acting like a child, for what he was doing, what he was doing to us, what he was doing to me, even for leaving me behind in our home.

"The first time, every escalation, every new thing, every new erotic moment, was your fucking idea," I hissed at him.

"I know," he said.

"Get out of my sight," I told him. "I'll let you know when you can come back for the rest of your things."

"I don't want to get the rest of my things. I just want a little time," he said.

"Get out."

They say that when you're run over by a train, it's not the caboose that kills you. Not always true. Within a week, I'd also left the house on Queen Anne Hill. I took my clothes, my jewelry, my toiletries. I found a place downtown not far from my original Seattle apartment but of course much, much nicer. In anger when I made that decision, I decided to spoil myself a little.

"Jessica, all anger is a form of fear," my grandmother once told me. "Identify the fear, only then can anger leave."

Before Mark, it was me fighting to be who I was. Then it was Mark and me against the world. For more than two years I'd been vulnerable to Mark and never had to deal with him defensively. Suddenly, the person I'd been protecting and who had been protecting me was the threat.

Now I was unarmed. Not only was Mark the source of my pain, he was also the man I loved. I couldn't protect myself without definitively ending our relationship. I wasn't ready for that, so I had to wait it out, passively, not protecting myself.

Mark and I never had "the talk." He shut me out, and honestly, I put up some walls of my own. I didn't know how to break those down, or find an emotional space where we could at least be honest. Honesty requires vulnerability, and we both hurt so badly that neither could take the necessary first step.

One day I received divorce papers in regular mail, not even certified, with a letter from Max Moore, "not representing Mark in a legal sense, but helping him through this difficult time," expressing regret at the breakup, platitudes about change. Also enclosed was a check that represented "a possible difference between Mark's income and your income for a period of three years."

It was an exceptionally generous check. Either Mark was making much, much more than I knew, or they thought I was making much less than I was. But they never asked for numbers and neither did I.

Not wanting conflict, wanting the pain to go away, I signed the papers immediately and sent them back without even a note. I did put the check in my bank.

When papers came to list the house on Queen Anne Hill, I recognized the name of the real estate firm and I signed and returned those, too; with no comment, no muss, no fuss. When the house sold, we made a stunning profit. I signed and returned the escrow documents without comment.

When papers came to sell the house out in the San Juan Islands, I signed and returned the listing agreement, then the escrow when it sold. We lost a little money, but not enough to fret about.

I received title to my Porsche in the mail. I didn't even know Mark had the title; I hadn't remembered it was in both our names. He signed his interest over to me for $1, and he certified that $1 had already been received. I sent a $1 bill back to him, folded in the same envelope and both inside a business envelope. No note.

Everything passes, everything wears out, everything breaks.

Chapter 25

My father usually felt sorry for himself and was chronically angry, so it wasn't a surprise he blamed me for the breakup with Mark. But his vehemence hurt and his repetition was insulting. Since Mark could not do wrong, Mark could not have been at fault.

Of course I couldn't tell the whole story and was still miserable with loss. Finally I was just sick of it.

"Why are you putting this all on me?" I asked my father. "What about what Mark could do? What about Mark's responsibility? I'm your fucking daughter, for Christ's sake. What about being my fucking father on this one?"

"Don't talk to me like that," he said.

"Why don't you just answer the fucking question instead of criticizing how I asked it?" my voice dripped with anger, scorn, hurt.

"Jessica!" said my mother.

"How about you, Mom? Want to be on my side?"

"Sweetheart, I'm sure Mark has some responsibility. He may be in the wrong, too, but I'm sure it has something to do with pressure at work. He's got some big cases coming up, doesn't he? He's a wonderful man. We don't want to lose him. Sometimes, we just have to reach out when things get difficult."

I just looked at her in disbelief. Then at my father. They had turned my loss into their loss and somehow made me responsible for it. I didn't have anything left to say. I gathered my things, got in my Porsche, and drove off.

As always, I went to my grandmother's house. She had not answered the phone when I tried to call, but she frequently didn't. I was convinced she would be the last person in the Pacific Northwest to get a cell phone. Even getting her an answering machine was a battle.

"Why do I need one of these?" she asked.

"So someone can leave you a message," I said.

"If what they want to say is important, they will call again."

"Maybe they just want to say hello."

"That's so important that I need to spend this money?"

"I'll buy it for you, Grandmama."

"You may not buy it for me, but you must choose the best one that is easy for me to use."

So I left her a message that I was coming over. When I got to her small house two blocks off the main street of town behind the Safeway, the house was dark. I knocked on the door because the doorbell had not worked for a decade or two. My father apparently could not be bothered to fix it.

Finally, the door opened and as soon as she appeared, I started to cry.

"Oh, Jessica!" she said. She swung the door wide and held out her arms. She felt smaller than the last time I'd held her, even more like the tiny birds she fed in her backyard. We hugged for a long time.

"It's so good to see you," she said at last, pushing me back.

"Hi, Grandmama," I said, wiping a tear from my cheek.

"Oh, baby," she said, looking right through me. "You are so sad."

I gave her a rueful smile and nodded my head. No hiding anything from her.

"*Tout passe, tout lasse, tout casse*," I said.

"Let's have café," she said. We went into her wonderful kitchen where herbs hung from the cupboards, flowers dried on a wood rack, the ever-present basket of fruit sat in the middle of the table.

She threw several glances in my direction while she put water on to boil.

"Grandmama, you need a microwave," I said.

She pursed her lips and let out a small burst of air. "I don't need, I don't want a microwave. It ruins the aromas, the flavors," she said.

I wasn't going to argue. In the kitchen, she was almost always right.

"Trouble with Mark?" she asked when she sat down with two cups. I nodded.

"I just don't know what to do," I said.

"Another man, another woman?"

"It's complicated."

"Yes, love is so simple and always so very complicated," she said with a half-smile, but her respect of propriety and privacy kept her from asking more. "Perhaps, with some time, it can be fixed."

"I don't think I can fix it," I said, as if the divorce was not already final.

"If you don't think you can fix it, maybe it is not yours to fix," she said. "If you did wrong, you apologize. If you did not do wrong, an apology from you just causes problems, if not now then in future. If he did wrong, he must apologize. If he did not do wrong, you must not expect an apology."

"We did something we should not have done," I said.

"There is no 'should!' " she snapped, then realizing how sharply she spoke, immediately softened.

"You do what you do, and you own what you've done. That is the only 'should,' my dear one," she said. "You face the consequences and try to change, or accept the consequences and do not change."

"We did something we knew might cause a problem, but did it anyway."

"If you broke it together, it is yours to fix together. That is the only way."

"And if he can't, or won't try to fix it?"

"*C'est la vie*," she sighed, putting her hand on mine.

"You can't do for him what he has to do," she said. Then she surprised me. "He is not as strong as you, Jessica. He has a place inside him that can't be filled."

"Why do you say that? How would you know that?"

Mark had sat in this kitchen only a half-dozen times, and at my parents' house with my grandmother a few more times over various holidays. I had no idea how she could presume to see inside him.

But she just shook her head, looked into my eyes and did not take her hand from on top of mine. When I started to cry again, she scooted her chair over and somehow managed to take me into her arms, saying nothing. She did not try to tell me what to think or what I should believe or what I should be feeling. She let the emotions wash over me in the safety of her arms.

She knew when I was ready, I would pull away.

It was raining hard when I left. I wasn't sure if I would make it all the way back to Seattle, but there were no motels I wanted to stay in on the way. I had to stop for gas once. When I finished filling up, I got back in my car, started the engine and pulled out to the exit but then just sat there, lost, lonely, and alone. I didn't try to wipe away tears washing down my face faster than raindrops ran down the windshield.

Finally, the car behind me gave a polite little honk on his horn.

"Exactly," I said to him with a little wave of acknowledgment. "Get a move on," I said to myself, and pulled back onto the highway.

My appearance began to change in the months after that. I don't know if the style sense of some of my clients or that of my younger assistants Lily and Sarah — even though they weren't that much younger than me — was starting to rub off, or if it was just Seattle.

But I acquired a bit more "edge."

Warm browns and soft yellows in my wardrobe went into storage, and my suits became black, gray, and white. I would wear a fuchsia or teal blouse to add a splash of color, but the suits leaned more to the dramatic, the cut sexy, and much less like some knock-off of a man's Armani. There seems to be an unwritten code that female lawyers must dress as much like men as possible. I pretended that I didn't get the memo.

But really, it was the hair. The next time I got my hair cut, my usual stylist was on maternity leave and the new one asked if I wanted to try something different. I said, "Sure."

She cut it quite a bit shorter than it had been, distinctly shorter on the left side.

"It should be darker," she said.

"Sure," I replied.

They say clothes make the man, or in my case, the woman. Maybe. But there is something very different about hair. It's so much more personal, so much more about identity. We can change our clothes and dress up or down, but changing hair is a much stronger statement. A woman with half her head shaved or dyed purple can change clothes ten times a day, but she'll still be making a very different statement than a woman with long, succulent waves — light or dark — who wears the same outfits.

I did not shave half my head or die my hair purple, but I did stop pretending any one shade was "my own." At times it was spiky, and sometimes my bangs draped over one eye. It was always thick like my grandmother's, and I experimented.

I can't say I was a hundred percent aware of this while it was going on, but others noticed.

"Nice look," said Tony one day.

"Good for you," said Claire, nodding approvingly when I came in with fresh black hair and a new white pantsuit one morning when we were scheduled to have an important court hearing. The full jacket had one button quite low, the pants had wide legs so that the whole statement was of excess. It wasn't cheap in any way. Some outfits cost about two Armanis. But it was style.

I worried a little about the impact when I became more aware of it. Once in the courthouse on an issue a little more serious than usual, a young prosecuting attorney I'd not previously met came up before the appearance and said "You probably should not be out here without your lawyer."

"I am her lawyer," I said, and held his gaze until he dropped his eyes and walked away.

Another time I had a client, Elise, who had grown up in Spokane and fled the farm life of her family, which owned orchards. Her father accompanied her on the first visit.

"I expected someone more … mature," he said after Claire led them into my office.

"Did you mean mature or conventional?" I asked

"Maybe a bit of both," he said, and I gave him an immediate ten credits for honesty and let it drop.

Elise got a more direct lesson. She'd been busted for selling heroin at the restaurant where she waited tables in Belltown. Tips were quite good, she said with a smug smile I would have to eliminate before it was seen by a jury. But I was talking about clothes and explaining how I wanted her to dress during trial.

"Why do I have to do that? Look at you!" Elise said in a snotty tone that I imagine she had been getting away with since she was twelve, and that I was already tired of.

"I'm not trying to avoid five years in prison, Elise," I said calmly, with no attempt to soften the tone or the message, and as if her attitude didn't matter to me one way or the other. The snottiness disappeared. In fact, she became a model client, and after I got her off we'd meet once a month or so for coffee. Elise asked questions about the law and law school, and I learned more than I wanted to know about the local drug trade.

It was Tony's theory that my new look worked to our advantage.

"Next to you, these girls look even more like hometown kids led astray," Tony said. "I think your edginess gives you more credibility when you explain how these girls ended up in their tragic situations. It's like you know the ropes from personal experience. I think it works," he said.

"Plus, I like it," he added, smiling as he walked away.

Only once, in front of Judge Burns, did my new look come up in the courtroom. True, the outfit was cut a little deep under the arms, but I thought the higher neckline might let me get away with it.

"You might want to rethink your personal presentation," he said to me when he called me to the bench after putting his hand over the microphone that taped proceedings. "You flirt with the edge of propriety."

I toned it down maybe a quarter of a notch, but not more than that.

Chapter 26

Empathy is not spread evenly among us. Confronted by another's loss, some say "it was inevitable," as if they had special — and unshared — insight. Others offer unfathomable platitudes: "Everything happens for a reason." Those who say: "He didn't deserve you!" forget, somehow, that the reason it hurts so bad is because it was so good.

Fortunately, I wasn't surrounded by many of these. One morning, just as we wrapped up one of our daily meetings, Claire put the tip of her index finger on the ring finger of my left hand, where the one-carat diamond had been. I'd sent it back to Mark.

"I'm sorry, dear," was all she said, knowing I would talk if I needed to talk. I loved her for not asking questions.

"Are you okay?" Sarah asked. I shrugged a reply. Lily looked at me with an invitation in her eyes to talk, which I declined with a little shake of my head. Because she was Lily, she acknowledged that with a slight nod.

And that was the announcement in my office.

A week or two later, Tony Stevens was true to form, and in a weird way, I kind of appreciated it.

"Sorry about you and Mark," he said in his first breath. "You want to grab a drink after work?" he asked in his second.

When I laughed out loud, at first he looked perplexed, then said, "I mean to talk about it. Really. Unless … never mind," and he walked away. Tony would not have been my first choice for a shoulder to cry on and he knew it.

I wasn't in the mood to cry on shoulders anyway.

For a long time, and no, I really don't know how long because to figure it out would take time I'd rather spend doing almost anything else, I did not go out. I went to the gym. I ran, and even did well in a couple of marathons. Not great, but I set a personal best in the second one. Of course I did. I'd set a personal best in the first one, too.

I didn't travel much, because there was no place I wanted to go alone, and there was nobody I really wanted to go with. I just wasn't up for it. After a while, I'd go with Sarah or Lily or both to a movie. Sometimes I'd go listen to music with other friends.

Tony used to say some women broadcast they are available for sex or a relationship just by their body language. During this time men could tell I was not available, regardless of how nice or accommodating or charming I tried to be. And they were right. I wasn't interested.

I'd sit alone at a table for lunch reading the current week's *The Sound,* still hyping an exposé of the anonymous benefactor they now called the "Prince of the Poor of Pike Place Market," in a scandal they named "Meals at Midnight." Street people would gather from behind fences or under the bridges and get a hot meal handout that seemed to appear from nowhere. *The Sound* speculated that someone from Microsoft or Amazon was the donor.

If a man came up to me while I was reading, I'd wait silently with my newspaper for him to go away. My "be polite" gauge was set to low. I refused invitations and isolated myself. I was healing, but slowly. I thought about adopting a dog or a cat, but I wasn't inclined to walk a dog twice a day or ever, ever scoop up cat shit.

After a while, I had the occasional date with someone I'd met through a chance encounter, or with someone who someone else said I just had to meet. It took a while, but I began to see guys for coffee, then dinner. More occasionally I'd agree to a sleepover, always at their place, or a weekend trip to Friday Harbor or Port Townsend or Vancouver or Victoria, B.C., and I occasionally had sex. Never great sex but okay sex, good enough sex, certainly.

Most guys are not content to be told the sex was "okay." They need to hear that it was mind-bending, the best ever, cataclysmic, galactically orgasmic, change-of-consciousness great. Which is stupid. If everything is always the best ever, then there can be no best. Everyone can't be above average, and all that.

And every time we have sex, it does not have to be the "best ever" for it to be satisfying, good, or even damn good. So it became pretty obvious when men asked me if the sex was good, or above average or whatever, the question was not really about how I felt about the sex.

It wasn't about me at all.

It was about them. It had little to do with the sex and nothing to do with sharing, even affection. They wanted me to judge their performance, but at the same time, they wanted nothing of the sort. They wanted accolades.

An honest, even a half-honest, response was not going to satisfy them. That was not as easy a lesson for me to learn as you might think. The fact is, for the most part the sex wasn't that good.

We'll start with the obvious. Men often thought they had to "lower my inhibitions." I think we've dealt with that issue here. I really don't have many inhibitions, but they would push alcohol at me.

I wanted to say, "If you want me drunk, it's about you, not about me. And what it's about I don't like all that much. You don't want me fully aware, fully participating, fully consenting with all my faculties? Too bad for you."

Secondly, many men are just not good at sex. Once in the bedroom, they bounce between "can't shut their mind off" to "can't think at all." Maybe when they have an erection, all the blood leaves their brain.

The real mystery here is that these are men who study every stroke of their golf game and buy books on how to swing a club, how to hold a putter, how to read a green. "Keep your eye on the ball. Swing relaxed. Concentrate on the ball in front of you, forget the last shot."

Some of the same techniques apply to lovemaking, right?

Or those who take driving lessons.

After my divorce I'd gone down to Seattle Raceway for a day of driver training in my Porsche. Just for fun. They taught us to look where we wanted to go and not at the wall, to drive with relaxed hands, and warned that we'd lose control if we weren't smooth or tried to do too much.

Some of the same techniques apply to lovemaking, right?

If men are willing to spend thousands of dollars on golf lessons or driving lessons, why won't they spend a few hours learning to be better lovers? Anyone can improve, and the practice is so much less tedious!

My first few attempts to help drew various levels of resentment.

If I said that perhaps five or ten minutes of overly athletic pumping right after a meal wasn't quite enough foreplay, I was called demanding.

If I said I liked giving and receiving oral sex, both as an appetizer and dessert, I saw in their body language they thought that was a bit gross.

If I took forty-five minutes to reach orgasm for any reason, I was called greedy or cold.

If I wanted more spontaneity, suggest we have sex after a concert while driving home on the Alaskan Viaduct, I was called perverted.

Other times, they turned it around on me, and actually attacked me for answering a question they had asked. I tried elevating my vocabulary. Even when I said it was "great," they knew I was also saying, "but not the best." They would not call again, even if I made it obvious I wanted them to.

Maybe the worst were the "hurt feelings." Somehow, by not saying something that bolstered their self-esteem, I had betrayed them. All of which quickly brought me to the conclusion that if I wanted a child in my life, I would have had children.

Every now and again they tried harder, sometimes they gave up. Other times I gave up, too, which was okay because I wasn't emotionally invested.

A handful of men were good. They were fun and adventurous and sensual, but something always screwed it up. Often it was their fantasies. Several times I was asked what I thought about bringing another woman into the bedroom.

Mateo was a good example. He was a banker whose parents were Spanish, but Mateo was born in the U.S. God, he was handsome. Maybe it was his Latin blood, he was a great lover, too.

One evening after dinner and a second glass of wine at a restaurant over in Bellevue, he asked if I would like, or "consider" I think he said, bringing another woman into our sexual relationship.

I'd heard this before and had a ready reply.

"I would definitely consider it ..." I said, then paused and looked off, slowly rotating my wine glass in my fingers as if reviewing the sensual possibilities at that very moment.

I saw his eyes light up as endorphins soared and blood rushed from his brain to between his legs.

"But of course we'd have to have a quid pro quo. Do you know any men who'd be willing to join us on occasion? If not, I may have a phone number or two."

The light drained from his eyes as if I'd splashed him with ice water from a glass on the table. His lovely eyebrows knit together. He shook his head. "I don't think that's my thing," he said at last.

"Too bad," I smiled and shrugged, leaving him wondering whether I was jacking him around or if I really wanted a couple of men for my entertainment. I knew the discussion would not end there.

For fun I decided to be noncommittal when he brought up the subject of whether I'd had more than one man at a time. He tried to ask in so many ways without appearing to be asking at all. I'm a lawyer, I knew how not to answer a hidden question. By the time we returned to his place he was "very tired" and ready to sleep.

I was good with that. As pretty as he was and as accomplished a lover, we didn't have a lot in common. I let myself out and didn't hear from him again.

Then there are the jealous men, or those who feel that because we'd had sex once, or a half-dozen times, they need to "take care of me," that somehow they had "responsibilities." I know they can't help themselves, but a half-hour of quiet thinking on the subject would do them a world of good.

I just wanted to say, "We had sex. It was fun. Don't make assumptions about the future without talking to me first, okay?"

Chapter 27

There's a spectrum to sex. Sexuality, sensuality, erotic are different for each of us but overlap, and there's much that we share. That's why we linger over the underwear advertisement with the healthy and beautiful yet rugged man making eye contact and inviting our hand to slip down that exquisite "V" between his hips and beneath the fabric. Just the possibilities tantalize, even without touch.

I went to SASA.

I enjoyed sitting at the bar or on a couch or at the foot of one of the tented alcoves where couples made love, or put mouths on and all over, or where someone was spanked or tied to a section of chain link fence fastened to the wall and anonymous others invited to touch. It was arousing.

Wherever I sat, I was soon surrounded by men. I always felt fairly safe because of SASA's strict "no touching without permission" rules. But in that environment you don't expect much personal space. There's touching … and then there's touching.

Men would lean close to talk, and I would feel the pressure of their leg, or an erection, on my thigh. Sometimes they would put a hand on my shoulder as they inched closer, pretending to be heard above the music. I could smell them when they did, and usually it was a nice smell. I didn't flinch, I didn't tell them no, I didn't discourage them.

In truth, I liked the feel of a hand on my shoulder, fingertips on my skin where the strap of my dress had slipped, ever so slightly. I liked the pressure of a stranger's erection on my thigh, feeling it throb and knowing they wanted nothing more than for me to reach down, unzip their pants and take that cock in my hand.

When I shifted in my chair, sometimes I sat so I could put even more (inadvertent, of course) pressure on a hardness being offered. They liked that. And I liked it even more when there was one of them on each side of me. I liked being there, I liked knowing that I could have anything I wanted. But I never did anything sexual until a Friday night when I showed up at SASA around 10:00 p.m.

The music downstairs was too loud, so I grabbed a glass of wine and went to the play room where guests could sit on both sides of a long bar and watch volunteers at a brass stripper pole.

As often happened, after a while a man sat down next to me. When I looked, I recognized the owner of SASA. I didn't think he recognized me. I'd never seen him in the club before, and it had been a long time since we'd met at that informal conference when Mark and I found each other on opposite sides of the table. That encounter didn't last long and had enough other drama going on.

And I looked quite different then.

"Hi," he said. "You're here alone." It wasn't a question.

"Yes."

"Looking for anything in particular?"

"Just enjoying the atmosphere," I said, nodding at a couple starting to make love on a couch ten feet away.

"Would you like to be part of the atmosphere?"

"How's that?" I asked.

"Just a second." He came back with a bright white, freshly laundered sheet from one of the many stacks of them scattered everywhere in the club. He unfolded the sheet and lay it out on the bar. "Sit up here," he said."Remember," he said, "No means no. You're in charge." And then he walked off.

I kicked off my shoes and sat up on the bar. I sat there until I started to feel silly and was about to slide off when a couple of men came over and sat at stools on either side of my legs and introduced themselves. Brad, on my right, leaned his shoulder against my calf while Charles on my left leaned close, looked up at me and asked, "Would you like to go into one of the rooms?"

"I don't think so," I said.

"Do you mind if we sit with you here at the bar?" asked Brad.

"That would be lovely," I said.

We made small talk while Brad ran his fingertips from my knee to where the hem of my dress ended at mid-thigh. I did nothing to discourage him. What he was doing was causing a serious pounding in my heart. We talked for another 15 minutes, with the hem of my dress being slowly pushed toward my hip. The rest of the fabric followed when I shifted position, and Charles so gently put his lips on my left thigh.

A man wearing a dark sport coat, his necktie from work stuffed in the pocket, walked up.

"May I buy you another glass of wine?" he asked, nodding at my nearly empty glass.

"Why, thank you," I said. "Chardonnay."

"Pleasure," he said with a smile, and put his glass down on the bar.

"Let's give him a little room, do you think?" I asked the other two. Probably not happy about the addition, they smiled anyway and slid down the bar, leaving one stool empty next to the post that ran to the ceiling and supported the end. I shifted sideways and leaned against the post, but adjusted myself to makes sure I was not sitting on my dress.

"Here you go," said the new man when he got back to where I was sitting.

"That's your seat," I said to him, indicating the stool at the end of the bar.

"Why thank you," he said and sat down.

"Well thank you …?" I asked.

"Rick."

"You look familiar."

"I get that a lot," he replied. "I've just got one of those faces. But I've never been here before, and I'm new to Seattle."

Well, Rick, this is Charles," who was now stroking my thigh, "and Brad."

"Now we're all friends," I said, feeling more relaxed than I had any right to feel. We listened to the music for a bit and I sipped my wine. The four of us laughed about silly things, commented on a voluptuous woman who had volunteered to do a dance with the pole.

"She's a really good dancer," said Brad as she wrapped her leg around the pole after a quick shimmy up and hung upside down.

"She's not paying enough attention to the music," said Charles.

"Charles, this music is impossible to dance to!" I said.

"Music? Dance? What are you guys talking about?" said Rick, who was joking, but really had not taken his eyes from my face and body since he came back with the wine.

I raised the left leg Charles was petting so Brad could begin running his fingertips up the inside of my right thigh. I stayed that way on the bar, sitting sideways and leaning up against the post, sipping my wine, until Rick asked, "May I help you off with your dress?"

A quick jolt of electricity ran from between my legs to my throat, barely pausing to throw a loop around each nipple on the way. I exhaled. Inhaled. Exhaled. Inhaled.

"Thank you," I said. I turned so he could get to the zipper of my dress. He slowly, ever so slowly, unzipped it to my hips. His fingertips brushed my skin all the way down in a way that was completely unnecessary but oh, did I like it.

He started to slip the straps forward over my shoulders, but I asked him to wait.

"I'd like to savor this," I said to his questioning eyes. As I turned to look around the room, every move I made loosened the dress a little more.

Finally, when I reached down for my wine glass, the straps fell from my shoulders and the loose top fell in a bunch in my lap. I'd not worn a bra and my breasts were caressed by the gaze of at least a dozen men and a half-dozen women who were now watching.

"Brad, do you think you could stand and help me off with the rest of my dress?" I asked after another five minutes. He was on his feet in an instant, and gently slid the dress down and over my butt when I lifted my hips. Of course his hands touched my skin, but he wasn't obvious. When the fabric passed my knees, I put my butt down on the sheet and lifted my legs so he could easily slip the dress over my feet.

I was wearing a thong. I must have known I was going to be on display when I left home.

"My God you're beautiful," said Charles. "You are a very lucky man," he said to Rick.

"She's not mine." said Rick.

"Charles, I feel a little naked. Would you help me with my shoes?" I asked, without answering the question he wanted to ask. He took each ankle in turn and carefully slipped a shoe on each foot more gently than any shoe salesperson I'd ever known.

"That was very sweet," I said to him.

Then I slid down a bit and leaned back on one arm and then the other, my breasts exposed to the room, the V between my thighs certainly visible to the three men sitting at my side.

Appearing from nowhere, the club owner stepped from the darkness and put down a sheet rolled into a pillow. "In case you need to relax," was all he said, and again disappeared.

"That might a good idea," I said, and scooted my hips down further so I could put my head on the roll at the end of the bar. When I turned my head sideways, Rick's face was about six inches from mine.

"May I kiss you?" he asked, his voice husky with lust.

"Please?" I asked back.

So very gently, he brushed his lips against mine, held them there. I could smell the gin and tonic he'd been drinking, clean and fresh. I reached over and put my right hand on the back of his head so he wouldn't pull away. I put my left hand on the side of his face. The kiss lingered.

I'd been with a number of men since the implosion of my marriage. Nothing was as erotic as kissing this man while nearly naked on top of a bar in a room full of men and women.

"Jesus" said Rick when we broke to look at each other.

"Oh yes," I agreed.

"Charles?" I didn't need to elaborate and when I lifted my hips, Charles slid his hands under my butt to take the top of my thong down, smoothly over my knees then I straightened my legs so the wisp of fabric could be pulled over my shoes. I kept my thighs together, but extended my left foot so my body was completely visible to the room, which had become silent except for the last notes of another song spun by the DJ who was catering to the dancers on the floor below.

Charles put his lips on my hip bone.

"Charles." I said gently but with a hint of command. He stopped instantly and looked at me. "I'd like your fingertips from here," I pointed at my left breast, "to here," and pointed at my pelvis. He smiled into my eyes and nodded.

"Brad, I'd like you to work from the other direction."

The two of them touched me like I was made of silk. I kept my thighs together and neither tried to enter me. Charles stroked the outside of my breasts, the under-curve, then my nipples which almost ached when he brushed them — and then down to my belly.

I reached over to Rick and said, "I need you right here," and drew his mouth to mine. Once again the eroticism astounded me. But now I wanted something a little more. I opened my mouth, which caused him to open his. My tongue found his.

"That's wonderful," I said when we broke for my first full breath of fresh air.

"Unbelievable," he exhaled.

"Touch me," I said, now between a request and command.

Rick's fingertip went to my left breast as Charles' hand was at my hips. I couldn't stop the moan from my throat, nor my hips from rising off the bar. But my thighs stayed together. Rick's fingertip went from my breast to my collarbone, to my neck, my throat. When it traveled near my cheek, I turned my head and took it into my mouth with more hunger than I'd felt in a long time.

Eventually, Rick found more of me with his hands, and mouth. Brad and Charles changed chairs a couple of times and they were welcomed, too. The experience lasted for a long, long while; the DJ spun songs; many people came close to watch, left, were replaced by others. I gave as good as I received, and what I received was incredible.

Eventually there was nothing left to give. I lay there for a minute, until Rick asked if I wanted a drink.

"A glass of champagne would be wonderful," I told him. He went downstairs to the bar.

"Would you like to get together sometime?" asked Charles. I laughed while putting my hand along the side of his face. "That's very sweet, but not something I'm going to think about at this moment."

Rick came back with the champagne. I didn't expect Perrier-Jouët of course, but the flavor was so off that I knocked it back quickly, hoping it wouldn't take skin from the roof of my mouth.

"Rick, would you mind getting me a bottle of water?"

"Of course," he said, and, while I started to dress he headed back downstairs to the large tub where the club kept bottled water on ice. When he returned, he unscrewed the cap and handed me the bottle. I emptied it in two long pulls but still had the taste of the awful champagne in my mouth. I went for some mints in my purse.

It was late, and between the sex and the hour, I was suddenly very tired. I sat down in one of the chairs at the table next to the bar and bent over to put on my shoes, which had come off at some point. When I raised back up, I felt extremely dizzy and almost like I was looking at myself from the outside.

I looked up at Rick, and said, "I feel strange."

"Would you like me to take you home?" he asked.

"No, but maybe you could walk me to my car? I'll be fine as soon as I get away from the music and into some fresh air."

Rick took my arm and we wove through the crowd. More than one couple thanked Rick and me for "sharing." He was gracious. I just gave a weak smile. I heard Mike the doorman say goodnight.

And that was the last thing I remember until I woke up, three days later.

Chapter 28

The only thing that's "real" is what's happening right now, in this moment. The past is an incomplete painting by imperfect memory, the future an imagined stage upon which hope plays against fear.

"We are waiting for you, Jessica."

My grandmother's voice was layered with the scent of eucalyptus. A Pacific storm lashed rain against the windows in my room at her house, as it so often did, but I was warmly wrapped in the down comforter she'd made for me. I was hiding from someone. Maybe they wouldn't find me if I stayed very still. I did not want to wake up yet, to go to school, or law school, or work, wherever. I wanted to stay right where I was, warm in my bed.

"We are waiting for you, Jessica."

The dream began to fade, and slowly I opened my eyes to a very different place. It had ugly pale-green walls. A TV hung from the wall past the foot of my bed. What I thought was rain was the breathing of an odd machine next to my head.

My mother and my grandmother were there. My mother was crying over in the corner; my grandmother was sitting on the side of my bed wiping a cool, damp, scented cloth on my cheeks, across my lips. Along with lavender, eucalyptus was part of her cure for everything. When I was little and had strep throat, my grandmother would sit there just like that and dip a cloth in a small bowl and wring it out, and the eucalyptus scent would return, fresh and strong.

"We are waiting for you, Jessica," my grandmother murmured again.

"Grandmama?" I started to sit up but she put a hand on my chest.

"Not yet," she said.

Which coincided with a stunning flash of pain from my forehead and right leg.

"What …?" I started to say.

"Shshshsshh," said Grandmama. "Be still, Jessi. For a moment. You have been sleeping."

"Grandmama, I'm awake now. Where am I?"

Just then a man I did not recognize came into the room, along with a nurse dressed in pale green that seemed to match the walls. My mother stood.

"Is she awake?" the man asked my grandmother.

"Not yet," she said fiercely. "Leave her be."

"Marie," said my mother to my grandmother. "The officer is just trying to do his job."

"Not yet!" said my grandmother.

"Check her out please," the man said to the nurse, who came over and took my blood pressure, shined a light into my eyes. She turned to the man and nodded her head.

He walked over to the side of the bed opposite my grandmother.

"Jessica Marie Love?" he asked.

"Yes?" I replied.

"I'm Officer Larry Brown, with the Seattle Police Department. You are under arrest on four counts of possession of a controlled substance, reckless endangerment, driving under the influence, speeding …"

"None of that is true," I said when he finished.

"You have the right to an attorney …" Officer Brown continued. I knew the litany and waited it out.

"Would you like to make a statement?" he asked.

"I'd like to speak with my attorney," I said, if for no other reason than to have some time to think.

"You may not leave Seattle without permission of the court. Is that clear?" asked Officer Brown.

"I have no intention of leaving Seattle," I said.

He left the room, and probably just in time to keep Grandmama from hissing at him like a goose.

Claire, Lily, and Tony came into the room.

"What's going on?" I asked.

"You had an accident," said Claire.

"Okay, but what was all that?" I waved to where the officer had stood.

"You had some drugs in your system," Claire said. She was looking not just *at* me, but *into* me.

"I don't do drugs. You know that."

"You had some drugs in your car," said Tony. "Significant quantities."

If anything, his gaze was even more penetrating than Claire's. I could feel his eyes searching for truth.

"But I don't do drugs!" I said.

It was only ten seconds, but then Tony smiled.

"Yeah. We know that."

"Sarah is at the police station waiting for charges to be filed so she can write a check for bail," said Lily.

"Is there enough money? We have payroll tomorrow."

"You're covered," said Tony.

"What is this, Tony?" I started to wave my hand at the room, then stopped. Any movement caused pain in my head to drown out the pain in my leg.

"Jessica, you almost died," said Lily.

"How?"

"You were in an accident. On Alaskan Way," Tony said. "You hit a parked car, an abutment of the viaduct, and a bus shelter. You broke through the railing and landed on a barge below the road, which probably saved your life. Ten feet in either direction and the car would have been in fifteen feet of saltwater."

"I don't remember anything about that!"

"Not surprising. You had large amounts of heroin in your system, along with cocaine, and a blood-alcohol content that was far beyond the legal limit. Nearly fatal by itself."

"What about all those charges. Those were serious crimes."

"You had significant quantities of illegal drugs in your purse that seemed to be packaged for sale, along with packaging materials in the trunk of your Porsche," said Tony.

"I've never taken heroin and haven't touched cocaine since college! Let alone packaged or sold it. Somebody set me up!"

"There were no witnesses," said Tony. "Police were notified by a call from a jogger who ran past at about 5 a.m. They don't know the exact time of the wreck."

"None of that is true," I said. "I didn't do those things. I don't do those things."

"Where were you earlier in the evening?" asked Claire.

"What is the last thing you remember?" asked Tony.

"Were you with anyone?" asked Lily.

My grandmother, still sitting at my side, was looking at me intently, my mother watched me from her perch at the window.

I didn't say anything at all at first, and just stared up at the ceiling and the walls. Of course, they all thought it was because I had just come out of a short coma.

Finally, I lied to them all and said, "I don't remember. Where's my car? I want to see this!"

As I tried to sit up, the pain returned. I reached up to my head, but instead of skin, felt a bandage. My right leg was in a cast. I had bandages around my midsection.

"What the hell?" I asked.

"Jessica, you were hurt. Pretty badly," said my mother. Those were the first words she'd spoken since I woke up. "You had a pretty bad bump on the head. Your left leg is broken. And there was some… damage…"

"What does that mean?" I asked.

But my mother could not answer.

"I'll be outside," said Tony.

Just then a rather short woman with short dark hair, wearing a stethoscope around her neck came in. She was not wearing doctor clothes, but a nice pair of slacks and blouse.

"Hello, there," she said in a calm voice, but emotionally neutral. "Welcome back. I'm Dr. Elaine Corso."

"Hi. What's going on with me?" I asked.

"Well, you were in a bad wreck. Apparently you were not wearing your seat belt. You hit your head against the windshield, but did not suffer brain damage," she said, "but we had to wait until the drugs were flushed from your system to be sure.

"As best as we can tell, you came out of your seat when the Porsche hit the barge nose first, your left leg was pinned and you took the steering wheel to your middle."

For a second I panicked, but looked down and could wiggle my toes, though the pain of even that was more than I could believe.

"Well, it doesn't look like like I'm paralyzed. So I'll walk again, right?"

"Yes, I don't see any problem with walking. However, there was impact damage. We had to concentrate on saving those functions that were necessary for a comfortable life. You will not be able to have children. I'm sorry."

It took a moment for this to sink in. Mark and I had decided not to have kids, but that was a choice. Having that choice made by other circumstances was hard to face.

But not catastrophic. I wasn't going to dwell on that, not now and not in this room. There was no point. It was what it was and I'd deal with it later.

"What's the treatment plan? A few more days in the hospital, a couple of weeks at home? How long until I can go back to running? Go to the gym? Get back to work?" I asked.

"Three months. Minimum," said Dr. Corso.

"Three months!?"

"Don't overdo it," she said. "We'll talk again before you're released." Then she left the room.

Everyone filed out, then. Except for Grandmama, who had not moved during all this conversation. She reached over and picked up the cloth, dipped it in the bowl of cool water scented with eucalyptus, and drew it across my forehead.

"Sleep, now Jessi. Rest."

I closed my eyes and slept for another complete day.

Chapter 29

We can't prove anything is true. Truth we take on faith, but that still has power. What others believe is true is often more important than what we know to be false.

After I was discharged from the hospital, Sarah and Lily drove me down to my grandmother's where I stayed until the cast came off my leg and I could move without risk of tearing sutures in my abdomen. It was a simple break, and though the muscle atrophy lasted a while, I was up and around before long. The adhesions from surgery were dealt with by a local physical therapist. Of course, the most serious injuries were not physical.

"These things are not true, Grandmama," I told her one morning over coffee.

"Yes. I know this," she said in that matter-of-fact voice that often drove me crazy.

"Why? Why do you believe me when everybody else has doubts?"

She put her hand on my cheek as she did when she wanted to add emphasis to what she was saying, when she wanted to teach me something.

"A rose does not one day become a blackberry, just because each has thorns. My Jessica does not give up self-control, and does not run away to hide in drugs or love or any illusions."

"Love is an illusion?"

"Love is different things for different people. The illusion is that it must be permanent to be real."

"*Tout passe, tout lasse, tout casse*," we said at the same time, causing us both to laugh, which hurt where the incision marked my midsection.

Wounds healed, I headed back to Seattle. Cases I'd been handling had gone to Tony, along with my staff to handle the workload.

"Jessi, you can't represent clients while under indictment," Tony said. "It's really that simple. You know this."

Yeah, I did. But that stung.

It made a great story in *The Seattle Times* and *Source of the Sound*: "Drug Dealing Lawyer? Attorney defends dealers, drives drug Porsche into bay!"

They loved it.

Tony offered to represent me, but I didn't want to burden him even more, and worried the taint of my case would expand.

I put feelers out to Max Moore's firm, but they were rejected via back doors. I assumed Mark's association there was the reason. I could have trusted other lawyers, but did not. I chose to represent myself and had a fool for a client, as they say.

I did not tell anyone where I'd been that night. I wasn't ready to add that cloud to the doubts about my character possibly held by others who would not understand.

I went back to SASA to see if I could learn anything.

"First time I ever seen you shit-faced," Mike, the big doorman/bouncer, said. "That's really why I remember it. And the accident. Word got around about the accident."

"Was I with anyone?"

"One of the guys you were playing with said he was taking you home when you left, but came back in sayin' you had come around and insisted on driving yourself. I told him he should've taken your keys. Said he tried, but you tricked him and drove off. Guess I was right, seein' what happened."

"Do you know him?"

"Nah. Never seen him before, not seen him since. Only time was that night with you, and when I went out for a smoke and he got out of one of those Chryslers with a fancy grill the drug dealers drive."

"What color? What year?" I asked.

"I'm not a car guy. If it was a Harley, I could tell you. Anyway, you'd taken off. He was hoping to have a little more fun, he said, but a dealer offered a taste after you left so it wasn't a complete loss."

"Can I get his name, Mike?" I pointed to his computer.

"You know I can't let you have that."

"Mike, it's really important. This is a really big deal to me."

Mike wouldn't budge, nor would his boss Elizabeth, even after hearing my story.

"I'm sorry, sweetie," she said. "I know you're in a jam."

I finally got to the owner, the man I'd met when he was represented by my ex-husband and Max Moore, and who had provided me with sheets and a towel the night of the accident.

"No," he said.

"No? That's it?"

"That's it."

"I really need the information."

"No."

"People slip drugs into cocktails here."

"Prove it."

"You have the proof on your security tapes."

"They're purged every 48 hours. You get nothing without a subpoena, and even with a subpoena there won't be anything to get."

While I kept pushing where I could push, I was trying to do all this while concealing my presence at SASA that night, so I had no leverage. I was also a favorite target for the local legal system that I'd given an occasional bloody nose. Prosecuting attorneys put a little extra effort into making sure I'd be found guilty of something. They piled on the charges, a common tactic but even more focused, layer after layer of multiple counts.

There was no doubt I would win most of them. But juries want to be "fair." They want to give a little something to each side to reward effort made, and because they don't want to seem unreasonable. I'd used that desire for "balance" to my client's advantage on more than one occasion.

But given my line of work, even a partial win would be a significant loss.

There was something else I hadn't counted on. Since Mark and I had split, I'd changed my hair more than once and worn different clothes, or my old clothes differently. As investigators interviewed those around me, it became clear they were making a case that I, myself, had "changed."

While I was preparing to argue that everything in my history indicated I'd never do the things I was accused of doing, they were preparing to argue I wasn't that person any longer. They also made it clear they would subpoena everyone around me, bring them into court. Cast shadows on them, too.

I was offered a deal. I would not admit guilt, but agree they had enough evidence to convict. They worked to make it fit in my case, but they had a cost/benefit to worry about, too. They could lose, something they wanted to avoid at all costs. A deal would get me out of the profession and destroy my reputation. Some ideas of "justice" aren't always what's in the law.

At first I told them no. I said I'd beat them in court.

"You know, even if you're willing to fight to the bitter end, what about those around you?" asked one prosecutor during a negotiation.

"What do you mean?"

"Well, I don't mean to imply" — which meant he did — "anyone in your office might have had a stake in your drug 'enterprise,' but it was pretty obvious by the way you changed that 'something' was going on. Why else would they not intervene to halt your obvious slide into the world you'd been exposed to as a lawyer?"

"Because I wasn't sliding into anything!" I said.

"I guess that will be determined after our investigation, and then in court," he said, so smug I wanted to reach across the table and change the shape of that stupid smile with my fingernails, stretch his face until it split. They made it clear that unless I said yes, they would go all-out on all the charges. They were using the process itself to punish me before a verdict. They were using extortion to force a guilty plea for something I did not do.

There aren't words to express the rage I felt.

But eventually, I adhered to advice I'd often given to clients. Yes, I might win on everything, but that wasn't likely. My potential downside was to lose big and serve a minimum of five years. I took the deal and began serving a six-month sentence in the King County Jail in downtown Seattle.

Chapter 30

Sometimes we fall, stunned and uncertain if we can take one more breath. Sometimes we find out what we thought would be unbearable isn't so bad. Jail was unpleasant, but not hard. Besides, there are lots of things one can learn in jail.

I signed up for the writing course that eventually led to this book. I helped fellow inmates with correspondence to the courts, to their victims. Hell, I helped them write to their lawyers, some of whom seemed to have forgotten all about their clients.

I learned that one woman can call another a "bitch" or "whore," and it can hurt even if both are prostitutes. I learned that, for some women, blow jobs are much less intimate than making love face to face in a bed.

I learned that "justice" is a word, a term, an ideal, a hope, an excuse, a sham, a pry, and a blanket. I learned that thirty percent of the hookers on the street may be black, fifty percent of the hookers arrested may be black, and seventy percent of the hookers in jail are black.

That is not because black hookers commit more serious prostitution.

There are some good public defenders. But lawyers on the 45th floor of the U.S. Bank Building make seventeen times the money that public defenders make. Money buys talent. Money contributes a "halo effect," where the good-looking guy in an expensive suit who dines on fresh salmon will be given more respect by a jury than an overworked lump in a baggy suit who gets too little sleep and stinks like gritty coffee, cheap booze, and gas-station burritos. This is a fact of life.

Look at their shoes: The shoes of a top lawyer cost more than the whole suit of the attorney representing most of the women I met in jail. I already knew this. I'd worn expensive shoes.

I also knew the promise of sex will turn a man's mind to mush, but hookers in jail added the lesson that just by introducing the "possibility" that another man might have an interest, a higher price can be negotiated. Biology.

Worse, I learned that some men who pay sometimes forget they are also part of the transaction and dehumanize a woman through acts or words of violence. Those hold a mirror only to their own depravity. Psychology.

I learned that all sorts of people become jailers. Some of them are kind or want to be kind. Interestingly, those are the ones it's sometimes hardest to get to know. They build thicker walls so they don't get burned.

Others, easier to know, are not so kind. Give the worst bully you ever met in middle school the keys to your cell. Give her a gun. Give her the power to write down on a piece of paper something that will keep you from your hour outside or from a job where you can talk to other people, just because you looked at her and didn't smile.

Or you looked at her and did smile. Or because she and her boyfriend were fighting. Or her car was slow to start. Or her kid got busted. Give her self-loathing and a chance to take all that hurt out on you, she will. There was a study done how being a "jailer" brought out the worst in people, even in upper-class college kids. It's certainly true of those who live with hurt every day. Happenstance.

There's a lot to be angry about in jail, besides the fact that people "outside" are able to do things you aren't able to do. But in jail, I also learned that outrage is a liability because it blinds. Being focused on yourself and not seeing what's really happening is just being stupid. Those who feel outrage over things that don't hurt them immediately are just jacking off.

"I want to damage that woman so badly," I said one morning at breakfast after a sleepless night of outrage, having come to the conclusion that Agent Deborah Riddle was the one who set me up. "Anyone want the job?"

"Shut the fuck up, right now!" hissed Vicki Wilson, a woman I was helping to find a lawyer because her "boyfriend" had used her as a drug mule. "You don't know who's listening."

"Shit girl, that woman slips on ice ten miles away, someone will come looking for you," said Angela, a tall, beautiful black woman who had decided she was done with her ex-boyfriend beating on her 8-year-old daughter from a previous relationship. She told him twice, then convinced him with the blade of a six-inch knife. He lived, but she was sorry for that.

So, I met some quality women while I was in jail. Some of them are still good friends. Some of them would help me later in ways I'm not going to talk about.

I was still in jail when the Washington State Bar revoked my license to practice law. I was surprised at my reaction to the news. My identity wasn't wrapped around being an attorney. I enjoyed the work. I enjoyed the income. But it wasn't all of me or even a big part of me. Still, like losing my ovaries, having it taken away like that without my consent hurt, even if I didn't know why.

Tony was great after I was released.

"Let's have lunch," he said. We wandered down through Pike Place Market to The Bomber, a small hole-in-the-wall where they served nothing but burgers and beer.

"Hey, Tony," said the counter person when we walked in.

"Hey, Kathy," said Tony. "Got a table?"

"Back in the hole," she said with a smile and motioned with her head toward the back of the place.

"That's my favorite," said Tony, and led me back, past the line where waitresses picked up baskets of burgers and fries, to a single table that had a complete view of the inside of the kitchen.

"This is the staff table when they aren't busy," said Tony, wiping it off with a napkin.

"I'll get that, Hon," said Kathy walking up with a wet rag that smelled like bleach.

"Usual?"

"Yup."

"I'll have the same," I said, without looking at a menu.

"Got it," said Kathy, looking at me with a smile.

Walking past the kitchen she called to the cook, "Two B17s, bacon and cheddar, no pickle, lots of tots extra crispy." A minute later she came back with two dark brown beers, set them down, and turned to the high stainless counter where orders were plated just as a cook shouted "Order up!"

"You still have a job," said Tony, when she was out of earshot.

"I don't know how, Tony. I can't practice law, and you can't afford to carry me," I said. "What's in it for you?"

"I'm a good guy," he said, not looking at me but into the kitchen where cooks and dishwashers danced.

"I don't trust anyone who doesn't act in their own self-interest." I meant this to come out with some humor, but it didn't. It came out flat and bitter, and I didn't like sounding sorry for myself.

"Me either," said Tony, neutralizing my hurt. "You run the show from the back room, we hire someone to make the presentations in court, we grow the whole thing, and it's win-win-win."

"Tony, that will take a while. And it might not work."

"Might not. But might," he said.

"Can I get back to you? I really need a break," I said.

"Take all the time you need," he said.

We finished lunch and headed out.

"Hey, Tony, comin' by tonight?" asked the cook as we walked past.

"I'll get back to you," was all Tony said.

It was hard cleaning out my desk in the Seattle Tower. It was even harder when I watched Claire clean out hers.

"Honey, this isn't on you," she said. "Besides, I've got a new gig. It won't be as much fun, but it will more than pay the bills." She was headed over to one of the software companies that were ramping up along Lake Union. "They need someone tough to keep the geeks on task," she said.

Sarah was going home to Spokane to care for her dying dad. Lily was going to stay on with Tony, who had plenty of work and enough other lawyers on staff for her skills to be put to use.

"I really do want to be useful," she said. "That's as important to me as the money."

That night at home, I read in the *Times* about the engagement of my former husband, Mark Love, Seattle, to Ashley Moore, daughter of Max and Claudia Moore of Bellevue, Washington. *Tout passe, tout lasse, tout casse.*

One evening, I got a call on my cell phone that I didn't answer. My family hadn't been very supportive while I was in jail. But I listened to the message, and when I heard the tone in my mother's voice, I called her back immediately.

"Jessi ..." she started to say, then stopped.

"Mother?" I asked. I'd stopped calling her "Mom" after the blow up over my divorce from Mark.

"Grandmother has passed away," she said.

I didn't really know her mother that well, so I said, "Mom, I'm so sorry for your loss..." hoping that reverting to the familiar would lend sincerity to my words. Then suddenly I realized it wasn't *her* mother she was talking about, but *my* grandmother, Grandmama, Grandmere.

"Oh God. Mom, what happened? Why didn't I know?!"

I'd been about to open the refrigerator, but I stepped backwards as if the handle had become a snake, as if by stepping back I could step away from what I was hearing. I kept stepping back until I came to the wall of my kitchen.

"None of us knew, honey," said Mom. "She kept getting a bit more frail. We suggested she see a doctor, but she just blew up her lips and said 'No doctor. I know medicine. I am old. I know what to do.' You know how stubborn she could be."

"How ... who ...?" was all I could get out, but Mom knew what I was asking.

"I took her a bowl of chowder this morning. You know it's the only thing I cook she will eat. She didn't answer the door. I went around back, and she was sitting in her kitchen chair, but her head was down. I knew something wasn't right. The doctor said her heart just stopped and she didn't even know."

By the time my mother stopped talking I had slid down the wall to the floor. I could not breathe. My eyes felt like they had been rubbed with sand, then salt.

"Honey?" My mom said.

"I'll call you back," I whispered, and clicked off the phone.

"Oh. Fuck. Oh fuck. Oh fuck. Oh fuck ohfuckohfuckohfuckohfuckohfuck ..." I slowly knocked my head against the wall as I chanted, trying to knock back the grief that was starting to overwhelm me.

It wasn't working.

So I tried that one last thing, and whispered "*Tout passe, tout lasse, tout casse*." That just opened the gates to a loss that clawed into me and tore me apart as nothing had in my entire life.

Chapter 31

Detachment may be what's left after everything we're attached to is ripped away.

I wasn't there yet. But I was also outside myself, watching as my mind looked for an anchor. After the loss of love and loss of career, the loss of my Grandmere set me truly adrift.

At first I tried to attach to guilt. When I could finally breathe, I stood to make tea but filling the kettle brought an image of Grandmama filling her kettle as I had watched her do so often, then sitting in her chair in her kitchen, then alone when she died, which put me right back down on the floor sitting against the wall, my face in my hands.

"I should have known! I should have been there!" I cried. "I should have seen her more often! I should have …"

"Jessi!" said Grandmere, sharply in my ear. "There is no should!" It was as clear as if she were right in front of me. Startled, I opened my eyes. She wasn't there, but I could feel her presence, her hand on the side of my face.

"Come see me now," she whispered. "I am waiting. I have something for you."

The paralyzing despair of the last hour — or hours — lifted slightly. I stood, washed my face, threw some clothes and toiletries in a bag. I called my mother and told her I was on my way, jumped in a rented Porsche. The trip home over backroads was slow as I sought to remember each of the moments Grandmere and I had spent together. Some brought more tears, some made me laugh. All brought feelings of gratitude and love.

Every time I used the clutch, my left leg twinged where it was broken in the "accident." I drove right to her house, hoping to decompress before seeing the family.

That didn't work. At the house were my father's truck, the Japanese car my mother drove, my sister's minivan and the pickup her husband bought from my father because, he said, "I know it's been taken care of."

When I walked into the house everyone stared at me. At first I couldn't figure it out. My father provided insight.

"Jesus, what the hell has happened to you?" he asked.

"What?"

"What do you mean, 'what'? Look at you. Look at your hair, your clothes. No wonder they wouldn't let you back into a courtroom!"

"Oh. Yeah. We should probably talk about that, but not right now, okay? Where's Grandmama?"

Like I said, in jail I'd learned that outrage was something that can be channelled.

"Honey, they took her to the funeral home about an hour ago," said my mother.

"Well, I suppose that's where I should be. What are you all doing here?"

"Waiting for you, Jessi," said my sister. "We thought we should all go down there together."

"Okay," I said, trying to avoid friction right off the bat. That was a fail, of course. As soon as we were in my mother's car, my father behind the wheel, he started in.

"Did you call her? Did you know? Did she call you? What's with the hair? Your eyes are pretty dark. Is it supposed to be some kind of style or is it because you've been crying? What did …"

"Hey, James. Enough with the twenty questions, okay?" I'd never before called him by his first name.

"Don't you …" he started to say, but my mother's hand on his arm quieted him for the rest of the trip.

There is only one funeral parlor in town. We thought we were going to pick out a casket, but the funeral director, an older man but very dapper, sat us down.

"Your mother visited a week ago," he said looking at my father. "She made all the arrangements. She gave me these," and he handed an envelope to my father, another to my sister, one to my mother and another to me.

"I have no idea what's in these, but she directed me to hand them to you, just as I have."

We all sat there for a moment, trying to take this in.

"She was here a week ago?" said my father.

"Yes, that is correct."

"And you didn't call me or notify the authorities?!"

"There was no need for authorities, and your mother requested that I not communicate with you until now."

"What kind of operation is this? A sick, frail woman on the verge of death and you do NOTHING?!" My father's voice was rising.

"She appeared neither sick nor frail, sir. We have people come in to make arrangements all the time. It's what we do."

Though his demeanor was sorrowful and compassionate, there was steel in this man.

Grandmere had been here just a week ago? She knew she was going to die. I thought about that for a moment and wondered if she had taken her own life. If so, she was ready to go. There were few accidents around Grandmere.

"There is no sin in deciding time and place when one is about to die," Grandmother said to me. This time I resisted the temptation to look around.

That was so like her. She would have abhorred the ruckus and humiliation of dying at the grocery store, or on a walk downtown. Her kitchen chair would have been exactly where she wanted to be.

My father tore his envelope open, as did my sister and mother. As they read, they started looking at me. I wasn't ready to open my envelope and didn't want to in front of the others. I put it in my messenger bag.

"Did you know about this?" my father asked.

"About what?"

"Why don't you open your envelope?"

"I don't feel like it right now," I said.

"Have you been talking to her?" There was accusation in his voice.

"Um, I live in Seattle," stating the obvious just to get under his skin.

"On the phone. Did you talk to her on the phone?" he asked.

"Oh! Yes! Grandmama was such a chatty person on the phone. Hard to break off the conversation sometimes." My sister laughed and her husband sniggered. Even my mom hid a smile at the absurdity.

"Look at you. Look at you. You are just like her," he said, throwing a thumb over his shoulder to someplace inside the building.

"Why, thank you. That's the nicest thing you've said to me in years."

"Don't take it as a compliment," he snapped back.

"James!" said my mother.

"Dad!" said my sister.

"It's okay," I told them, keeping my eyes locked with my father's, which could not conceal a smoldering anger.

"*Tout passe, tout lasse, tout casse*," I said.

"Don't you do that," my father snarled at me. "I had to listen to that garbage from that whore from the time I was born!"

This time everyone gasped.

"James!" said my mother.

"My father told me everything," said my father. "From the time I was ten, he told me how he'd been wounded in France, how she tricked him into marrying her by getting pregnant with me, how he had to bring her back home!"

"That was not true," said the funeral director quickly, with surprising force.

"What do YOU know?!" my father nearly shouted.

"Your mother and I played backgammon every Friday," said the funeral director.

"Where, right here? I'll bet you did," said my father. The words foamed out of his mouth like bile. I always thought his quiet reflected some sort of wounded reserve. Instead, I was learning it hid a boiling pot of venom.

"Actually, no. Across the street at Tommy's café, after your mother left church." The director nodded slightly toward the Catholic church on the same side of the street. "After my wife died, your mother and I would go over to Tommy's and play. She usually beat me two games to one, or three games to two. She was exceedingly good," he said.

"What's this have to do with my father and how they met?" said my father.

"I was in France, too. With your father, in fact. A number of us who enlisted out of Washington ended up in the same unit in Europe. Your father was wounded in a small town in France when the Germans shelled our position. Your mother was a nurse. She cared for him. They fell in love, and she came back with him," he said.

"That's not how my father told it," said my father. "He said…"

"James." I'd never heard that tone of voice from my mother to my father. It was quiet — but anything but soft. It seemed to fill the room.

"Your father was an angry, drunk man who lied often and blamed anyone and everyone else for his own failings. He often came home late when he came home at all," said my mother.

"He worked nights!"

"Your mother told you he worked the night shift. That was a lie to protect you. He was out in bars, and tomcatting around. Your mother and I talked often before he died."

"Those are lies she told! He was a good father!"

"Just because he taught you to throw a baseball does not mean he was a good man. When I asked why she never left him, she said she had made her own decisions and she had to own them."

"You weren't there. You don't know anything!" shouted my father.

"James, your father made passes at me on more than one occasion," my mother said. "Now would be a really good time for you to stop talking."

I was stunned by what my mother was saying, and the strength in her voice that I'd never heard.

My sister sat with her mouth gaping, her eyes open nearly as wide. Her husband was cleaning his nails.

"Your mother will be cremated tomorrow at noon, according to her wishes," said the funeral director to my father. "She asked me to read a few words and the priest will be here to say a prayer. She has already purchased the urn."

He turned to me. "Jessica, her ashes go with you. I imagine you will want to read your letter."

With that, he stood from the table. He was tall, very straight of bearing; an elegant elderly man in impeccable black, and I knew instantly why Grandmama would have sought his company. They were alike in so many ways.

The car was silent as we drove back to Grandmama's house. My mother made noises about me coming back to the house, but I told her I would stay at Grandmama's.

"Yes, dear, that's how it should be," she said.

"Thank you," I whispered to her with a kiss on the cheek as I got out of the car. She brushed my face like Grandmama had done so many times.

"You want company?" my sister asked in the driveway, already knowing my answer. I just shook my head and smiled, and she and her husband drove away. At last I was alone.

Except for the presence of my grandmother, who stood silently at my side.

Chapter 32

Does experience of an afterlife require belief in God? There's much we experience that can't be explained. God isn't necessarily the best answer. Of course, that doesn't mean God *isn't* the answer, either.

Not once that night, in that house, was I alone. It was like Grandmama had let go of her body so her spirit could be where it needed to be, and that was near me.

"*Ma chère*," began the letter she'd written to me in her careful, elegant script. "I have passed. I know you will grieve, but do not feel lost. Nothing is other than it should be. Everything passes. People, too. But love is immortal, as long as we allow it to reside within us. And you know my love for you."

She had left nearly everything to me, though there wasn't much, really. She'd lived a very simple life, but this was one reason my father was so upset, I supposed, and why the family looked at me so intently in the funeral home.

"There is a dress in my closet I would like you to wear to my funeral. There is another for travel."

Travel?

In the envelope was also a small key, which she wrote would open a wooden box on her mantle. Which I did. Inside, were fragments of the shattered teacup I had dropped decades before, and another box.

"*Ma chère,* do you remember this teacup? I saved it not because I want you to feel pain at that memory, but because I want you to be free. Please take this cup, the small box, and my ashes back to France. There is a small town not far from Bordeaux named for my great-great-grandfather, who helped acquire lands in the New World for France. Some places in Louisiana and Canada have our last name.

"My brother is still there, making some of the world's great wines. He is married to a woman of wisdom. You will enjoy her, and learn many things, I think.

"My brother survived the war but suffered injuries. If he has passed, his family will still be there. Give them the little box. They will take care of the rest."

The small box was latched, but not locked. Inside was another small envelope addressed to her brother, and the pendant that Grandmama had me wear on the day I was married. It seemed to shine on its own, with a light of the deepest blue.

I held it up to look at it. It was as if Grandmama were looking back at me from its depths. I put it back on the velvet lining where it was cradled.

"Please place the cup fragments in the earth above the chateau and scatter my ashes nearby. I have so missed France, but I had an obligation to raise your father, and then to raise you. You are my reward, Comtesse. You are my blood, my spirit, my family as no other could be."

She included one phone number and one address.

I wanted to drive over and shove this letter into my father's face with my fist. But her hand was on my shoulder. "No," she said, stern but with a smile in her voice. "He is not important. You are important."

I went upstairs to the tiny house's bathroom, the one we shared when I lived there with her. I looked into the mirror and saw the wreck my face had become from all the crying. I looked at all the wonderful soaps on the counter, not one of which could be purchased in the local Thriftway. I had no idea where she got them. When I lived there, I'd never asked.

I washed my skin as she had taught me, thoroughly but gently, until all traces of tears and dark makeup were gone. I put on cream that smelled of lavender, then pulled the oddly uneven strands of my last modern haircut to where I could cut them off with scissors I found in the top drawer.

I brushed my now-short, dark hair straight back from my face, where it was held with gel from a jar labeled in French.

It was amazing how much I looked like her. And her mother, whose photograph was in a frame by the mirror.

In Grandmama's closet were several suits and a few dresses, besides the house-dresses she wore at home or in the garden but never outside her own gate.

"Better a few of the best quality rather than many of no quality," she used to say.

At one end, with my name safety-pinned to their hangers, there were two black dresses that fit me like they were tailored. I wondered how she knew they would fit me so well, but next to them was the wedding dress she'd made for me. The black dresses *were* tailored, I smiled.

She hadn't said anything about shoes, but the black ankle boots I wore down from Seattle would do just fine.

That's how I arrived at the funeral home the next day, just before noon.

"Oh, my dear!" said my mother, tears filling her eyes. "You are so beautiful. So much like her!"

My father looked at me, and then away, anger or shame darkening his eyes. I didn't care which.

"Oh my God!" said my sister. "That's incredible! Are those her clothes, too?"

The ceremony was as short as the funeral director said it would be. A priest I did not know said words about Heaven, the Lord and His many houses. It was obvious this was a formality and the priest did not know my grandmother well. When all was done, the funeral director handed me the urn of her ashes in a box crafted out of walnut and cedar. I felt her warmth still in the wood.

"She was right about you, all along," he said looking deeply into me, and I felt the love he had for her.

"I'm sure she would like you to have this," he said, and with tears in his eyes, he gave me the small backgammon board on which they played every Sunday afternoon after church.

"I can't take this!" I said. "Please, keep it. To remember her."

"I shall never forget her," he said. "But I am old, too, and there is no one I could pass it to …" he paused and took two slow breaths, "… to whom it will mean as much. *Tout passe, tout lasse, tout casse*," he said, with a sad smile and tears in his eyes.

Chapter 33

There is an aura of grace about those who have aged well, who have learned acceptance along with earning the wisdom of their years. Perhaps acceptance is a part of wisdom.

"Ah, yes," said Grandmama's brother Marcel when I told him who I was and why I was calling. "I've been expecting this phone call."

"Did she tell you she was ill?"

"No, but we all become old."

"She knew she was dying but didn't tell anyone."

He laughed softly. "I'm not surprised. Marie was always the strong one."

"She wanted me to scatter her ashes in the orchard there," I said.

"Of course. When would you like to come?"

"Soon?"

"We will make up your room. Take the train or plane to Bordeaux, and I will pick you up. Just let me know the time of your arrival."

I booked a flight on Royal Dutch Airways from Seattle to Paris. It wasn't the cheapest flight, but it was direct. I'd found a high-speed train to Bordeaux from which I could absorb the countryside. The ride was smooth and startlingly fast. Some of what I could see felt like the Pacific Northwest, but different. Other places seemed very foreign, yet familiar. Hard to explain.

When I walked into the train station, Gare de Bordeaux-Saint-Jean, a distinguished man walked up to me and held out his hand. "Madame Love?"

"Yes?"

"I am Marcel DuBois. Your grandmother's brother. We have a car nearby. Let me take your bag."

We didn't speak much as we walked through the crowd leaving the station. Eventually we arrived at his car, a long, sleek wagon.

"What is this?" I asked to start a conversation.

"A Citroen C5. Made not far from Paris."

"I didn't know the French made automobiles."

"Probably not much longer, unfortunately," he said. "It is hard enough to compete against the ruthless efficiency of the Germans and Japanese. When the Chinese start selling cars, I think French automobiles will be only a memory."

"How did you know it was me among all those people at the station?" I asked.

He looked over at me and smiled.

"I will show you when we get to the chateaux."

As we drove northeast out of Bordeaux, then east along D243, Marcel DuBois pointed out various wineries, talked about how the character of the wines once reflected the families that produced them.

"This has changed since many wineries have been purchased by corporations. Instead of making wines they love, they make wines to please the market. Maybe this is necessary, but something is lost."

I didn't recognize many names until we passed through Saint-Emillion, but then we kept heading east.

"Your English is perfect," I said.

"Thank you. My mother insisted. She went to school in England before the First World War, and loved the people and the language. She was even engaged to an Englishman, but he was killed fighting Germany.

"She eventually married a local boy but never lost her love for things English. There was no money, so she taught me at home. She was a very severe teacher."

"My grandmother didn't speak nearly as well as you do. She never lost her accent even though she lived in the U.S." I said.

"My sister put most of her effort into the kitchen instead of her studies," he said with a laugh. "But then again, this was what was expected, back then. And my mother knew, I think, it would be easier teaching me. My sister was very headstrong."

"I'm looking forward to learning more about where Grandmama came from," I said.

"This is where she grew up," he said as we pulled into a long, graveled drive. At the end was a lovely stone house, two stories and shaded by tall, leafy trees. Not at all like my idea of a "chateaux," but timeless and elegant in the middle of a vineyard.

"We'll leave the car here for now," Marcel said, putting on the parking brake.

A woman came out of the house wiping her hands on an apron as we got out of the car.

"You are Jessica!" she said, with an exclamation I didn't understand.

"Yes."

"I am Genevieve, Marcel's wife. I will *not* say I am your great aunt. That makes me feel entirely too old!"

Her laugh had music to it. Her English didn't flow like Uncle Marcel's — as I had already decided to call him — but it was still quite good.

"It's nice to meet you, Aunt Genevieve."

"Genevieve will do," she said, but with a smile. "Please come in. Marcel, take Jessica's bag up to her grandmother's room. Everything is ready."

Uncle Marcel looked at her, then looked at me. "But of course, my love," he said in English. "Jessica, you see who is the nobility here at Chateau DuBois."

"Oh, Marcel," said Genevieve, immediately taking his face in both of her hands and kissing him lightly on the lips. To me she said, "Men are so sensitive, and Marcel more than most."

At that moment a feeling of familiarity took me like a long embrace. It felt like I'd never before been at home. This was my grandmother's family — this was my family. I was nearly overpowered by the feeling that I belonged to these wonderful people!

"Would you like to rest or wash up?" Genevieve asked me.

"I would like to take off my shoes and wash my face," I said. I'd also worn the same pair of black slacks since I left Seattle, which now seemed a so many miles and a lifetime away. I wanted to be in the long, loose dress in my bag and a pair of sandals that would let my toes feel the sun.

"Of course. I'll take you up."

The stairs were very narrow, with a landing half-way that let them double back. At the top we turned left.

"We've upgraded a couple of times, but not since our own children left to their own lives. It may be somewhat old-fashioned from what you're used to," said Genevieve.

"I love every inch of it!" I said, with no exaggeration.

"This was my daughter's room," said Genevieve, opening a door at the end of the hall, "and your grandmother's before that. And yours, for as long as you will stay," she said, stopping and putting a hand on my shoulder.

How could these people I'd never met be so gracious to me?

"I don't know what to say," I said.

"Welcome home," she smiled, walking into the room. To the left just inside the door was the head of the bed which faced outward to windows draped with heavy white curtains. To the right was a bureau, and past that another door which Genevieve opened.

"The bathroom is right here," she said as she walked through to a huge bathroom in the corner of the building. It didn't have a door into the hall, its only entrances were from the two bedrooms that shared it. There was a toilet, sink, bidet, and a huge tub beneath the corner windows with a shower wand and curtains to contain spray. "If we have other company, the doors can be locked from the inside.

"We'll be out on the veranda when you want to come down. Take your time. A glass of wine will be waiting for you."

I took a quick shower to wash off travel grime, changed, and grabbed the small wooden box from my grandmother and went downstairs. I followed voices outside to a warm veranda by the front door.

"Hello, ma chère. May I pour you a glass of wine?" said Genevieve.

"Thank you." But before I sat down, I walked over to where Uncle Marcel was settling back into his chair and handed him the wooden box. "What's this?" he asked.

"Grandmama left me a note that I was to give this to you, or your son or daughter if you had passed away," I said.

He looked at me, and at the wooden box. "Did she tell you what it was?"

"She had me wear it for my wedding."

The lid stuck just a bit as he opened the box. Inside was the small envelope and underneath that, the pendant. That seemed to startle him. He opened the envelope and took out the two sheets of paper inside. I could see my grandmother's handwriting.

Uncle Marcel had not read for more than five seconds when tears began to run down his cheeks.

"Marcel?" said Genevieve.

"*C'est bien*," he said softly.

When he had finished reading, he handed the letter to Genevieve. Her eyes stayed dry, but very softly and looking at me, she said in English "How beautiful, how sad."

"What's that?" I asked.

"Genevieve …" Uncle Marcel cautioned.

"Marcel, I make these decisions for myself," said Genevieve, firmly but with kindness.

"We shall talk after I have thought about this," she said to me, and got up and went to the kitchen, where something wafted incredible aromas out to the veranda. I sipped my wine and enjoyed the golden warmth of sun on my face.

"What do you know of your grandmother?" Uncle Marcel asked at last.

"She was very hard to know," I said. "She was private. She didn't talk much about what she was feeling."

Uncle Marcel smiled. "That was always the case," he said.

"Our family goes back many generations, hundreds of years before the founding of your country. In fact, this very farm was bestowed on the family for exploration and the securing of French holdings in the New World. And this …"

Uncle Marcel reached into the box and pulled out the blue pendant. It glowed, as if it knew it had come home.

"During the chaos of 1792, this was looted from the crown jewels. It found its way to our family, who returned it to Paris. But then it was bequeathed to our family for safekeeping by one who did not want it to fall into the hands of the Corsican. He said that a family who would return such a thing to its rightful owner could be trusted forever."

"May I?" I asked, reaching for the jewel.

"May you? Of course you may. It's yours," said Uncle Marcel, looking at me. But he did not hand me the box.

"Mine?"

"Our family tradition is that that the holder of the blue stone passes it on to one she feels would protect it, and honor our tradition. My mother was the holder, but never told us where the stone went before she died, and we assumed it was lost."

"You didn't know Grandmama had it?"

"Even when she was quite young, your grandmother and my mother had a difficult relationship. I think it was because they were so much the same, and each so private in many ways.

"During the Second World War, my mother wanted us to stay far away from the fighting. She said nobody knew who would win, and it was best not to be identified with either side." He paused, taking a sip of wine.

"I still remember the last argument. It was in the kitchen of this house. The Nazis were in Paris. Your grandmother knew I was in the Resistance, but I had not told our mother. My mother found out when Marie said she would not let her brother fight and die without doing what she could to help good defeat evil.

"My mother looked at me in shock, then said Marie and I were both naive. She said war did not know the difference between good and evil, only the strong and the weak, and that Marie's duty was to her family, not to some idealistic *merde*. She threw one of a matched pair of tea cups against the wall near where Marie stood. Marie grabbed the other, stormed out and joined the Resistance. She became a nurse. I still remember hearing my mother cry deep into the night. Marie never returned.

"I did not know until now the pendant had already gone to my sister. I'd hoped as much, but it was not right to ask my mother. I remember my mother demanding something be returned, and my sister saying there was no such requirement in the tradition."

"But why does that make it mine?" I asked.

"Your grandmother passed it on to you."

"No, she asked that I return it to you," I said.

"*Non*." He held up the two-page letter. "She passed it to you. This is what she says here, quite plainly." He handed the box to me and the letter.

I looked into the sapphire blue depths and tried to understand everything I had learned since my grandmother died, changes I had no ability to anticipate.

"But why? I'm hardly an heir of the DuBois name or lineage."

"She felt you were." Uncle Marcel said this simply, as if there were nothing else to say, and stood up to pour me a bit more wine.

Chapter 34

We think of hours and minutes as constructs so we can meet schedules or make plans, but the body has its own clock and calendar.

"Good morning!" Genevieve said when I walked into the kitchen the next day. I wasn't entirely certain if it was early afternoon or late morning, my cell phone did not work in France. I'd slept hard and well, but had no idea for how long.

"Is it still morning? I couldn't get to sleep and then I couldn't wake up!" I said.

"It's just ten. Coffee?"

"Yes, please."

"Marcel will be back for lunch at noon. Are you starving? Would you like something to eat now?" She nodded to a plate of pastries, and I took a croissant off the top.

"Is the coffee too strong? We know Americans often prefer something a little lighter."

"No, the coffee is just right. Thank you. May I walk through the vineyard?"

"Of course. Would you like a guide?"

"Thank you, but I'll find my way back before Uncle Marcel gets home."

"He likes to hear you call him 'Uncle Marcel.' It allows him to feel closer to Marie." Genevieve smiled. "You've brought more than you know."

I walked from the porch past a flock of chickens. There was a rooster who lorded over the hens and smaller males, his plumage crimson and gold.

"Why, Sam, aren't you magnificent. But do you have to be so bossy?" I asked him.

It didn't occur to me in the moment that I'd named the rooster after the boy of my childhood who had changed my life, who was the reason I'd moved in with my grandmother, who had gone off to die in Afghanistan, who started my metamorphosis from girl to woman.

I walked past a shed with mechanical equipment and ancient wooden rectangular bins. Once I got to the hillside behind the house, I took off my sandals and let my toes sink into dark, soft earth, already warm.

Uncle Marcel's words of last night, Genevieve's this morning, the dirt beneath my feet, and the morning sun blended into a serenity I had never experienced.

Rows of vines, strung along fences that guided their growth and supported branches heavy with grapes, were separated by alleys I assumed were for equipment and moving the harvest.

Nearly to the top of the hill I stopped, but not for a reason I understood, then sat on a patch of grass beneath a giant oak tree left standing in the vineyard.

"Thank you," I said, intending that for Grandmama. I felt her beside me, smiling out at the valley that lay before us. The connection was so strong that for a moment I did not know if I was thanking her for bringing me here, or if she were thanking me.

As the sun neared its apex, I took out the shards of the teacup she had sent home. I pushed the shattered porcelain into the earth, except for some small chips and one piece that had a complete blue flower.

"May I keep this?" I asked Grandmama.

"Of course. I want you to have it," she replied.

I headed down. When I neared the porch, Genevieve came out the kitchen door wearing a warm and wide smile.

"You can wash your feet there," she said, and pointing to a small washbasin and hose on the side of the house.

Uncle Marcel appeared behind her.

"How did you find their tree?" he asked.

"Whose tree?"

"That oak," he pointed up the way I had just come. "Your grandmother sat under that tree whenever she needed calm. My mother, too, sat under that tree for guidance. And her mother as well."

His smile matched Genevieve's.

Through the afternoon and over dinner that night, I heard stories of the family of Chateau DuBois. I was humbled by my family's history.

"What about your father?" I asked late in the evening.

"Ahhh," Marcel exhaled. "My father was an excellent maker of wine. But he was not strong. When the Nazis came to our town, my father felt our future would be best if we simply went about our lives and accepted their presence. As a reward, the Nazis made him mayor.

"Those who were caught resisting the Nazis suffered horribly in the war. After the war was over, there was a very turbulent period in France, what we called a 'savage purge.' *Collaborateurs* were hunted and killed. They killed my father. Because your grandmother and I were in the resistance, they allowed our family to keep this home, although there was a price."

"What was the price?"

"The price was that Marie and I had to be present for his execution. They did it here, behind the shed where we keep equipment for the vineyard."

"Why did they punish you? You were in the Resistance!"

"Unfortunately, the French learned some wrong lessons from the Nazis. Our presence at the execution wasn't to punish us, but to add cruelty to my father's last moment. It was not successful. Before they pulled the trigger, my father did the most noble thing of his life. He looked at us, especially at Marie, and said 'What I did was wrong, but was what I thought was best for my family and for France. *Tout passe, tout lasse, tout casse.*' Then they shot him."

"Oh my god. Revenge is so awful."

"*Non*. My father made his decisions, and died because of them. It was not really revenge, but a purge. The French needed to purge the evil of what Nazis had done to us, purge that from ourselves, from our towns, from France. This was necessary for us to recover. It was hard, this is true, especially for Marie. Those who pulled the trigger had been compatriots, friends, men she had saved by bandaging their wounds. Not long after we buried my father, she left France with your grandfather and never returned."

I was awake a long time that night wondering how my Grandmama felt in the moment her father was killed, and how that influenced who she became.

The next morning I woke early when I heard Uncle Marcel leave the driveway in the Citroen. Genevieve was also up, even though dawn was just throwing a glow into the eastern sky.

"Marcel has work in Bordeaux," she said when I told her I'd heard the car. "We are negotiating with one of the *grand crus* to buy our grapes this season, instead of bottling our own wine. It has just gotten so expensive," she said.

After breakfast, she invited me out to feed the chickens. I loved the way she said "chick chick chick," and they came running from wherever they were in the yard to be fed grain.

"Where's Sam?" I asked.

"Who?"

"The rooster. I named him Sam. The red one," I said.

"Oh, no. You never name them," she said.

"Why?"

"Because naming them makes them into something else, makes it too easy to have a relationship with them."

"What's wrong with that?"

Genevieve looked at me with a mixture of sadness and mild frustration.

"This is something about Americans. Your idealism is wonderful, but you ignore reality. Sam, as you call him, was dinner last night."

I looked away so she would not see the expression on my face.

"That just seems cold," I said.

"Jessica. We French are aware there are consequences if we do not control our feelings, if we let them control us. This can be a matter of survival. So, we do not name animals we intend to eat. We do not fall in love expecting it to last, but know it must become something else. We love our family and mourn when they pass, but accept that the world can be indifferent."

"*Tout passe, tout lasse, tout casse,*" I said.

"Exactly," said Genevieve, putting a hand on my shoulder. "But that's only part of the saying."

"I'm sorry?"

"That's how the saying is most often given, and what most people know. But there is also another ending: Everything passes, everything wears out, everything breaks, everything is replaced."

"I never heard that ending."

"I'm surprised. That's why Marie stayed in America and raised you. So you would know these things. But perhaps she intended for you to learn that here."

"What? Why?"

"Oh. Marcel did not tell you this? I should not have said anything."

"Please …"

"This, too, was written in the letter, in the box you brought. This was her decision, to stay in America, and care for you. She felt from the time you were born that you were her legacy. That you needed her nearby, and that someday she would give to you the stone."

I was instantly overwhelmed. All the times I'd asked Grandmama why she did not return to France, and not once had she said this to me.

"I think I need to walk up through the vineyard," I said, and headed back to the oak that looked out over the valley. I spent most of the day there, aching to understand. The answers were incomplete, limited by my own lack of texture, or history.

That evening at dinner I asked Uncle Marcel why my grandmother stayed in America, especially after her husband had died. He looked over the top of this wine glass at Genevieve, and out of the corner of my eye I saw her give a small nod.

"She felt that you needed her nearby, that she had things to teach you that you could not learn otherwise."

"But why was that so important, when she could have been here!" I was nearly in tears from a mixture of guilt and gratitude.

"It was more important for her to be there for you," he said with the Gallic shrug, indicating the answer was obvious.

"My God, I let her down."

"*Non*, I think not," he said, with a slight smile.

"I lost my license to practice law. I lost my marriage. I've been wandering around with no job, no purpose, angry at society and everything about it. I've not done much to earn the sacrifice she made."

"This is not how she saw it," said Uncle Marcel.

"How do you know?" I said, with some skepticism, thinking no one knew my Grandmere like I did. I'd forgotten somehow I was talking to her brother.

"Well, the letter she sent with you for one thing. And this letter is not the first correspondence she and I have had, you know. She was very proud of you."

"I lost my marriage."

"My sister felt that was a victory, of sorts. She thought your husband was, how did she put it, 'hollow,' I think she said."

"She didn't know I lost my law license."

"Yes, this is true. But it would not have mattered. She believed you would overcome such a setback."

"It was more than a setback. I never fit in and was crushed by society. It won."

"*Non*, this is not true," he said shaking his head. "This can not be true."

"Why?" I asked.

"Society can't 'win,' as you say. Society is not an adversary. Society is simply water in which we swim. It is not conscious; it can't be an enemy. Yes, it has rules. You may accept those rules. You may break those rules. You may seek to change those rules. Each choice has consequences. But society does not 'win.' "

"I broke some rules. They said I broke laws and took my law license. Didn't society win?"

"To feel helpless is a choice as well, I suppose," he said with his shrug. "But if you fight and you lose, society does not win. There are people; there are rules. You fight the people; you change the rules. This was my sister. She broke rules, then showed her allegiance to our family by caring for you and sending you here, saving something she did not want to be lost."

"Uncle Marcel, I didn't deserve that. That she should live out her life away from all this …"

"This was not your choice to make," he said, with a soft, sad smile. "I asked her often to come home. But it was not my choice to make either."

"Why don't you two go outside and have this conversation while I do the dishes?" said Genevieve. "Marcel, aren't you in the mood for a cognac?"

"I'll be right back down," I said. I went up to my room then returned to the dining room with the small wooden box. Uncle Marcel and Genevieve were still at the table, talking softly.

"I want you to have this. To pass on within the family," I said, putting it on the table in front of him.

"You are sure of this?" was all he said.

"Yes. I have no children, and I think it belongs here, in France. You know best who would protect it."

Uncle Marcel nodded. "I want you to meet her," he said.

Chapter 35

Connection to others often feels like magic, but that's because we just don't understand how connection works. Is it biology, psychology, or happenstance? Yes.

I knew who the blue pendant would go to as soon as she got out of the car.

Uncle Marcel's grandson, André, had brought his wife, Claudette, and two children down from where they lived near Tours. Soleil was twelve years old, I guessed. She had a direct gaze, thick dark hair. She looked much like I imagine my grandmother looked at that age. She looked much like I did at that age. She wore a quiet wry smile that was invitation to communicate, defense against being harnessed, and cloak behind which she could spin away.

The blue pendant had been passed by women of my family from one generation to the next for 250 years. My grandmother knew who I'd become before I did. I could see Grandmama reflected in Soleil's strength and serenity, if not my own.

Their English was quite good, and I was picking up a little French. When we stumbled, Marcel or Genevieve translated easily and quickly enough for us to share an immediate bond.

With more of the family in town, we had the ceremony for which I had ostensibly come to France. Except for a small urn I'd kept for my own private ceremony, we took Grandmamas's ashes to the small graveyard behind the chateau. There they were put in a small plot next to those of her mother and father.

Afterwards, Soleil and I took my urn up to the oak in the middle of the vineyard where I mixed ashes into the earth. We sat there for some time. I did not mind that Soleil could see me cry, and she did not attempt to intervene in my grief.

"This is a very special place," she said when I was done.

Soleil followed me around the house over the next several days, watching me intently, asking questions in English that made us both laugh, as we came to understand we had so much in common.

"You are like a sister I've known forever," she said to me one day.

"You are more like my sister than my sister," I replied. When I went for walks, Soleil went too. When I sat under the oak, she sat nearby, not saying much, as we gazed out over the valley.

One afternoon, Andre, and Claudette invited me out to dinner.

Chez Bonet was a small restaurant in a two-story building of sun-baked stucco with a tile roof. Small windows in the second story had curtains, hinting there were living quarters upstairs overlooking the main street of the village.

Our table was set for eight, and we were the first to arrive.

"This restaurant has been in the same family for five generations," Andre said as we were seated by a pretty young woman dressed in a full-sleeved, simple but elegant blue dress. She was quite chic for what seemed to be a roadhouse café.

"It has won many awards, including from Michelin. The current proprietor was a friend we grew up with," Andre said, looking at Claudette, who looked away.

As if called to the table, a dark-haired man emerged from around a corner carrying two bottles of wine. About six feet tall, he had a prominent gallic nose, and dark, deep-set eyes. But what caught my attention was the smile he gave Andre and Claudette. It was pure joy, and gave way to a quiet laugh of delight.

"How long?" he asked of Andre. "How long have I been asking you to come?"

"I've been busy, Charles," said Andre, embracing the man.

"You've been busy creating children with the love of my life," Charles replied, moving to embrace Claudette with what did seem more than a friendly hug.

"Charles and Claudette were dating for a while," Andre said to me.

"Dating!? Were were nearly engaged!" said Charles. "But, she fell in love with a better man." He said this with mock despair and low bow to Andre, and we all laughed.

"You were 'nearly engaged' to half the girls in the village!" said Claudette.

"What brings you south?"

"Our cousin from America. Charles Bonet, this is Jessica Love. She is the grandniece of my grandfather, Marcel DuBois."

I stood to shake his hand. Charles was about four inches taller than me. His demeanor changed as our eyes met.

"You do not look American," he said. "You look as if you grew up in this valley. I am pleased to be introduced to such beauty." He did not release my hand.

"I think you say that to every woman," I replied. I did not take my hand away from his.

"No, Madame, I do not."

"Mademoiselle," corrected Claudette.

He was looking into my eyes, and I was looking into his. Neither of us spoke. I don't know why I felt the instant, intense connection. There was a pause as something passed between us.

"Ah. Yes. Please excuse me, I must get back to the kitchen," he said, finally, as if just to me. "We have a new sous chef. He is excellent, but a bit temperamental. I must go make sure he is happy."

Only then did he release my hand. Only then did I realize he was still holding it, and remembered to sit down.

"Very seldom have I seen Charles at a loss for words," said Claudette when he was gone, looking at me with a smile.

Other guests began to arrive. We were all about the same age, and they all spoke English as often as they could to include me in the conversation.

Next to me was a petite woman with brown eyes, darker and beautiful in a different way than the others. She looked like she was from somewhere south of the Mediterranean. Michelle was a jeweler. "It is not easy, being an artist and trying to live this far from the city," she said. "Sometimes I go to Bordeaux, or Paris, when I have to sell something to live."

I told her about my idea to make a necklace out of the piece of the china cup I had broken as a little girl.

"What a wonderful idea! May I help you bring this together?" Michelle said. We agreed to meet at her studio the next day.

She and Charles had a couple of cool exchanges in French during the meal, which started with an appetizer of fish and a bottle of cold white wine.

"Are you two still playing together in life's symphony?" Andre asked Michelle.

"I cannot seem to stay, and cannot get away," shrugged Michelle. "But I have a friend in Paris I hope will solve this problem."

"He does not give you what you truly need," said Charles, reaching for yet another bottle of wine. "You have too much passion for such a man."

"You know so little about so much!" flared Michelle.

"It is better than knowing too much about so little," he shot back.

Obviously, whatever had burned between them still smoldered.

Dinner was an incredible parade of flavors and textures, surrounded by laughter, questions to me about Seattle and America and honest curiosity.

There were other tables in the restaurant, but they were served by other waiters and assistants. Charles brought each course of our entire meal and cleared each course away with the help of a young man who seemed to anticipate every request made of him.

Finally, Charles brought a chair.

"Can you make room for me?" he asked both me and Michelle. We scooted our chairs apart so he could sit between us.

"How long will you be in France?" he asked as Michelle made a point of engaging the man on her other side, clearly not wanting to be close enough to hear our conversation.

"I don't know. At some point, I need to get back to Seattle."

"I hope that is not soon. I would like to see you again. Will you let me show you this beautiful region of my beautiful country?"

"I would like that."

"Perhaps tomorrow?"

"Let's wait until Andre and his family leave. I don't want to miss time with them."

"Yes, of course," he said. "Andre — how long will you be here? Do we have time for a climb in the hills?" he asked.

"Until Sunday," Andre replied. "I have to return to work, and the children need to be back at school."

"Let's have a picnic tomorrow. Bring your children. We will go to that place on the river where we have all had such a wonderful time. I will bring food, you bring wine from your uncle's cellar. I know he has special vintages hidden down there!"

Andre looked at Claudette, who looked at me, then at Charles.

"Would it be alright if we brought Jessica?" she asked, with a smile. "I know Soleil would love for her to join us."

"If you would like to come," he said to me, his eyes looking into mine in a way that would make me say "yes" whenever I was with him.

Chapter 36

A home reflects it occupant. My grandmother's house was spartan, my father's poorly built. The house with Mark in Seattle was dramatic, Uncle Marcel's chateau is timeless.

Charles lived not far from where we'd had our picnic. His house was small, and could have been built in any century. It had a small living area that opened wide, almost an entire side of the room, onto a wide stone patio that looked out over the river just below. The floors were of the same flat, thick stone. The walls were of white plaster thickly applied with ridges and whorls and yellowed with time.

His bedroom with an adjoining bathroom was on one side of the living room and on the other side was a spacious kitchen with copper and stainless cookware suspended from a steel band that hung over the stove from dark rafters that looked like they'd been cut by hand.

"It was a summer retreat built by my great-grandfather," said Charles. "Today it takes 20 minutes to get here from town. Back then it took all of one day."

I'd told Genevieve I was going to join Charles for dinner and not to wait up. From the dirt of his garden we pulled a couple handfuls of small white potatoes which he washed in a shallow pan on the patio just outside the door. We gathered rosemary which he crushed with his fingers to rub on lamb that was warming to room temperature on a huge butcher block work table in the center of his kitchen.

"It is fresh and strong and just right," he said, sniffing a dusty green sprig, which he then offered to me. I pulled his hand to my face to enjoy the herbal scent, but then kissed those fingers and then the hand while moving forward into his arms. When he kissed me I realized, with some shock, that I'd not been kissed in a long, long time, since before my accident in Seattle. And perhaps never with such soft, intense sensuality.

His lips found my throat, and his finger tip traced the "V" from my collar bones to just between my breasts, following the line the white blouse made against my skin darkened by summer sun.

I'd not had sex since the night of my accident. I'd not had an orgasm of any sort. I realized I was afraid that the accident may have done something to me. I'd not had sex because I didn't want to find out if it had.

"Charles, I don't know."

"What don't you know?"

"Whether this is a good idea. If I can," I hesitated.

"We don't have to, but not to would be such a waste," he said.

"I was hurt in a car wreck. There was an operation. I don't know if I can."

"How long ago was this?"

"About a year."

"You have not made love in a year!?!"

"No."

"I will look at this, if you will let me?"

I made no protest as he unbuttoned my blouse and kissed the top of my breasts, then again kissed my throat, the side of my neck. He had his shirt off before I knew it, and my fingertips sought out the satin of his skin, rubbing the length of his muscled back, the soft fuzz above his belly.

Soon I was on top of him, he pulled the shirt off my arms. I bent forward to kiss him hard on the mouth, my tongue seeking his.

"Charles." I said, when he gently rolled me to my back and began to unbutton my slacks.

"We must see. YOU must see what is possible," he said. "One may have to avoid or change our ways if there is trauma, but one cannot be without sex just because one does not know. We shall see, then you will know."

He waited for me to agree, which I did with a kiss. He removed my slacks and panties. Fear was in fierce competition with the urgency I felt as his finger trace the scar on my abdomen.

"Is it ugly?" I asked, looking not for a description but for his opinion.

"*Non*. It is small, and it is fading," he said, and then he kissed that, too. His fingers slid down and touched the yearning between my legs and I gasped. A year of sexuality was boiling up within me.

"Jessica, does this hurt you?"

"No. I just want you so badly."

Our bodies clicked completely. There was the smallest pain for a moment, then nothing but sensuality and passion blended into a cocktail of joy.

We lay together for long minutes afterwards, my hands moving up and down his back, feeling his soft skin and the mass of him over me. His face was buried in my neck, my hair nearly hiding his eyes.

Finally, he pushed up and rolled off to my right side, and he brushed his hands over my body, caressing me as I had caressed him.

"You are alright? This was alright?" he asked at last.

"Oh, yes."

"We must have dinner. I am famished!"

He got up, slid through his shower and out to his kitchen. I followed that path when he said, "The towel on the right side is yours." As I dried my skin the air moving through the house from the river was soft and fine, a cashmere breeze. The lamb and potatoes were wonderful.

We made love once more that night before I fell into a deep and grateful sleep with my head on his chest, one of my legs draped over his.

On my way back to the chateau the next morning, I stopped at the gallery/jewelry store owned by Michelle. It wasn't that far from Charles' restaurant, on a quiet narrow street with pavers deeply worn over the centuries.

I had the small shards of teacup in my purse, but I wasn't certain that's why I wanted to see her again. A small bell jingled when I opened the door.

Michelle had me sit down, took the porcelain from my fingers and turned it over, and back.

"Do you have other pieces?" she asked.

I reached back into the pouch and put the bits I had not put into the earth at the oak tree on the table.

With the nail of her index finger, she pushed the pieces of blue and white porcelain about on the smooth brown leather that was her work surface.

"What do you think?" she said at last.

"It looks like a butterfly!"

"Yes, metamorphoses. I think this porcelain represents change."

"*Tout change*?" I asked.

"*Tout passe, tout lasse, tout casse,*" Michelle replied. "But everything finds its place. Which this means, too, I think."

Tears came to my eyes.

"Jessica?"

"No, it's alright. Yes, that looks lovely. Will it be hard to make?"

"No, not at all. Give me a few days."

As I was leaving, I turned.

"Michelle, the other night, at dinner, Charles."

She held up her hand.

"We were lovers. It was one of the most glorious times of my life and I love him still, in many ways. But we will never be together. If he has shared love with you, you are very lucky. There are not many men like him."

I didn't say more.

It had been an amazing few days. I wondered if I'd found a new home, if there was anything left for me back in Seattle.

I drove the small white Volkswagen Golf I had rented back to the chateau.

"I guess dinner went a little later than anticipated?" Genevieve said with a smile as she came out the front door before I'd made it to the first step.

"Yes, well, we …"

"Charles is a lovely man," she interrupted. "His father was a lovely man, and his grandfather, too. In fact," and her voice dropped to a whisper, "I spent one of the most wonderful weeks of my life with Charles' grandfather. Probably where you spent last night." She gave me a hug.

Chapter 37

Happenstance often seems like part of a Grand Design. Maybe. Of course things happen that change our lives. But we're the ones who remember some things, forget others. Maybe we are the pattern, maybe we author the grand design.

A car came into the driveway a week later as Genevieve and I were sitting in the kitchen shelling peas from the garden, as I had so many times at the table in my grandmother's house. We had been talking about where love goes, and why does it leave, or stay.

"A delivery man, probably parts for the winery. Marcel will attend to it," Genevieve said. But a minute later, Uncle Marcel came into the kitchen.

"Jessica, someone in America is trying to reach you," he said.

The envelope had my name typed on the outside, and was addressed simply to me, care of Chateau DuBois, with the address.

I opened the envelope. Inside was a typed sheet with just a few words.

"Contact me at your earliest convenience at the number below. I think I know who tried to kill you —Agent Deborah Riddle."

"Uncle Marcel, is there an easy way for me to call a number in America?" I asked him.

"You may use the phone in my office."

"I'll pay for the call."

"*Non*, you will not. It costs very little, now with the Internet. I am always calling friends with wineries in California, Chile, Australia. Your call will not be noticed."

"Grandmama could have talked to you at any time? And did not?"

"She preferred to write longhand," he laughed, then led me down the hall to where his office looked out on the vine-covered hillside behind the chateau. He sat down at the computer on his desk and made the connections, showed me how to dial, and put a pad and pen in front of me on his desk. When he closed the door, I dialed the number.

"Hello?" came a voice heavy with sleep.

"This is Jessica Love."

"Shit. It's 5 a.m."

"You have information for me?" Deborah Riddle wasn't someone who made me want to be either polite or sympathetic.

"I'll call you back after I've made some coffee."

"That won't work. This is not my phone."

"Where are you?"

"In France. You sent me a note, right?"

"Yes. I got the address from your family."

"So, who tried to kill me?'

"I don't want to discuss anything on the phone."

"This feels like a trap. Haven't you damaged me enough?"

"What do you mean?"

"You were unhappy about the Ashley Moore trial. Your last words to me were that I'd get what I deserved. You or some buddies in law enforcement set me up, framed me with drugs. I lost my law license, almost died."

"I had nothing to do with that, but I think I know who did."

"Send me an email."

"I won't be putting any of this in writing. You want to know more, you meet me in Seattle."

"Where? When?"

"I'm available almost any time. You have my number. Call when you're around. I'm going to find some coffee, now." She hung up the phone.

I sat for another half-hour at Uncle Marcel's desk, looking up at the oak tree on the hill where my grandmother's ashes were mixed with the soil.

There was a soft knock at the door.

"Jessica, is everything alright?" said Uncle Marcel.

"Come in. Yes, I think everything's alright. But I don't really know."

He walked over to his computer and shut it down.

"May I ask you a question?"

"Yes, of course," he said.

"That phone call was from somebody who I think hurt me. She says no, but that she knows who did."

"Yes?"

"I don't know if I should let it go. Put it behind me. Or whether I want revenge, or just answers."

"Jessica, how long will you stay with us?"

"You've been so generous. I know I can't stay forever."

"*Non*. That is not what I am saying. You are welcome here for the rest of your life, if you'd like. But what are your thoughts, your plans?"

"I suppose I'll go back to Seattle before long."

"Yes, I think so too. I hope you will return to France, but think you will go back to Seattle, at least for a while."

"Then I don't understand your question."

"You must look at this as if you were already in Seattle. How will you feel about it when you are there? And later, some time in the future, how will you feel if you 'put it behind you,' as you say?"

"I will want to know. So I will try to find out."

"And when you find out, what will you do?"

"Revenge seems stupid, but I'm tired of feeling like a victim."

"I don't like the word 'revenge' very much. Victims feel more pain because they feel helpless, and live in fear of that helplessness. Balancing the scales states that one is not helpless."

"Balancing the scales is the purpose?"

"It has purpose beyond itself. It is perfectly rational to confront one's fear by confronting one's enemies. There needs to be no other purpose." He sat back in his chair, apparently with nothing else to say, and I saw how he and my grandmother were from the same vine. I saw how my soul was related to theirs.

Later that afternoon, I drove to see Charles. After we'd made love, I told him I was returning to Seattle, and told him why.

"You have to do this? Is it not better to let the past be the past?" he asked as we lay together. I hoped it would not be the last time.

"I don't think I can move forward without knowing who did this to me," I pointed at the thin white scar on my tanned belly. "Some things have to be brought to a close."

"Even if this means opening them again, just so you can close them?" I nodded. The white rough sheets on his bed felt good against my skin, his fingertips on the underside of my breasts and across my belly were gentle, soft, welcomed but not arousing after having made love in the warmth of a long afternoon.

"There is risk?" he asked, eventually.

"It doesn't matter. Some things just have to be done."

"You sound French, sometimes."

"I was raised French, just in America."

"Will you come back?"

"I will lie here again with you."

"Okay, Jessica. You go take care of this business of yours. I will be here and cook fine meals, and think of you constantly."

"I don't expect you to wait for me."

"*Non*, I will not wait for you. But neither shall I frivolously pursue others until I know you are not to return."

"I'm coming back."

"We shall see. Life takes us to many unexpected places, and our intentions often don't matter."

Charles leaned over and gave me a long, full kiss on the mouth.

"I will miss you for however long you are gone," he said, then pushed off the bed. I heard him in the shower. While I was in the shower, I heard his car leave the drive. We'd had as much good-bye as either of us could stand.

"Thank you for coming, for bringing your grandmother home to rest," said Genevieve the next morning as I loaded my bag into Uncle Marcel's Citroen. "Please come back any time. This is your home." She gave me a quick kiss on each cheek.

On the way into Bordeaux, Uncle Marcel asked "Do you have a plan?"

"There is much to learn. Then we'll see," I said.

At the airport, he extended his hand. "You are changed, I think, from when you arrived."

"I don't know how to thank you."

"There is nothing to thank anyone for," said Uncle Marcel. "You simply received what was already yours."

The flight to Paris was short and easy. The flight from Paris to Seattle was interminable, and surreal. It felt like I was returning to a dream, one I'd nearly forgotten, while at the same time, France and all it meant seemed to recede, dream-like, as I flew west.

I pondered what Deborah Riddle might have to say. I wondered if I could believe she was not responsible for the accident that nearly killed me. I looked forward to the chance to meet her again, face to face. Something would happen, even if I didn't know what.

For most of that long flight, my fingers rubbed across the wings of a blue butterfly that hung from a platinum chain around my neck.

Chapter 38

We don't see things as they are, but as we believe them to be.

Deborah Riddle agreed to meet at a café that had really good coffee. I also knew a back way out, down the hall and past the ladies room shared with other businesses. I arrived a half-hour early so I could choose the table, not that it mattered any more than my knowing the exits. Riddle was a federal cop who could drop a net around the entire block if she thought it was needed.

Riddle's eyes swept the restaurant as soon as she came through the swinging glass door. Though I made eye contact, she kept looking around, so I stood up from the table with my messenger bag as if I were headed out, but stopped in front of her.

"Looking for someone?"

It took about one full second for her to say, "Jesus, look at you." I walked back to the table where I sat with my back against the wall. She took the chair opposite.

"Keeping an eye out?" she asked.

"Somebody tried to kill me in this city. One tends to be a little more aware of the environment."

"I doubt they'd recognize you. That's a good thing, though."

"Travel will do that." I didn't actually remember how I'd looked the time I'd last seen Riddle. I knew my hair had grown, I was wearing a lighter shade of lip gloss, my dark green, long-sleeve blouse was probably more flowing. My comfortable trousers billowed, a contrast to the tight jeans and yoga pants worn by others my size in the city.

"So, it wasn't you who set up my so-called accident?"

"No."

"Convince me."

"After our case blew up at trial, we went looking for answers. Not many people have access to our evidence lockers, especially if it involves narcotics. I suspected you had something to do with it."

"Thank you."

"Not unfounded."

"If you say so," I said.

She just shrugged.

"We found nothing on you. What we did find was the agent who handled the bags, the one you humiliated in court, had written large checks from his bank account over the last couple of years."

"How do you tie that to me?"

"The payments were made to a law firm."

"I never represented a federal cop."

"No, but Max Moore defended the cop's son. Kid had gone all Miami Vice and was popped for dealing and assault. Moore got him off, but it was a long trial. Moore is very expensive. Our cop could never afford him."

"So?"

"Payments to Moore's firm stopped after the Ashley Moore trial."

"Maybe your cop paid off the bill."

"Not likely, but maybe he was granted a credit for work done."

"What did he say when you questioned him?"

"We didn't get a chance. We set up an interview in the federal building where he worked, told him we had some questions about evidence management, told him we'd like him to bring copies of his bank statements."

"You already had them."

"Yes, but we wanted him to provide them. If he tried to hide or modify them, there would have been more for him to explain."

"Ah, the wheels of justice."

"You ought to know."

My turn to shrug. "So what happened during questioning? What ties this to me?"

"The night before he was to come in, our cop died in a car accident. On the Alaska viaduct. Drunk, with a trunk full of drugs. So drunk our team didn't think he was able to drive. Just like what happened to you."

"Copy cat. If it was related, they wouldn't have been so stupid to stage the same accident in the same place."

"You'd be surprised at how many perps do exactly that. Sometimes it's laziness, sometimes intentional. The smarter they are, it's like they're taunting us, letting us know there's a link and daring us to find it."

"Pretty slim. What else do you have?" I asked, thinking I was not interested.

"The wife of our dead cop is Claudia Moore's hairdresser."

"Really." That came out as a statement, not a question. "How do you know this?"

"That's not important," Riddle said. "We think the cop's wife told Claudia about the son's troubles, Claudia leaned on Max to take the case, Max did but brought our cop under his thumb."

"There are too many leaps in there, not enough for an arrest warrant let alone a guilty verdict. Cop calls expensive lawyer he can't afford to defend wayward son. A half-decent alibi and he's in the clear."

"Yeah. You'd have poked holes all through the case. That's why we haven't gone any further. And why I thought you'd be interested."

"Why?"

"Because if this is the way it happened, then Max Moore is the one who set you up, planted drugs on you, and tried to kill you."

For a few seconds, I looked down at my coffee. The surface reflected the lights above our table. I used to drink it with cream, before I went to France. Now I drink it black, sometimes with a bit of sugar. That wasn't the only thing that changed during the trip, of course. "Give her time, Jessica," said my grandmother softly in my ear. "Let her convince you."

"I've spent a lot of time hating you, and thinking you set me up," I said out loud.

"I believe in justice, not revenge," she said.

"I've hated you, going way back to when you convinced me to lie that I'd been raped when I was 15."

"That was a long time ago. I don't remember much, but I was pretty gung-ho back then."

"You were a cop. You had me lie. A boy was killed because of that lie."

"Like I said, I was pretty gung-ho. That was part of the reason I handled those cases, aside from being the only female in the department kids would talk to."

"Why was it so important to you my boyfriend be charged with statutory rape?"

It was Deborah Riddle's turn to look down into her coffee. Finally, she looked up and I was surprised to see her eyes were wet.

She told me about growing up, not attractive, not many dates, and of falling in love in her senior year. The boy was smart and had well-to-do parents. They didn't often go out with other kids but spent a lot of time exploring each other. When she found out she was pregnant, she was both scared and thrilled, so scared she waited too long before she said anything. When she finally told him, he changed instantly. He was angry, he ridiculed her. He told her he wasn't going to be a father, and to rub it in he said he didn't believe he was the father.

"He said not to tell anyone, but the next day, I swear it was all over the damn school. Kids would look at my belly, they pointed and laughed at me. He never even looked at me again. I was ashamed. I dropped out of high school."

Her mother convinced her to have an abortion, so they went out-of-state, down to Portland. It didn't go well, complications and infections. Eventually she was hospitalized and doctors removed her ovaries and uterus. She earned her GED in Oregon while living with an aunt, studied law enforcement, and returned to her hometown, my hometown, where she became a cop. It wasn't long before she was called in on sex cases.

"I took the side of the girls, always. I thought the boys deserved whatever happened to them. I guess I was getting my revenge one boy at a time."

"I'm sorry," was all I could think of to say.

"It's okay," said Deborah Riddle. "I had a partner until recently, and we loved each other."

""Him, her? What happened?" I asked.

"Him. Bobby passed away. It was an unfortunate situation and I'd rather not talk about it." Her expression was grief, along with something else I could not name at the time.

I sat quietly for a moment, to show respect.

"So it's not revenge you're after now?" I asked.

"Max Moore killed a cop, or had him killed, one of *my* cops, and he tried to kill you. He shouldn't get away with it."

"You believe this because the accidents look the same? That's a long leap from one dead cop."

"Maybe not."

"Yes?"

"The drugs they found in the car the night our cop died? They matched exactly the drugs found in your car the night of your accident. Not just similar. They were exact matches, of each drug. Each came out of the same container, at some point. There is no way they were not from the same person."

"Which means what?"

"Which means, whoever killed him is the one who tried to kill you," she said.

After years of hating Deborah Riddle for what happened to me, it took a bit for me to accept that she was not the one who set me up, but that it was Max Moore.

"Why? Why would he want to kill me?"

"I don't know. I thought you might."

"Why not gather more evidence?"

"I'm trying, that's why we're talking. But we'd never make anything stick to Max Moore. Someone who had a grudge, a private citizen, might be able to even the odds a little bit."

"So, you're using me?"

"Don't act shocked. You've seen worse."

"What do you expect me to do?" I asked.

"I don't know. I don't want to know. I just thought you should have this information."

"So I can even the scales of justice for you?" I asked.

"And maybe for you. You don't deserve what happened to you."

Chapter 39

The problem with going to friends for support is the possibility they won't support you.

"Tony, why do we always meet in the restaurants down here? Not a judgement, just a question."

"Good food. Good friends. They go together, don't you think?"

We were in a tiny Chinese restaurant, sitting in a cramped booth with cracked plastic benches and a table that had been built out of plywood coated with varnish. A thin metal band had sprung loose from the edge and caught my sleeve when we sat down. The restaurant was so overheated we couldn't see out through windows streaked with rivulets of condensation.

"How've you been Jessi?"

"Good. I spent the last two months in France with relatives. They're amazing people."

"It was good for you. You look absolutely great. You fall in love?"

"Why do you ask?"

"A woman in love has an air of fulfillment, there's a peace about her."

"Men don't?" I asked.

"Men don't stay fulfilled long enough for that kind of peace."

"Oh, Tony. You make such sweeping statements." I laughed. It was so good to see him.

"Whatever. We see the world we've experienced. What's his name?"

"His name is Charles, I have no idea if it's going to go anywhere, and that's all you need to know."

"Okay. So what was so important that you needed to see me right away?" he asked.

I recounted Deborah Riddle's theory about the federal cop in charge of evidence for the Ashley Moore trial, his payments to Max, how the accident that killed him was just like mine. Tony's expression changed when I mentioned Claudia, and I remembered that time they saw each other in my office.

He didn't say anything when our food arrived except to thank the waitress. Occasionally he stared out the window, then back down to his plate.

"What do you think?" he said at last.

"If Max Moore tried to kill me, I want justice."

"No, what do you think about lunch? I think it's pretty good."

"The Hunan chicken is excellent. The pot stickers need some work," I said, put off that he wasn't engaged with what I wanted to talk about.

"Yeah. I think that's right," he replied.

"Tony, what about Max Moore?"

"What do you want from me?" he sighed.

"At the moment, I think I want you to be my lawyer. Let me know where the boundaries are, advise me, attorney client privilege and all that."

"Don't tell me if you are planning something illegal," he said.

"I know all that. I promise not to tell you if I plan anything illegal." I thought he was being funny.

"Why anything at all, Jessi? Revenge? You're in love, probably on course for a new life … why go back there?"

"What happened to me was wrong."

"Justice? You were a lawyer long enough to know better. Where's your real self-interest?"

The waitress came and collected our dishes at the same time she put down the bill, upside down in one of those little plastic trays an inch longer than paper currency. Tony pulled out his wallet and put a $100 bill on top. She put her thumb over the paper and walked back to the kitchen, dishes stacked on her other arm.

Then the cook came out. He was apparently the owner, as well. He was black, wearing kitchen whites and huge. He put the plastic tray back on our table. The $100 bill was still on it.

"Lunch was good, Tony?"

"Jessica says the pot stickers were not the best, but everything else was great."

"You know, she's right. We have a new supplier, not local. We'll have to raise the price but we're going back. Don't tell anybody we don't make them here, okay?" he said this looking at me. I nodded my head.

"Hey," he said to Tony. "You overpaid your last bill. By quite a bit. We need to settle up." He pushed the tray with the $100 at Tony.

"Let's talk about it another time," Tony said, pushing the tray back.

"Okay, another time. Don't take so long to come back. And thanks for feedback on the pot stickers," he said, looking at me.

He pushed the tray back at Tony, the hundred still on it as if our input had been worth giving us lunch.

Tony wormed out of the booth to stand. "Let's go for a walk," he said to me.

"What was that about?" I asked.

"Let's go for a walk." He headed for the door.

It was between rain showers. He led me down to the waterfront and we talked about the redevelopment of the area. Men with jackhammers were breaking up concrete, backhoes were scooping the rubble into dump trucks that were hauling it away. More would be lost than gained, in his opinion. Then Tony made me stop at a section of sidewalk next to the water and we looked out over the bay.

"Jessi, tangling with Max Moore is too risky. You don't know if he was even involved. I think you have more to lose than to gain. Let it go."

"No," I said in a flat voice.

"Why?"

"I want to know what happened to me and why. I will not live the rest of my life feeling someone thought they could throw me away."

"That's overstating it."

"You know, Tony, as insightful as you are, sometimes you just don't get it. Is it a male thing? Somebody, maybe Max Moore, took something important from me without my permission. He destroyed it. I'm supposed to 'let it go' and live with that forever and he gets away without even a wrinkle on his conscience?"

"So you want to wrinkle his conscience? That's not going to happen, especially with Max Moore, if he was even involved."

"I think he was."

"But you can't prove it, Jessi. No lawyer could and certainly not the district attorney in this city. You don't have a motive, and Max wouldn't go to the effort or risk without a pretty good one. You were the lawyer for Ashley Moore, and the dead federal cop was involved in that case too, in the role of handling evidence. You each have an accident involving drugs. Not much of a link and not nearly enough to file charges and I don't think Max will just hand you a signed confession."

"What if I had more facts?"

"Jessi. This is Max Moore. It's not just about facts, you know that. It's about story, and he could come up with a pretty good one that might put you in even greater jeopardy. What happens if you lose?"

"What story? What could he do that he hasn't already done?"

"What if you're right? What's to keep him from taking another swipe at you?"

"That's an even better reason to take him down."

"What do you have that would take him down?"

"They were identical drugs from the same source."

Tony stood a little straighter and turned to look into my eyes.

"Yeah? Maybe you and the dead federal cop were both users and you got your drugs from him. Better yet, maybe you were the dealer and supplied drugs to the cop in exchange for his tampering with the Ashley Moore evidence." He looked not just at me, but into me, then.

"Is that what you believe?" I was shocked to hear this from Tony.

"No, but it doesn't matter what I believe. It's about story and you don't have one that Moore couldn't destroy in front of a prosecutor or jury. You can't change the past, Jessi. What happened happened. Revenge doesn't work. You need to let it go."

"I will *NOT* let it go!" I took a step back and faced Tony. "You don't get it. 'What happened happened' is just a bullshit excuse for being weak. I am not an expendable obstruction in the way of whatever his purpose might have been. My doing something changes the outcome. It means I no longer have to think about that day with anger and fear. Impacting him as he impacted me *does* change the past, because it changes how I feel about it!"

Tears of rage were running down my face.

Tony opened his arms for me.

"No fucking way," I said, and turned to face the bay. He leaned on the rail next to me. We didn't speak for minutes.

"Okay. You've made your point," he said. "I won't be your lawyer, but maybe I can help. But you need to understand that you'll probably never find justice."

"You're wrong."

Chapter 40

It's surprising how many shades of black there actually are. Many people think black is black but that's not any more true than believing the world is just black or white, right or wrong, good or evil.

I look pretty good in all black, too, and my slacks and shirt matched in shade. I admit the black outfit was an affectation. I didn't really need to wear it. Actually, it was an idea Tony tossed out there. I thought it would be fun, so I went with it.

I'd parked my car around the corner from the L'Escargot, the same restaurant in the stylish old mansion in Bellevue where Claudia and I had met once before. It was cold and rainy, so I waited in my Porsche until my phone beeped with a short text. I climbed out and was a little wet by the time I arrived at the front door.

I asked the hostess for a napkin to dry my face and she unrolled one that had wrapped silverware from a tray behind her.

"I'm supposed to meet Claudia Moore. Can you tell me where she's seated?" I asked.

"Oh, yes, I'll take you," said the hostess, who was wearing an outfit nearly identical to what I had on.

"That's okay. Just tell me where they are, I'll find the table."

"Third floor in the alcove closest to the street," she said.

They'd turned the original garage on the bottom floor into an elegant bar and lobby. The second floor had the kitchen, and what had been bedrooms on the third floor were now filled with tables of elite diners. I walked through narrow hallways impressed with servers who maneuvered trays into the small vestibules.

There were 42 steps from the garage at street level to the third story.

"Excuse me," called one matron to me as I walked past a doorway. I looked at her, waved and kept walking. She'd survive another minute without the glass of wine or basket of bread she obviously didn't need anyway. I wish I'd caught her expression, though.

Tony and Claudia sat at a table nestled in a bay window overlooking the old town and the park. I draped the purloined napkin over my arm and walked up.

"Are you ready to order?" I asked.

With barely a glance, Claudia said, "My order is known. Please find someone who has worked here for a while."

Tony looked up at me and gave a slight smile. "I'll have my usual," he said.

"Dark beer, tall glass?" I said.

This startled Claudia, who then actually looked at me.

"Who are you?"

"We've met. I'm hurt you don't remember."

"I can't be expected to remember every waitress."

"Actually, at the time I was a lawyer. Your daughter's lawyer."

I enjoyed the surprise and dismay that flashed across her face.

"You set this up!" she hissed at Tony.

"Of course," he replied.

"You manipulated me!"

"Claudia, isn't that what we all do? We're just more subtle than most. But sincerely, I'm trying to help both of you."

They were sitting across from each other, so I took the chair between them, facing the room.

"Sorry," I said. "I'm just not used to standing on my feet all day. I suppose I'll get used to it, though."

I reached over and took a sip of Claudia's water. It was an unnecessary flourish, but I couldn't resist.

She turned to me. Maybe turned *on* me is a better description.

"What do you want? Why are you here?"

"I want to ask you a question."

"I don't feel like answering questions."

"I think you want to answer this one."

"What?"

"When you told your husband about the conversation you and I had about the second bag with Ashley's clothes, what did he say?"

"We don't actually converse that much. Why do you think I told him anything?"

"Because you thought it was important."

"You don't know that. You have no idea what I talk about with …"

"What about Robert Miller, the husband of your hairdresser? Did you talk to your husband about him?"

"Which hairdresser? I've had more than one."

"Doreen Miller, a hairdresser who's a widow now, with even more damage to her life. Did you know her husband died? You might remember her son was arrested for drugs and robbery. You convinced Max to represent him."

"I'm not responsible for every individual I come in contact with! Doreen told me her story. I gave her a solution!"

"Claudia." The way Tony said her name had a mixture of strength and gentleness in it.

Actually, it had a plea, too, and a bit of love, or maybe it was just compassion. He packed it all in there, and it had an incredible effect. Her head swiveled from me to him, and then back to me, then to him. She stared at him at length, and a tear began to fall. That would have been a newsworthy event if a camera had been around.

"What did Max say when you told him about our conversation?" I asked again.

"He said he'd take care of it," she finally whispered.

"Did he say how?" I asked.

"No, but he did say you were a nuisance, not a threat."

"He didn't say how? That he would fill me with drugs and send me off the road?"

"Oh, god no. When I learned what had happened to you, I was shocked."

"How did you find out?" Tony asked.

"God, it was everywhere! In the *Times*! I walked in and put the paper down right in front of him. 'Did you do this?' I asked. He said, 'Claudia, that's not our agreement. Please don't question how things are done.'

"I was speechless. And afraid. He could also have me killed in an accident that no one would question."

"Claudia," I said, "your husband tried to murder me. He destroyed my life."

"I didn't mean for that to happen. I just wanted to protect my daughter. I know so little about what he does, or how he does it."

"I'm going to get my life back. There may be consequences for you, too."

"Don't even think about going to the police," she said. "He has half of the Seattle police and the DAs office on his 'owe me list,' he calls it."

"Is there some way I can get his attention without announcing myself?"

"That shouldn't be difficult. You're very much his type, from what I've been told," she said with a wry smile that spoke less of pain than scar tissue.

"Claudia, you need to make some decisions," Tony said, in that same, compassionate voice, still full of love, and now sadness. There was a long pause. She looked for her water glass, but seeing it in front of me, reached over and took a sip from Tony's instead.

"Yes, I suppose I do," she said. "It may be time to travel," she said. "Maybe I can find someone?" she looked at Tony.

He reached across the table and took her hand. "We missed that chance a long time ago. You know that, right?" he said.

"Yes, I know that, you sweet, brilliant, beautiful, frustrating, stupid, stupid man," she said without pulling her hand from his hand, her eyes from his eyes. After a minute, I realized they had forgotten I was there.

"I should leave you two," I said, and started to stand.

"No, you stay," said Claudia, coming out of her trance. "You may have my lunch. It looks like you need to eat. It will be put on my tab. It's the least I can do."

To Tony, she said, "Walk me to my car?"

"Hopefully it's parked on the other side of the Bellevue Inn?"

"I believe it is, though actually, I've forgotten exactly where. It may take a while to find."

"I've got all afternoon," said Tony.

"Perfect," said Claudia. As they walked out of what once had been a bedroom, I assumed they were off to another, Tony's hand gently placed in the small of her back. Good for them.

Claudia was right. I was hungry. I ate her lunch and drank Tony's beer.

Chapter 41

Men do not often see what a woman really looks like unless she wants them to. Between what we do with shading and texture of eyes and lips and hair, men are prone to see what they want to see, and we can be almost anyone.

I went to Sullivan's a number of times hoping for an opportunity to get close to Max Moore. Claudia said I was his type, but I didn't want him to recognize me. I'd painted my lips to appear fuller, de-emphasized my French cheekbones, and changed my hair to a business-like cut. I would set up my laptop at the bar and look just like all the other lawyers from upstairs with work to do and an eye out for a possible date.

About a week after Tony and I met with Claudia, a good-looking man about my age asked if he could buy me a drink. I'd actually met him a couple of times when Mark and I were still married — a lifetime ago it now seemed — first at a fundraiser for the Seattle Children's Hospital and again at the Boats Afloat Show on Lake Union when Mark and I were thinking of selling the island house and buying a boat.

Steve came up to me at the end of the bar where I was "working."

"If you're not on deadline with that, may I buy you a drink? If you are, may I virtually buy you a virtual drink?"

I laughed, said sure and closed the laptop. I'd worried a little that Mark would come in. I didn't think different makeup and hair would fool my ex-husband, but Mark usually went to the gym after work and besides, with his status as a married man, I doubted he spent much time in bars.

I told Steve my name was Rebecca Wilson. He asked which firm I was with and I told him I was up from San Francisco on a special project that I really didn't want to talk about. There's enough interchange between Silicon Valley and Seattle firms that guard their plans like nuclear secrets that my explanation didn't raise a ripple.

I asked him who he was with and he said "Moore & Associates." I shook my head as if I'd never heard of them.

In that way some guys affect when they want you to know they are both important and self-effacing, he added, "The firm's a big dog in Seattle law, but I'm just a mutt. I do real estate contracts."

It was about that time Max Moore walked up to the bartender, who quickly gave him a drink and pointed to the other end of the bar where a man stood alone, his back to the room, talking on a cell phone. He put his phone away when Moore walked up but didn't turn around.

"Steve, do you know those two men at the other end of the bar? Don't look right now, but I think they are realtors working on the same deal I'm working on. I thought they were at a meeting in Bellevue."

Steve turned to look, then turned back to me with a smile.

"No, those aren't realtors. The taller one is Max Moore — the Moore of Moore & Associates. The other one's 'of counsel,' up from Los Angeles."

"What's his specialty? Real estate? Tech?"

"He hasn't made much of a splash with the firm. Rumor is that Moore uses him for work he doesn't want to attract attention. He's kind of hard to know. I bought him a drink once and he barely said 'thanks.' A lot of people here don't care much for Rick Meyers."

I inhaled sharply as the man turned and I recognized Rick, the man I, well, one of the three men I'd made love with — had sex with — at SASA the day of the wreck that destroyed my career. The man I'd looked for before my trial. I inhaled like the air had been sucked from my lungs then replaced with pure oxygen. I repressed an urge to walk over to them.

"Jessi, do not challenge before you are ready," my grandmother had told me about backgammon. As Moore and Meyers talked and laughed, I feigned interest in Steve's stories about his role in the boom of Seattle real estate.

Memories of the night of my wreck flooded back. Then, a picture woven of guesses, insights, and logic spun into focus. It was overwhelming. I put my drink down on the bar and stared at Steve.

"Oh. My. God." I said. "Oh. Shit."

"You okay?" asked Steve, and he started to turn around to search for the source of my outburst.

To stop him, I put my hand on his thigh, always a way to capture a man's attention. Once a man's blood starts flowing to the penis, it immediately empties the brain.

"I'm fine," I said. "I just realized I'm late for that meeting in Bellevue."

"You won't make it at this time of day in Seattle traffic," Steve said.

"I can conference in. They knew I might be late," I said. Technology made lying so easy.

I reached for my purse.

"I've got this," said Steve, which was sweet as well as hopeful.

"You sure?" I asked.

"Yeah. May I see you again?"

"That would be nice," I lied, maybe. "Do you have a card?"

He gave me a business card and I quickly left Sullivan's, my back to the two men who had just proven I had work to do that depended on events and people that were mostly out of my control.

In the lobby I changed into a pair of running shoes and headed down to the Edgewater Hotel. I gave the valet a $100 bill and my phone number, and told him I'd give him another $100 if he'd send me a text when a certain fancy car showed up.

Two days later, the text I was waiting for hit my phone. One word: "Bentley."

I lived close by. Twenty minutes after the text I arrived at the Edgewater in a cab, gave the valet another $100. I got a room and was sitting in the bar two tables away from Max Moore chatting with a man and woman I didn't know, each of whom seemed enamored.

I was pretty sure I could send the right signal to Max Moore, and all things considered, I was pretty sure he would interpret it correctly. If a woman wants a man's attention, she can usually get it. Depending on the man. And the woman, of course. After all, I was his type.

When his companions rose and left, Moore walked over and asked if he could buy me a drink.

"That would be wonderful," I said.

I worried he would see through the darker eye shadow, the colored contacts, the shorter and much, much darker hair, the lips that were lined to look fuller than they ever were. I'd tried for the look between a high-priced call girl and a runway model. As far as I'm concerned, both are honorable professions but most models are underpaid.

We made small talk, and I told him I'd just arrived at the hotel and was in Seattle on business.

"What do you do?" he asked.

"What is it you want me to do?" I shot back.

"We may be traveling a slippery slope," Max said.

"Not yet, but it could be," I said.

Then I laughed and said I was just teasing and told him I was a pharmaceuticals representative from New York, newly hired and working with West Coast reps to introduce a new product.

"I've heard that's a great career," he said.

"Depending on the company, it pays well and I get to travel."

"Which company?"

"I'd rather not say, especially now that I've told you we're launching a new product. And you?"

"I'm a lawyer," he said, simply. No name, no posturing. If I didn't know what I thought I knew, the attraction would have been intense. We chatted, and I asked him what I should see while in Seattle. He was smooth and for a while I worried he would not make a move. But men are men, and I mean that in a good way.

"Let me show you some of the sights. Will you have dinner with me?"

"I've heard it's possible to get decent seafood in Seattle?"

Moore laughed and said that was true.

We each had another drink, then left for dinner. As we walked out he tipped the valet, who looked at me with a sly smile when I thanked him for opening the door of the Bentley.

"Nice ride," I said when we settled into the opulent machine, and he started an engine that only murmured its power.

"I enjoy it very much," was all he said about a car that costs a quarter million dollars.

Max took me to Canlis, a Seattle restaurant with views as fantastic as the meal. We talked about Seattle, New York. I was glad I recently had been to France, because that was a good part of my contribution to the conversation. Eventually our meal was over, and I told him I should probably head back to the hotel.

We went to the room I'd booked, and I let him kiss me. Cognitive dissonance is a survival trait, as is denial. His face was weathered, but his blue eyes were alive. He was very gentle as he lifted me and put me on the bed as if I weighed no more than a pillow.

I had not planned this part out. My immediate goal was to get close to Moore — success — but I was completely unprepared for whatever came next. How was I going to implicate him in my "accident?"

I let him unbutton my blouse, but I was getting uncomfortable. I was not going to have sex with this man. I needed to derail this, but hesitated.

"You are just spectacular," he said, looking at my breasts and kissing my neck.

"What's this?" he said when he got to the scar on my belly.

"I had an accident. It's healed," I said.

"Serious?"

"Not anymore."

"Good."

I wrapped my arms around him to stop his hands from undressing me. That he was involved with Rick made me afraid. That he'd been responsible for my wreck, damage to my body, destruction of my career made me twist up as if he'd turned into a gargoyle. I wanted him off me, and now.

"We have to stop," I said.

"What? Now? Why?"

"Because it's late, because I have to get up early, and because I think I just started my period."

"Really? No," he said. "I don't mind that. We have a shower and lots of towels."

"That's very nice, but I'd be self-conscious. Please? Can't we wait just a little longer? It'll be worth it." I tried to smile suggestively but didn't think I pulled it off.

"You have me going." he said, waving at the hardness now disappearing beneath the fabric of his slacks. I think he was suggesting I do something about it, but that wasn't going to happen, either.

"Let's wait until we have plenty of time. Please?"

Asking him like that, putting him in control, seemed to mollify him. He smiled and stood.

"Alright. When do I get to see you again?" he asked, pulling on his shoes.

"In just one week." I said. "I'm coming back through Seattle on my way home. I arrive Tuesday, the 25th. How about Wednesday the 26th?"

"That's too long," he said, sliding into his jacket.

"But since that's what it has to be, may we set aside some real time to enjoy each other?" I asked, giving him the slightest kiss on the tip of his nose. He agreed and stepped into the hallway. When I closed the door after him I locked it, then locked the night hasp, and leaned against the door. I was shaking.

Not from fear, at least not only from fear. Max Moore and Rick Meyers had taken more than my uterus and ovaries, and left more than a small scar on my belly. They'd left other scars, too, that at that moment were open wide and bleeding.

Chapter 42

Emotions often take priority over rationality. Emotions even create rational explanations for the most irrational behavior.

I had several priorities over the next week. First, I booked adjoining rooms at the Edgewater for the 26th of the month. Then I called people I knew when I was a lawyer, former clients mostly, and friends I'd made while in jail. I'd kept up with a few.

"Hi, Staci, this is Jessica Love."

"Oh God, how did you find out?" she said.

"Find out what?"

"That I needed a lawyer."

"Staci, I'm not a lawyer any more. I got busted, remember? They took my law license."

"So, why'd you call?"

"I need a few things," I said, and read off a list.

"Jesus, you going into business? A word of advice from a former jail mate? Bad idea."

"No, not going into business, and it'd be best if we didn't talk about this much. Can you get me what I need?"

"Yeah, I can probably pull it together. You're not working for the cops, are you?"

"No, not working for the cops," I said, but deep down I wondered.

Then I called the cop I might have been working for, Agent Deborah Riddle.

"Riddle," she answered the phone.

"What belongs to you but others use it more than you do?" I asked.

"Cute, but I've heard them all. Who is this?"

"Jessica Love."

"What's up?"

"I have an idea …" I told her that together, we might be able to get Max Moore to confess. She thought it was a good plan.

My last priority was not being seen by Max Moore. Seattle is a big town, but the Pacific Northwest is bigger and has a lot to offer. I went down to Port Townsend. I stayed in an ancient Victorian hotel there on Water Avenue, went to the wonderful Rose Theater, browsed incense-suffused texts at Phoenix Rising Books and petted Pavi, the owner's giant, beautiful poodle.

From there I went to Anacortes, took the ferry to Friday Harbor, then spent a few days in Victoria, immersed in the European flavor of that wonderful city. Hearing French occasionally spoken on the street took me back to France, Uncle Marcel, Genevieve, and Charles. I thought of my grandmother as a young woman watching her father shot by people she'd regarded as friends.

Victoria washed away some of the callous I'd built up while back in Seattle. The innate kindness of the Canadian people who say "sorry" when *you* are in *their* way, cars that stop yards (meters) away from pedestrians at an intersection, bookstores and coffee shops that seem … personal in ways that are lost in the states. Victoria felt more like home than home, and made me feel more vulnerable, but in a *good* way. Sensitive to what was going on around me.

I bought a cheap purse and a more expensive video camera. My plan had been to get close to Max Moore and discover things I could use to find justice. Now I recoiled from the thought of getting that close, of touching him, or having him touch me. Now I didn't have much of a plan. Tony said Moore was not likely to admit what he'd done to me, implying that was my only hope. I knew I had to confront Moore directly.

Chapter 43

Confidence impacts how others see us, how we see ourselves, often what happens. Uncertainty does the same thing but has the opposite effect.

I texted Max: "Edgewater 119 @ 7 p.m."

When he knocked, I opened the door wide wearing only a g-string and bra.

"Well, look at you," he said, holding a bottle of Champagne and two glasses.

"Please. But pour me a glass of Champagne while you do?"

He poured as I pulled a little black dress over my head.

"I thought we'd have an appetizer first," he said, nodding at the bed.

"What time is dinner?"

"They'll hold our table," he said with the confidence of a man who knows his patronage is valued over any small slight to a maître d', and the impatience of a man whose brain is infused with lust.

"I'm famished," I said. "Entrée first, dessert later."

I finished dressing while he sat in the chair by the window watching me, sipping Champagne. When I was nearly ready, he got ice from the machine just down the hall to keep the Champagne cold while we were at dinner. As we left he opened the door for me, as always, a gentleman. I was counting on that.

I was into the hall when I stopped.

"Oh! Would you hand me my makeup bag?" I said and pointed to the smooth leather case on the dresser.

"Of course."

When he brought it to me, I opened my purse for him to drop it in. "That's not much of a makeup bag," he said, and I gave him a kiss so he would not see the bag land next to lipstick and eyeshadow I kept in the inside pocket nor the washcloth on the bottom.

We took the Bentley to a wonderful Italian restaurant in the older portion of Bellevue. The waitstaff was not as deferential as the maître d, but the food was excellent. Some of the other customers looked at us, perhaps disapprovingly, sitting side-by-side and close together. It might have been the difference in our ages, or that I was dressed a little suggestively.

"The men are jealous of me; the women are threatened by you," Max said.

We talked about jealousy, biology and psychology. I asked if he came here often, he said no, but seemed familiar to the staff. He talked about his daughter, and I tried to avoid saying anything that would betray that I knew more than I should.

We finished dinner and refused dessert. We walked to the car and, as he always did, Max opened my door for me. While he was walking around the car's tight but still large exterior, I used the washcloth to slide my make-up bag under Max's seat.

Back at the room, I gave him the key card to unlock the door. Without pausing after it was open, I walked to the dresser and put my purse next to the TV. I pulled out my lip gloss and then fumbled around as I put it back into the purse I'd bought in Victoria with a hole now cut in the side, not quite covered with a fold, and turned on the video camera I'd hidden inside. I prayed the next hour would go as planned.

"Champagne?"he asked, gesturing toward the two chairs by the window. "The bubbles are gone but it's still good. Let's not waste a drop."

"That would be wonderful," turning back to my purse to face the camera towards the chairs.

"Jessica, what's the game here?" he asked, moving close and turning me around in a way that was not at all romantic.

"Who? My name is …" the words were barely out of my mouth before he slapped me hard across the face. While I was regaining my balance, he pulled what looked like a tiny toy gun out of his inside pocket, but it had a long silencer on the end. I knew it was not a toy.

"Max, what are you …?"

"Stop it, Jessica. Did you really think a haircut and makeup could disguise who you are?"

Fuck my arrogance.

He roughly pulled me to the closet where he pushed me against the wall while he pulled the belts from the complimentary bathrobes. Then he held me down on the bed with my face into the pillow and tied my hands and feet with the belts. Then he rolled me over and sat me up on the bed, picked up his phone, typed a quick message with one hand with the gun in the other under my chin.

"When did you know?" I asked.

"After our first dinner at Canlis. I knew we had met before, but couldn't place it. You have a way of speaking that's a little different from other people. When I saw the scar — you said you'd had an accident — it all fell into place. There was a risk, but I decided to play along. I wanted to know what your motive was and besides, you are very attractive. Playing along had other obvious benefits." he smiled.

"So, I'll ask again. What's your game? Thinking I might pay a little blackmail now that your circumstances are not as remunerative as they once were? Looking for revenge on your ex-husband by sleeping with his boss?"

"Maybe a little of both," I lied.

"And what were you going to use as evidence?"

"Nothing. I figured that if I …" His hand came up to slap me again. "No wait! In my purse. A camera."

He stepped over to the dresser where my purse sat and pulled out the video camera I'd hidden inside. He shook his head as if I were the dumbest thing he'd ever seen, and threw it out the window into Puget Sound.

"Saltwater will take care of that in a few minutes. You know, Jessica, I was hoping this would all work out. You were supposed to die in that car wreck. But you were lucky and then you disappeared. That was going to be good enough. France was it? Why did you come back? What did you want?"

"You took something from me."

"Your career? Children? You and Mark had already decided not to have children."

He saw the surprise on my face.

"Oh, Mark and I often talked. I was like a father to him. You see, I'd selected Mark to marry my daughter when he was still in law school. Smart, strong, athletic. Mark was going to to be my heir. He was going to take the firm national, he was going to sire my grandchildren.

"But you kept getting in the way and my daughter was stupid. He fell for you during that first conference in the SASA matter. You remember that case, I'm sure, when you first met Mark. So I offered you a job, thinking I could split the two of you up, but you wouldn't come to work for me.

"Then you got married, even though I tried to talk Mark out of it. I wasn't there of course, but remember the ride in my limousine you took after your wedding? The driver informed me that you had appetites. At the time I just filed it away. You built a good career, created a home … but I finally had a chance when you and Mark went to SASA."

"You knew about SASA?"

"Oh yes. The SASA matter was an expensive bit of legal work for our client. There was the settlement, and legal fees, of course. I suggested to the owner that he could bring me in as a partner instead of paying my bill, and I wouldn't take much of the profit. I really just wanted access to the membership roster. You'd be shocked at who some of the members are. Judges, police, CEOs, all joined my owe-me list.'

"Then you and Mark showed up and joined the club. I knew I'd be able use that. When the sex went too far for him, he was confused by your appetites. I sensed his pain and let him open up, suggested he sort things out by himself. He left you, but still had doubts until you had your "accident" and lost your law license. Now he's the father of my grandchildren and again my heir apparent, as I'd planned all along though it was a little more involved than I intended."

"None of this had to do with the Ashley trial? With SASA!?"

"Oh, your first conversation with Claudia about the trial made me realize you could tie facts together that no one else knew. That was too dangerous. You being sexually adventurous was just the opportunity."

"You're a monster." That's all I could think of to say.

"According to who? The Bible? Society? I think you left those behind some time ago, didn't you? I simply look for what I want and take it." Moore then sat next to me on the bed, gently brushed the hair away from my face. The gesture was frightening in its intimacy.

"I abandoned morality because I gave myself permission to explore sexuality while feeling safe and appreciated? I did nothing wrong!"

"I didn't say you abandoned morality. I said you left it behind. Important difference. We are much alike, you and I. We moved beyond what others think of as 'moral.' We live as we choose to live, by our own rules, creating our own fates, seeking our own pleasures, without guilt or shame. I don't condemn your sexual appetite, I applaud it! Is that why you came back? I never thought you'd make so much of it," Moore said.

"We are not alike. Maybe society fails to distinguish my 'immoral' behavior from yours, but there's a difference. My curiosity, my choice, my consent have nothing to do with you using people, harming others without regret. You hurt me. You demeaned me. You destroyed my marriage and ..."

"What about Mark? Wasn't he injured by your lust? You 'exploring your sexuality' as you put it? Are you really one of those who suffer from the disability of falling in love?"

"Disability?"

"With all of the debilitating symptoms of a bad allergy."

"Mark and I enjoyed our sexuality and he instigated much of it. I'm not responsible for why that changed. You used 'morality' to prey upon his insecurities, then you tried to kill me. You framed me with drugs. You destroyed my career. How dare you compare me to you, take so much and throw it away, then say don't make much out of it! Yes! That's why I came back!"

"Was it worth your life? You had a chance to live. Not like the federal agent."

"What?"

"When investigators got close to Robert Miller, he actually came to me for help!" Moore smiled. "They told him to bring his personal financials. I knew what that meant, even though he didn't. He thought his previous work entitled him to free legal services and tried to blackmail me. I couldn't risk he might buckle and turn on me."

"So you killed him."

"Oh, not personally. You've met Rick Meyers, who does that work for me. You actually met him twice before. He was the chauffeur who took you for that memorable ride on your wedding night. And then of course, that evening of fun in SASA."

My mind staggered trying to absorb the idea that Moore had extended himself into so many personal moments of my life. He stood up, pulled on his coat and walked over to the windows looking out on Puget Sound. I tried to free my hands, but he saw me reflected in the window.

"Don't, Jessica. I will shoot you in the head and the little bullet from my little gun will rattle around in your skull and probably kill you, but possibly just turn that wonderful brain of yours into cabbage. Regardless, it would be very painful."

"You don't play backgammon, do you?" I asked.

"Backgammon?" he turned to face me just as the door to the adjoining room crashed open and crashed against the wall. Deborah Riddle rushed in, holding a much larger gun on Max Moore.

"Drop the gun. Raise your hands," she said.

Moore let the little automatic fall to the floor and put his hands in the air.

"Who are you?" he asked.

"Federal Agent Deborah Riddle. The person who's going to give you exactly what you deserve."

"You need to read him his rights," I said.

"Shut up, Jessica. I'll get to you," Riddle said.

"She's right, you know. When we get to court, that will be important," Moore said. "She'll be a witness."

"Neither one of you will make it to court," Riddle said.

"Wait. This isn't what we planned," I didn't finish.

"No, Jessica, it isn't," Riddle interrupted. "I knew you'd lead me to Moore. You've set it up perfectly. He kills you, I kill him, everyone gets what they deserve and the world's a much better place."

"What ...?" I asked.

"You had Bobby open that bag on the stand, you knew it would blow up the case, you didn't care that it would put a target on his back. He and I had plans! We were going to retire and grow old together! You got him killed!"

"No," I started to say. "I didn't ... wait, your 'Bobby' was Agent Robert Miller?"

"Yes. Step away from that gun!" Riddle said to Moore. I turned toward Moore. He had taken a step forward, but now stepped back. Then I heard a loud click as the room door latched into place. Riddle and I turned at the same time, just as Rick Meyers brought the heel of his hand up and under the point of Riddle's chin. Her head snapped back and she crumpled unconscious to the floor.

In his other hand, Meyers was holding the room key I realized that Moore had never taken out of the door.

"Where've you been?" Moore asked.

"Seattle traffic."

"Claudia?"

"Bathtub. Overdose of barbiturates and white wine. Possibly an accident, possibly suicide, though no note," Meyers said.

Moore nodded, then said, "I believe you two know each other," to Meyers and me as if making introductions at a cocktail party.

Meyers looked at me on the bed. "I remember every inch of her."

"I need to go to the Olympic Club, talk to as many people as I can to build an alibi. Finish this up. I'll see you in the office tomorrow afternoon."

"What do you want me to do with the bodies?"

"Put Jessica on the bathroom floor, as if she was sitting on the toilet when she died. A needle in her arm, or nearby. It needs to look like an overdose. Make it look like she killed the cop. Put her prints all over your gun and leave it on the bed."

"I brought what I need," said Meyers.

"You don't have to do this, I won't …" I started to say.

"Shut up. I can make your last couple of minutes easy, or very painful," said Meyers. Moore just looked at me with a sad smile, and shook his head. Then he walked out of the room.

Meyers opened the briefcase he was carrying and pulled out a small black case which he unzipped to display a row of hypodermic syringes.

"You want to die from a plain heroin overdose, fentanyl, or heroin and demerol, maybe with a little cocaine?" I said nothing.

He finally made his own choice, filled a syringe and reached for my arm, even as I struggled. I heard a siren in the distance, far, far away.

Just as Meyers captured my wrist there was a tap on the door, not loud. Then another, a little more insistent. Meyers leaned close and whispered, "One word, one word and I kill whoever's out there and then kill you as painfully as I can. Got that?" He grabbed the cloth Moore had wrapped around the ice bucket and stuffed into my mouth. He pulled a small gun out of his waist band and walked to the door.

"What do you want?" Meyers said to the closed door. He tried to look through the peep hole, but apparently couldn't see anything.

"I have an urgent message from a Max Moore. Just arrived," said a voice on the other side.

"What does it say?"

"It's in an envelope from the reception desk. I'm not allowed to open it."

"Slide it under the door."

"I have to deliver it to a person in the room. In case it's urgent. You have to sign. Or I take it back to the desk and they'll come here with security and a key."

Meyers looked down for a second, then made his decision and opened the door an inch. To reach for the white piece of paper that barely peeked in, he transferred his gun from his right hand to his left. But as his fingers touched the paper, someone grabbed his wrist. The door crashed open, ripping the security chain from the wall and slamming against Meyers' head and shoulder. He recovered and began to bring his gun around but there was a "pop!" and Meyers fell, convulsing, to the floor.

I thought Max Moore had returned.

But Tony Stevens walked into the room, kicked the gun out of Meyers' hand then closed the door. He came over to the bed and pulled the cloth from my mouth.

"Max ..." I started to say.

"Max Moore will soon be in the back of a Seattle Police car being read his rights," Tony said.

"Claudia?"

"Claudia is going to be okay."

Suddenly the fear and the anger and the grim determination I'd been carrying for so long broke. Tony put down the gun and pulled me, still tied up, into his arms.

"We don't have time for this, Jessi," he said. "Police are on their way. I want you to lie back on the bed, unconscious. Let them wake you." He looked at the glasses and bottle on the table. "The last thing you remember was Max giving you a glass of Champagne. Do you understand?"

He picked up the phone with the wash cloth and when the operator answered, he whispered, "Gunshots. There's blood," and dropped the handset. He took the cloth, walked to the door and disappeared into the hallway. I heard the heavy exit door across the hallway open and shut. I lay back and closed my eyes and wished I could not hear Rick Meyers gurgle and writhe about.

Chapter 44

Armor comes in many textures and shades.

When scheduled to testify against Max Moore, I dressed in the black outfit my grandmother had made for me to attend her funeral. I wasn't nervous, but did find my right hand going to the small butterfly at my throat, made from the piece of teacup that had slipped from my hands in her kitchen so long ago.

Tony would not talk to me before the trial.

"The last thing you remember is Max giving you a glass of Champagne," was the only thing he would say when I called or texted.

I told the court that Max and I had gone to dinner, that I wanted him to acknowledge what he'd done to me so Agent Riddle could arrest him, that he'd given me a glass of champagne and I didn't remember anything else until police woke me. My testimony was bolstered by the tape Riddle made before she slammed into my room at the hotel.

"So it was all about revenge? You set all this up because you were angry?" asked Moore's lawyer.

"My grandmother taught me that anger is based in fear. I was not afraid of Max Moore, not then and not now. Yes, I wanted justice, but justice was done when he admitted he'd dosed me with drugs exactly like the drugs he used to kill an agent of the United States Customs Service, just like the drugs police found in his car."

Moore's lawyer yelped objections, some of which were sustained. I expected that.

The jury found Moore guilty of the murder of Robert Miller, the officer in charge of evidence in Ashley's trial; a half-dozen charges related to trying to kill me, twice; conspiracy to murder his wife Claudia; and the murder of Richard Meyers, based on the evidence: Meyers died from a bullet fired by the gun found in Moore's possession in the exit hallway where he fell and knocked himself unconscious while hurrying away from the crime.

They added possession to Moore's list of crimes because of drugs found under the seat of his Bentley: rohypnol, cocaine, heroin, along with a few prescription pharmaceuticals. What choice did they have? Moore was the last one out of the Bentley, his prints were the only ones on the small leather case. The car was locked in the parking lot (and watched over by the valet) the entire time he was in the hotel.

Law is about story, but that doesn't mean justice is denied. Moore will never get out of prison.

I was walking out of the courtroom when Agent Deborah Riddle came up to me.

"We need to talk," she said.

"Really? About what?"

"Please?"

It took me a long moment before I said yes, and we walked through a Seattle mist. Neither of us had an umbrella. I doubt Riddle owned one, and I was enjoying the feel of the cool moisture after the overheated courthouse.

"Why did you cover for me?" she asked.

"Whatever do you mean?" I said with a half smile of overstatement.

"I was going to kill you. You didn't tell the cops."

"I was afraid you were going to confess."

"I would have if I hadn't heard you tell the cops you didn't remember anything after Moore gave you champagne. At first I believed that, and thought no one would find out what I said in that room. Then I started to recall other things, that I had a gun on Moore, that you were on the bed. I don't remember who knocked me out, but I know you weren't drugged when I said what I had in my mind."

"Sometimes memories are just durable dreams," I said.

"Who knocked me out?"

"It must have been Rick Meyers."

"Then who killed Meyers?"

"A jury just determined it was Max Moore."

"Okay," she said at last. "But why didn't you tell them I was going to kill you?"

"Buy me a coffee. Double espresso." I opened the door to a small coffee shop with a table away from others in an alcove by the window facing the street. I sat as she asked if I wanted milk or sugar, I shook my head. I thought about what I wanted to say until she returned with our drinks.

"I told the police and testified in court that you and I had arranged to tape Max Moore's confession, if I was successful in getting him to make one. I testified I do not remember anything after Moore gave me a glass of Champagne. His giving me Champagne was recorded on your tape. You entering the room was after that, during the time that I testified I could not remember."

"You weren't drugged when I came into that room."

"This is your opinion."

"I know what I'm talking about."

"Look, what's the real question here?"

"You could have told them I was going to kill you. It would have been … what I deserved." As she said this, she looked outside through windows streaked with rain. The sadness in her eyes was complete.

"No. You would not have deserved that. There are no ultimate scales of justice setting everything right in the world. Bad shit happens to good people. Bad people can live long lives on silk sheets. Even if I remembered what you think you do, there would be no need for me to say anything to harm you."

"Turn the other cheek, revenge is wrong, no eye for an eye?"

"I didn't say that. What I'm saying is that I get to choose. Even if all you remember is true, and I'm not saying it is, if I chose not to say you were going to kill me, I would have done so because I understood your motives had very little to do with me, really. Perhaps I'd think you didn't deserve another rupture in your life. Perhaps I'd have been grateful you gave me what I needed to go after Max Moore. Perhaps I'd just want to let it go and not be forever angry at you for doing what you needed to do to ease your own pain."

"My anger would have become yours?"

"I would have been adopting your anger, which would be like adopting a friend's cat that I knew had no bladder control and liked to rip up the furniture. No offense."

We both laughed.

"I've got to go," I said.

"Who killed Rick Meyers?" Riddle asked, again.

"I testified that I was unconscious through all that. It's on the record. The jury determined it was Max Moore," I said, again, standing to collect my bag.

"Okay. But one more thing," she said, putting out her hand, which I took in mine.

"Thank you for talking with me. Thank you for everything. I am so sorry."

"Apology accepted, but don't be sorry. It's a good day," I said. "Justice was done today."

Chapter 45

So much is hidden in plain sight. What we see is an "event horizon," a surface that contains information about everything that *has* happened. But we are are chained within moments, and blind to the turbulence that defies time and constantly interferes with itself.

Tony finally called, about a week later. I'd left a half-dozen messages.

"Lunch?" he asked.

"Yes, lunch. This afternoon? Where?"

"Place Pigale?"

"Haven't been there since I was last there with you," I said.

We even sat at the same table overlooking Puget Sound where a lifetime ago Tony had given me my first real job. We didn't say anything after a hug and sitting down. I let Tony order our beer and the special of the day while I looked out at sunlight playing on the water and waves passing through each other, unaffected, as if they existed in different dimensions.

"How did you find me at the Edgewater Hotel?" I asked when the waitress left our table.

"Claudia." He said this as if it were an explanation.

"Yes?" I replied. Tony was holding back, protecting something.

"Tony, they were going to kill me. You saved my life. I'd never seen anyone die before, then I saw one that didn't stop convulsing until after the police got me out of there."

"Yeah, that was bad."

"Tony, you executed Rick Meyers."

"Yes."

"Why?"

"Because he was going to kill me. Because he was a psychopathic killer who murdered at least one person, tried to murder you and Claudia and would have succeeded except for luck. The law is too imperfect to contain people like that. With those you either win every encounter, because you can only lose once and eventually you will, or win once and for all. He was too dangerous to give another chance."

"How did you find me?"

He paused, but knew I had a right to know.

Tony told me that Max was home and still in the shower when I texted him from the hotel: "Edgewater. 119." Claudia and Max had long before stopped going to the effort of hiding their infidelities. She saw the text was from "Jessica," guessed it was from me and what I had planned.

The afternoon after Claudia, Tony and I had lunch, she'd told Tony that she and Max had an understanding about their marriage. What she didn't tell Tony then was that Max had set Claudia up with Rick Meyers. Of course, she didn't know that Max's ultimate aim was having Rick remove her from Max's life when the time came. Until then, Meyers and Claudia were having a comfortable and convenient affair.

But the time had come. After Max left the house, Meyers arrived. He made Claudia a cocktail, as he often did, though this one was loaded with drugs. While they were sitting together on the couch, Meyers put his phone down, but face up, to pick up his glass. He got a text from Max: "Edgewater. 119. Now."

Claudia pretended she hadn't seen the message and told Meyers she needed to go to the bathroom. She called Tony and whispered that I was in danger at the Edgewater, room 119. She went out and sat down next to Meyers, and that was the last thing she remembered until she woke in an ambulance.

"I could tell something was wrong with her when she called, so I went to her house, kicked in a back door and pulled Claudia out of the bathtub. She kept saying your name and 'Edgewater 119.' I called for an ambulance on her phone, then headed to the hotel.

"I saw Moore leaving your room and ducked behind the ice machine. When he went past, I knocked him out, hauled him through the exit door and left him under the stairs. I took his gun. You know what happened next. Then I went back to the exit hallway, cleaned the gun and put it in his pocket. That's about it."

It's all about story.

Tony was on his second beer, I wasn't halfway through my first.

"You have the town buzzing," he said finally. "Everyone's impressed you got Moore with those drugs."

"I have no idea what you mean," I looked him dead in the eye.

"Jessi, there is no way that Max Moore would have had those drugs in his Bentley. He's far too smart. Any drugs he was involved with could have been carried by a dozen different mules. That means it could only have been you. You had a reputation before, but every lawyer in town is a little afraid of you now."

"Every lawyer?" I asked.

"Not every lawyer," he said with a smile.

"I think the jury agreed with the prosecution's explanation, that Max Moore used those drugs to incapacitate victims."

"Whatever," Tony said. Then he offered me my old job back.

"We can set it up just like we had it. It might even be better. You're a little famous, now."

I thought about that and came to the conclusion that my world was a strange place, where what was right and what was wrong were not the absolutes that most of us were brought up to believe. And I was glad.

"Tony, I'm not going to work for you. But my office will be on the floor below yours. I signed a lease this morning."

"In the Seattle Tower? Why? The elevator takes a half-hour to go twenty-seven floors!"

"Because I like it. Just the same as you do."

"I'm only there because it's across the street from my apartment house."

"Yeah, whatever," I said in mock agreement. "But I'm going to open my own practice. I'll be glad to show appreciation for any referrals. I'd like to retain you on an 'of counsel' basis. We'll agree on terms."

"Want to walk back to my place and discuss those terms?" he asked.

I laughed at him, "You're not really that guy," I said. But it was time to go. As we walked past a rack of free papers, I saw *Source of the Sound* was still making a fuss about the mystery man feeding the poor of Pike Place Market.

Just then, the chef of Place Pigale stuck his head around the corner and said, "Tonight's our night, right, Tony?"

Tony threw a quick nod at the chef, then a fast glance at me and I could see a frown. Suddenly, I knew why.

"It's YOU!" I said in a soft voice. "You're the one feeding the homeless down here!"

"Don't be silly. Why would I do that?" he asked, but his voice didn't have the swagger it needed to convince me.

"Sit." I pointed back to the table we'd just left, and I ordered two more beers as we walked back by the waitress just headed to our table with a rag.

"It's you. Don't bullshit me."

"Jessi," he said in a softer voice, "a lot of people will suffer if you say anything to anyone else."

I leaned over the table. "Not a word," I whispered.

"Thank you."

"Where's your self-interest?" I asked him.

"What do you mean?"

"You know exactly what I mean. Why? Why do this? Why all the mystery?"

He took a long pull on his beer.

"The mystery is because it wouldn't happen if it was above board, in the sunlight. It would change, it would be channeled, it would get snarled with rules and good intentions and then even better ideas until those who needed it would have nothing to do with it. And I didn't want the publicity."

"Why not? It could have been good for business. It certainly could have polished your somewhat less-than-shiny reputation."

"Yeah. Maybe not. My father took off to Alaska when I was three or four, left Mom and me with nothing. And before you ask, no, I never heard from him again or looked for him. She and I ended up down here around this market. She became an escort, prostitute, hooker, take your pick. But it meant we had an apartment, food on the table, sometimes a Christmas. She did the best she could and I got used to the late-night company, though I'm sure it had some impact on my views about romance.

"It wasn't a bad life for seven or eight years, but she drank too much and at some point, someone gave her a taste for cocaine, which became crack, which became meth, which became a pretty ugly death."

Tony told me the state took him and placed him in foster homes, but he'd run away and end up down near Pike Place. It was home. He learned to hide well enough the authorities stopped looking for him. He was raised by drunks, hookers, addicts and the deranged, sometimes sharing a sleeping bag on cold nights, sometimes just some newspapers.

"Do you know what it's like to be so hungry that a dumpster smells like a feast?" he asked, staring into me until I shook my head and looked away.

Eventually he was big enough to wash dishes, had jobs in various restaurants, put scraps aside for himself and the others living over the edge of society. He went to school when he could, got a job delivering produce after a driver took him along on the route and taught him how to drive.

"Eventually I signed up for the military, and they trained me to do things we'll not talk about. I was a little ragged around the edges and it took a few years, but I learned how to seem 'normal.' After I got out, I went to the U of W, did well enough that I got a ride to law school. Here I am."

"Where does Claudia fit into this?"

"What?"

"You two have a history."

"She and I were together while we were in law school, but it wasn't easy. I had a lot of baggage from childhood and she had a lot of dreams. Max was my best friend. I didn't know that being my friend gave him cover for being without either honor or empathy. One time when things were really bad between me and Claudia, Max offered to mediate. I didn't hear from either of them for three days. She wouldn't talk to me when they got back and when I accused Max of using me to get with her, he just smiled and said, 'Never trust anyone who doesn't act in their own self-interest.' "

"Oh, shit."

"A lesson well learned," he said.

"Claudia is a lawyer, too?"

"No, she dropped out. She got pregnant, probably over the three days they were gone. She and I had always been careful, but that takes two. Max said he would give her everything she needed in life but her role was to support him and their child. He told her if she became a lawyer, he would take their child and she'd be on her own. He came from a very powerful family and would have probably succeeded."

"My God, Tony," I said at last. I gestured at the bustle of Pike Place Market, of wealthy buyers of fresh-caught salmon, fresh morel mushrooms, and handmade cashmere shawls from shop keepers who traveled for an hour from homes they could barely afford, all amidst homeless men and women who sat for hours on the ground or on park benches or on walls separating the market from the road and tracks below.

"This is where you came from, so this is what you do. This is who you are. It's incredible you turned out to be the person you are."

"We don't get to choose the fires in which we are forged," he said. "I saw the same in you, right here, the first day we met."

Chapter 46

Dynamic organisms are never static. Plants, animals, governments, law firms: They sprout, grow, reproduce and die. That's just the way it's supposed to be, if there is a "supposed to be." That's just the way it is.

A rather significant settlement was reached with the partners of Moore & Associates. The firm could not avoid responsibility for actions of its primary partner and the hiring of Rick Meyers. It was Tony's idea and he received significant compensation too, given that they disrupted our firm as well as damaged me personally.

I'm not a victim, but I'll be compensated by those who tried to victimize me.

The implosion of Moore & Associates put a lot of lawyers on the street, and a number of them retained a pretty good book of business. My former husband, Mark, named his firm Love and Watkins, PLC. The sign outside their office read "LAW, plc." Cute. I don't know if there ever was a "Watkins."

I ran into Mark at my favorite lunch spot one afternoon. I was there eating a sandwich and reading the paper when he came up to the counter.

"This is a coincidence," he said, sitting down.

"I doubt it. What's up?" I didn't believe him. Nor did it matter. He ordered a latte.

"Okay. Maybe not so coincidental. Jessi …"

"Yes?"

"I made a mistake."

"Yes." It was a flat agreement with his statement. Nothing more.

"You know, we could be great partners."

"Excuse me?"

"We could work together. It would be great."

"Think your wife would approve?"

"Ashley keeps pretty busy with the kids. You and I had great synergy. We'd make a potent team."

"Mark, I don't want synergy with you. I don't want anything with you. Leave me alone with my lunch, please. I'll pay for your coffee."

He looked at me, started to say something, changed his mind and walked out.

There's no such thing as closure, but that came mighty close.

I already had my support staff in mind. Claire came first to help me out.

"Was that your son?" I asked her about the team of cops that descended on the hotel. One of the officers had Claire's last name, and he fit her description.

"It was," she said. "He's something, isn't he? Just like his father, but he's as smart as he is handsome."

"And how did he think the arrest went down?" I was fishing. I knew what Claire's son had seen. I wanted to know what he said to Claire.

"Oh, he never tells me the details of his police work. Scares me too much, especially for his family and my grandkids."

For the first month, we were only in the office two days a week, then three. Then four. I mentioned to Sarah that I needed someone to help out when we saw each other at a very special occasion: She and Lily had just been married, and we were at the reception.

"I am so happy for you two!" I said when I got my turn for a hug and spent my minute with them. I asked if I could hire them both.

"No, but I'm available," Sarah said.

"It was one thing to work together before, but now that Sarah and I are married, I really don't think we can work in the same office," Lily said.

"Besides, we want to have a baby, and Lily is much more maternal," said Sarah.

The simple, factual way she said that, each of them looking at me and not to each other for confirmation, brought tears to my eyes.

We cap the work at four days a week, including court appearances, and leave the schedule flexible. I upped rates to the point where upper-end clients pay us well and I can provide services pro bono whenever a case catches my eye that deserves special representation. Sometimes I pay other lawyers to help people who can't afford their services. Tony, for instance.

And, being Tony, half the time he won't take the money. He keeps saying he'd prefer to work out a private arrangement. I love him for being exactly who he is, even if he hides that from everyone else.

The fee structure also gives me enough time to be nearly anywhere in the world when I want to be there, if I want to be there.

That's why I'm on this flight, on my way to visit Charles in France. He said he wants to give me something very special for my 35th birthday.

Charles is amazing. He knows how to treat me, and he knows exactly what I like, in every way. There are people in Europe who enjoy what you can only imagine. If I said more, I wouldn't be invited again. So I won't.

Some judge me as "immoral," to use that ugly word. But every time they look twice at me sitting there in the airport laughing and enjoying those I'm talking with, or walking down the street with short skirt and a light step, or in a coffee shop flirting with good friends or strangers, and they condemn me, it's because they fear.

They fear because, deep down, they know they are lying to themselves. They know I'm not that different from them, my desires are not that different from theirs. I just make different decisions, accept them as my own, and don't expect anything to last forever. *Tout passe, tout lasse, tout casse.*

I don't stifle my joy or sensuality just because there are men who apparently feel entitled to my time and attention. Men who believe that what they see through their eyes in less than a minute justifies an intrusion, regardless of my consent. It doesn't take much to convince them of their mistake. I try to be nice, but don't pander if they're stubborn.

Of course, I'll visit Uncle Marcel and Genevieve, and my wonderfully special niece. She is discovering her womanhood, her voice, and her desires. She's coming to the U.S. next year to spend the summer. That will be significant for each of us, especially since we now have the same last name. I changed mine after Max Moore's trial.

I'm not Jessica Love any longer, and never really felt like Jessica Jones. I took my grandmother's maiden name, *Du Bois*. I worried for a while that I didn't feel her presence as often as I did right after she died. Then I realized that was because there was less distance between us, that we had merged, or I'd been absorbed. She is with me still, reminding me often that the decisions I make belong to me.

At my throat hangs a porcelain butterfly. It brings me back to center, always a totem of Grandmere's strength and sacrifice.

End

About the author

Erik Dolson was raised in Oregon, graduated with a degree in Philosophy from Stanford University in 1973, then drifted around Europe and Asia for the next couple of years: he argued existentialism in Paris with other expats, drove a forklift in Israel during the Yom Kippur war, hid from Turkish soldiers on Cypress, befriended locals in Afghanistan who eventually became the Taliban, searched for God in India.

Dolson returned home to San Francisco to attend his mother's funeral, then waited tables in Portland, Oregon, for six years while writing unpublishable fiction. Leaving the city and its temptations, Dolson became owner, editor and publisher of the weekly newspaper in Sisters, Oregon, and helped raise his twin daughters who were adopted as infants from India.

After the girls were fledged and his ex-wife took over responsibility for the newspaper, he returned to writing fiction.

Dolson currently splits his time between a home on the eastern flank of the Oregon Cascade Range and his sailboat in the San Juan Islands, though he still travels extensively to other corners of the world.

In addition to *Indecent Exposure*, he has published a literary romance, *Chalice*; finished the first draft of the second Jessica Love book, *Dragonfly*; set aside the fourth draft of an extremely dark mystery set in the San Juans, *All But Forgotten*; has an incomplete mystery set in a place much like Fiji, *Butterflies*; and works occasionally on a small book about Adult Attachment Disorder, *It's Nobody's Fault*.

More about Erik Dolson, along with his blog and excerpts from the books, can be found at erikdolson.com and ontillmorning.us.

Please write a review

I'd like to make a request. Please return to Amazon and write an honest review of this book. It will help others decide if they should buy a copy, and hopefully result in the sale of more books.

Maybe even a sequel. Thank you.

Made in United States
Troutdale, OR
01/30/2025

28378762R00154